MURDER

SHORT STORIES

COMPILED BY
PATRICIA MOORE

UNABRIDGED & COMPLETE
LONG READING TEXT (NOVEL)

NEW DELHI (INDIA)

MURDER

SHORT STORIES

This English Edition, Published in India

Published by

MG BOOKS

An Imprint of

MAANU GRAPHICS

(PUBLISHERS OF GENERAL BOOKS)

5FF, Ganpati Bhawan, 21 Ansari Road,
Darya Ganj, New Delhi-110002
Ph: 43755225, 9315898404
E-mail : maanugraphics@yahoo.com
mgbooks.maanu@yahoo.com

Printed at
Satyam Enterprises, Delhi

CONTENTS

19TH CENTURY UNSOLVED MURDERS

AN enormous percentage of murders - perhaps as many as one third - remain unsolved. This is particularly true in the late twentieth century, when "serial killers" strike at random - for example, in America in the 1980s, the uncaught "Green River Killer" of Seattle killed at least forty women, eight times as many as London's Jack the Ripper, who killed five prostitutes in 1888. So it is understandable that we look back on the nineteenth century with nostalgia, and find a certain quaint charm even in its murder cases. In fact, considering the undeveloped state of nineteenth-century crime detection, remarkably few of its famous murder cases remained unsolved.

One of the few that defied the skills of the New York police force was the case of the death of a salesgirl, which so intrigued Edgar Allen Poe that he used it as the basis for his story "The Mystery of Marie Roget".

If the death of "Marie Roget" is now no longer quite a mystery, the classic Victorian poisoning drama, the death of Charles Bravo, is as baffling as in 1876.

And another, the case of Lizzie Borden, is the most intriguing American murder mystery that took place almost a quarter of a century later, in 1892, and is regarded by most aficionados of crime as a fitting climax to the homicides of the age of gaslight.

THE CASE OF MARY ROGERS

MARY Cecilia Rogers was born in New York in 1820; her mother, who became a widow when the child was five, supported herself by running a boarding-house in Nassau Street. Mary grew up into a tall, very beautiful young woman with jet-black hair. This led a cigar-store owner named John Anderson, whose shop was on Broadway, to offer her a job as a salesgirl. In 1840 this was regarded as an imaginative piece of business enterprise, for New York was even more "Victorian" than London, and young unmarried girls did not exhibit themselves behind shop counters, particularly in shops frequented exclusively by young men. Mary's mother objected to the idea, but her daughter's enthusiasm finally won her over. She drew many new customers to the shop, although - as Thomas Duke is careful to note in his *Celebrated Criminal Cases of America* (1910) - "the girl's conduct was apparently a model of modest decorum, and while she was lavish in her smiles, she did not hesitate to repel all undue advances".

She had been working in the store for about ten months when one day in January 1841 she failed to appear. Her mother had no idea where she was, and according to Duke, "Mr Anderson was unable to account for her absence". The police searched for her and the newspapers reported her disappearance. Six days later she reappeared, looking tired and rather ill, and explained that she had been visiting relatives in the country. Her mother and her employer apparently corroborated the story. But when a rumour began to circulate that she had been seen during her absence with a tall, handsome naval officer Mary abruptly gave up her job -only a few days after returning - and was no longer seen on Broadway. A month later she announced her engagement to one of her mother's boarders, a clerk called Daniel Payne.

Five months later, on Sunday, 25 July 1841, Mary knocked on her fiance's door at 10 a.m. and announced that she was going to see her aunt in Bleecker Street; Payne said that he would call for her that evening. Payne also spent the day away from home, but when a violent thunderstorm came on towards evening he decided not to call for Mary, but to let her stay the night with her aunt. Mrs Rogers apparently approved. But when Mary failed to return home the following day she began to worry. When Payne returned from work and learned that Mary was still away, he rushed to see the aunt in Bleecker Street - a Mrs Downing - and was even more alarmed when she told him that she had not seen Mary in the past forty-eight hours.

It was two days later on Wednesday morning that three men in a sailing-boat saw a body in the water off Castle Point Hoboken. It was Mary, and according to the *New York Tribune* "it was obvious that she had been horribly outraged and murdered". She was fully clothed, although her clothes were torn, and the petticoat was missing. A piece of lace from the bottom of the dress was embedded so deeply in the throat that it had almost disappeared. An autopsy performed almost immediately led to the conclusion that she had been "brutally violated". Oddly enough, Daniel Payne did not go to view the corpse, although he had earlier searched for her all over New York, including Hoboken. But after being interrogated by the police, Payne was released.

A week passed without any fresh clues, and a large reward was offered. Then the coroner received a letter from some anonymous man - who said he had not come forward before from "motives of perhaps criminal prudence" - and who claimed to have seen Mary Rogers on the Sunday afternoon of her disappearance. She had, the writer said, stepped out of a boat with six rough-looking characters, and gone with them into the woods, laughing merrily and apparently under no kind of constraint.

Soon afterwards a boat with three well-dressed men had come ashore, and one of these accosted two men walking on the beach and asked if they had seen a young woman and six men recently. They said they had, and that she had appeared to go with them willingly. At this the trio turned their boat and headed back for New York.

In fact, the two men came forward and corroborated this story. But although they both knew Mary Rogers by sight, neither of them could swear that the girl they had seen was definitely Mary.

The next important piece of information came from a stagecoach-driver named Adams, who said he had seen Mary arrive on the Hoboken ferry with a well-dressed man of dark complexion, and that they had gone to a roadhouse called "Nick Mullen's". This tavern was kept by a Mrs Loss, who told the police that the couple had "taken refreshment" there, then gone off into the woods. Some time later she had heard a scream from the woods; but since the place "was a resort of questionable characters" she had thought no more of it.

Two months after the murder, on 25 September, children playing in the woods found the missing petticoat in a thicket; they also found a white silk scarf, a parasol and a handkerchief marked "M.R." Daniel Payne was to commit suicide in this spot soon after.

A gambler named Joseph Morse, who lived in Nassau Street, was arrested and apparently charged with the murder; there was evidence that he had been seen with Mary Rogers on the evening she disappeared. The following day, he had fled from New York. But Morse was released when he was able to prove that he had been at Staten Island with another young lady on the Sunday afternoon. One odd story in the *Tribune* declared that Morse believed that the young lady *was* Mary Rogers, and that when he heard of the disappearance he assumed she had committed suicide because of the way he had treated her - he had tried to seduce her in his room. He was relieved to learn that the girl with whom he had spent the afternoon was still alive.

In the following year, 1842, Poe's "Mystery of Marie Roget" was published in three parts in *Snowden's Ladies' Companion.* But for anyone looking for a solution of the Mary Rogers mystery, it should be treated with extreme caution. Poe argues that Mary Rogers was not murdered by a gang but by a single individual. His original view seems to have been that the motive was rape; later he heard the rumour that Mary had died as a result of an abortion, and made a few hasty alterations in his story to accommodate this notion. He argues that the signs of a struggle in the woods, and the battered state of her face, indicate that she was killed by an individual - a gang would have been able to overpower her easily. He also speaks of a strip from the girl's skirt that had been wound around the waist to afford a kind of handle for carrying the body; but the evidence of two witnesses who dragged the body out of the water makes no mention of this "handle". In spite of this, there can be no doubt that Poe's objections to the gang theory carry a great deal of weight.

What was not known to Poe in 1842 is that Mary's employer, John Anderson, had been questioned by the police as a suspect; like all the others, he was released. But fifty years later - in December 1891 - new evidence was to emerge. By that time Anderson had been dead ten years; he became a millionaire, and died in Paris. Apparently he had told friends that he had experienced "many unhappy days and nights in regard to her" (Mary Rogers), and had been in touch with her spirit. His heirs contested his estate, and in 1891 his daughter tried to break her father's will on the grounds that when he signed it he was mentally incompetent. The case was settled out of court, and the records destroyed. But a lawyer named Samuel Copp Worthen, who had been closely associated with Anderson's daughter Laura Appleton, knew that his firm had kept a copy of the testimony in the Supreme Court of New York in 1891, and he made it his business to read it. He finally revealed what he had learned in the periodical *American Literature* in 1948. It revealed that Anderson had been questioned by the police about the death of Mary Rogers, and that this had preyed on his mind, so that he later declined to stand as a candidate for mayor of New York, in case someone revealed his secret.

The most significant part of the testimony was the assertion that Anderson had admitted to paying for an abortion for Mary Rogers and had got "in some trouble over it". But he had insisted that he had not "had anything, directly, himself to do with her problems".

This would obviously explain Mary's week-long disappearance from the cigar store, and the fact that she looked tired and ill when she returned. It probably also explains why she decided to leave the store a week later - not because of gossip about the naval officer, but because she needed more time to convalesce.

Worthen's theory is that in the six months after leaving the cigar store Mary again got herself pregnant, and once more appealed to Anderson for help. When she left home that Sunday morning she intended to go to Hoboken for an abortion. (In fact, there was a story that Mrs Loss, the tavern-owner, had admitted on her deathbed that Mary Rogers had died during an abortion; there is no hard evidence for this confession, but it is known that the District Attorney was inclined to the abortion theory of Mary's death.) She died during the abortion, and her body was dumped in the river to protect the abortionist - the dark-skinned man with whom she was seen on the ferry - and Mrs Loss's family.

How does this theory fit the known facts? The answer is: very well indeed, particularly if we make the natural assumption that the father of the second unborn child was Daniel Payne - for it seems unlikely that Mary agreed to marry him, then continued her affair with her former lover. (Nothing is known about this former lover, but Anderson is obviously a suspect.) We must assume, then, that Payne knew perfectly well that Mary was on her way to Hoboken to have an illegal operation. We may also probably assume that the pregnancy was still in its early stages, and that Mary anticipated very little trouble - after all, she had recovered from the earlier abortion in a week, though it still left her feeling ill. Mary's mother was probably also in the secret. Duke comments: "It was generally believed at the time that the murdered girl's mother knew more about her daughter's mysterious admirer than she chose to tell."

What of the evidence about the gang? It is possible, of course, that a young girl was actually seen entering the woods with a gang of men, and that this was nothing to do with Mary Rogers. But it is far more probable that the anonymous letter claiming that Mary had entered the woods with six ruffians was sent by Mrs Loss or one of her friends - it came from Hoboken. Then all she had to do was to persuade two of her relatives or friends to claim that they were the men on the beach, and that they had seen Mary enter the woods and seen the boat with three men that landed shortly afterwards . . . The result would be a perfect red herring, directing the attention of the police away from her own abortion parlour.

What of the petticoat found later in the woods? This, significantly enough, was found by Mrs Loss's children. We may assume that the petticoat, the umbrella and the handkerchief were left behind in Mrs Loss's roadhouse when Mary's body was dragged to the water in the middle of the night, and were later planted in the woods, in a place where the bushes were broken, to suggest evidence of a struggle.

And what of the evidence that Mary had been raped? This, apparently, was the coroner's report; we do not know whether she was examined by a doctor or if so what the doctor concluded. What we *do* know is that Mary's body was already decomposing, and that because of the hot July weather it was buried within a few hours of being taken out of the water; so any inquest would have been performed in haste. In 1841 the science of legal medicine was in its infancy, and it is doubtful whether anyone took a vaginal swab and examined it under a microscope for spermatozoa. What was probably taken for evidence of rape was actually evidence of an abortion that had gone wrong.

Duke reports that Daniel Payne committed suicide "at the same spot in the woods where his sweetheart was probably slain". Other writers on the case have questioned this (notably Charles E. Pearce in *Unsolved Murder Mysteries,* 1924). But Payne's suicide would certainly be consistent with the theory that he was the father of the unborn child.

It is a disappointing - if obvious - solution to one of the great "murder mysteries", that Mary Rogers died in the course of an abortion. Why is it not more generally known? Partly because Poe himself obscured the truth. In the 1850 edition of Poe's works published the year after his death "Marie Roget" appeared with a footnote that stated:

> It may not be improper to record . . . that the confessions of *two* persons (one of them the Madame Dulac of the narrative [Mrs Loss]) made at different periods long subsequent to the publication confessed, in full, not only the general conclusion but absolutely *all* the chief hypothetical details by which the conclusion was attained.

But this is obviously impossible. Mrs Loss only seems to have confessed that Mary had died in the course of an abortion in her tavern. Poe's theory was that she was murdered by a man "in a passion" who then dragged her body to the seashore. The likely truth seems to be that she died of an air embolism, and that the abortionist, with the aid of Mrs Loss, made the death look like murder by tying a strip of cloth round her throat; the two of them then probably carried it to the water. Poe's "Marie Roget", far from being an amazingly accurate reconstruction of the murder, is simply a bad guess. Poe may not have been a murderer, but he was undoubtedly a liar.

In a magazine called The Unexplained (No. 152) Grahame Fuller and Ian Knight suggest that Poe himself may have been the killer of Mary Rogers. A witness said he had seen her with a tall, well-dressed man of swarthy complexion on the afternoon she died; Poe ws of olive complexion, and was always well-dressed. But he was only five feet eight inches tall. Poe's biographers all insist on his gentleness and courtesy. On the whole, the notion of Poe as a demonic killer, writing "Marie Roget" to boast about his crime, must be relegated to the realm of fantasy.

THE BRAVO CASE

IT happened in the Priory, Balham, south London, where Charles Bravo, a thirty-year-old barrister, lived with his newly-married wife Florence. She was an attractive girl, who had been a widow for four years when Bravo married her in December 1875. Her first husband, Captain Alexander Lewis Ricardo, of the Grenadier Guards, had died of alcoholism, leaving Florence a welcome - and, she thought, well-earned - £40,000.

When Charles Bravo proposed to her, he was aware that she was the mistress of a middle-aged doctor called James Manby Gully, who had tended her when her first marriage was breaking up. Charles's sexual past had not been entirely blameless, so the lovers agreed to put all thoughts of jealousy from their minds. Charles was undoubtedly in love with her, and just as undoubtedly attracted by her money.

As she soon discovered, he could be overbearing and bad-tempered; but Florence wasn't the type to be bullied. She had a mind of her own - and a tendency to drink rather too heavily. She ran the Priory - an imposing Gothic pile -with the help of a widow named Mrs Cox. To begin with, the marriage seemed happy - even though Florence had two miscarriages in four months, and Bravo suffered from fits of retrospective fury about Gully, and once even struck her.

A dummy hanging by a noose at the Long Beach Amusement Park in California formed part of a "fun house" exhibit in the centre for over five years.
It was such a convincing piece that it was often used as a prop for films which were being shot in the Park. During the filming of an episode of The Six Million Dollar Man, one of the film cameramen became dissatisfied with the way in which the right arm was hanging from the body of the dummy and was attempting to adjust it in order to make it look real when the whole arm fell off. On closer examination a protruding bone was noted and he identified the dummy as a human but in not the and when sprayed as he an with had had been bought by the amusement park from a local wax museum.

On Friday, 21 April 1876, Charles Bravo ate a good supper of whiting, roast lamb, and anchovy eggs on toast, washing it down with burgundy. Florence and Mrs Cox drank most of two bottles of sherry between them. At ten that night, loud groans came from Bravo's bedroom; he had been seized with severe abdominal pains, and began vomiting. He vomited for three days, until he died.

Sir William Gull, Queen Victoria's physician (who was suspected by some twentieth-century criminologists of being Jack the Ripper), saw him before he died, and gave his opinion that Bravo was suffering from some irritant poison. A post-mortem confirmed this - there were signs of antimony poisoning. At this point Mrs Cox declared that Bravo had told her: "I have taken poison. Don't tell Florence."

An open verdict was returned at the inquest. But the newspapers smelled scandal, and openly hinted that Florence had killed her husband. Another inquest was held, prompted by Charles's brother Joseph, who was out to get a verdict of wilful murder - which would lead to Florence's arrest.

This time, the Dr Gully scandal came into open court -doing Gully a great deal of professional damage. Added to this a dismissed servant of the Bravos' testified that he had once bought tartar emetic for the doctor. But again, the jury decided that there was not enough evidence to charge anyone - although they agreed that it *was* a case of murder. So Florence was exculpated, and she died of alcoholism two years later in Southsea.

Ever since then, students of crime have argued about the case. The most popular theory, obviously, is that Florence did it. An inquest on the body of her first husband - conducted after the Bravo inquest - showed traces of antimony in *his* organs. However, Ricardo had by then been separated from Florence for months.

It seems possible that his violent attacks of vomiting were not due to alcoholism, but to slow poisoning with antimony. But why should Florence kill her husband? Possibly because he insisted on his marital rights, and she was terrified of further miscarriages; possibly because she came to realize that he was interested only in her money.

It is tempting to speculate how many of the great mysteries of the past might have been solved if the police had been able to use modern methods. The Ripper murders would fairly certainly remain unsolved;

in the few parallel modern cases I can think of the murderer has either remained uncaught, or was caught by chance. But some of the domestic mysteries would almost certainly not remain mysteries - a fingerprint on a bottle would have been enough. One of the great Victorian causes célèbres, the Pook case, would have been solved within hours if there had been tests for human blood in 1871. The victim, a servant girl named Jane Clouson, was found lying in a lovers' lane at Eltham, south London, her face and head horribly lacerated. She died shortly afterwards without speaking. The constable found a lathing hammer near the scene of the crime - a cross between a hammer and a chopper. This had made more than a dozen wounds, through one of which the girl's brain was protruding. It was discovered that she was two months pregnant. The young man who was believed to be responsible was Edmund Pook, the son of a Greenwich printer, in whose house Jane Clouson had been a servant for two years. Shortly before her seventeenth birthday, the girl had been dismissed through the agency of Pook's mother, who felt the girl was too familiar with her son.

Edmund Pook proved to be a spoiled, swaggering, altogether unpleasant young man. He flatly denied any intimacy with Jane Clouson, and said she was dirty. But he was unable to explain bloodstains on the cuff of his shirt, or on his clothes.

Fifty years later, it would have been a simple matter to test his later assertion that the blood was his own - he was subject to epileptic fits and nosebleeds. It is possible, of course, that his blood and Jane Clouson's were of the same group, but then, he certainly left fingerprints on the hammer.

In *How Charles Bravo Died,* author Yseult Bridges suggests that Bravo accidentally took the poison with which he had been dosing Florence. Crime novelist Agatha Christie believed that Dr Gully did it, or helped Florence to do it. Many other writers believe Mrs Cox was the culprit. Bravo disliked her, and is known to have wanted to get rid of her.

Gaslit London was a grim city in which mothers with babies at their breast slept out on the freezing pavements, a city of disease, violence and corruption. It comes to life in the pages of that curious work called My Secret Life by an unknown Victorian whom we know only as Walter. Walter often wandered around the slum streets, seeking satisfaction of his peculiar desires. He might have a sudden impulse to have sex with a pregnant woman, or with a young virgin, or even a child. On one occasion he picked up a woman and a ten-year-old girl, went back to a cold, dismal room with them, and spent the night possessing them both. Moreover, it was not the first time the child had been made to give herself to a man for money. Again and again, Walter describes possessing young girls for a shilling.

The Priory has now been turned into working-class flats, and has a reputation for being haunted; but no one has ever produced a satisfactory explanation of the mystery of Bravo's death.

LIZZIE BORDEN

AT 11.15, on the morning of 4 August 1892 - the hottest day of the year - Lizzie Borden called the maid Bridget Sullivan and told her that someone had killed her father. The seventy-year-old banker was found on the divan in the parlour, his face unrecognizable; someone had struck him several blows with a hatchet. Borden's second wife, Abby, was believed to be out visiting a sick friend - according to Lizzie - but she was later found upstairs in the guest room, lying face downwards. She had also been killed with blows from a hatchet - much heavier, more savage blows than those that had killed Andrew Borden. Lizzie's story was that she had been out in the barn, and had heard a cry from the house; she rushed back to find her father dead.

It soon became clear that Lizzie had much to hide. Her mother had died when she was two; two years later her father remarried; Abby Gray was six years his junior, twenty-two years older than Lizzie's sister Emma. Two days before the murder, Lizzie had tried to buy prussic acid. Lizzie's father and stepmother had been experiencing stomach pains for some time before the murder. Lizzie hated her stepmother.

Moreover, medical evidence proved that Abby Borden had died shortly after 9 a.m., while her husband was not killed until about two hours later. It was just within the bounds of possibility that an unknown assassin had entered the house and murdered the couple - but not that he had remained concealed for two hours, in a small house in which there were two women. (Lizzie's sister was away staying with friends.)

Lizzie was arrested and tried. The evidence against her was purely circumstantial; the prosecution merely attempted to demonstrate that she was the likeliest person to have committed the murders. But she was a respectable girl of unblemished reputation, and the jury found her not guilty. She lived on until 1927. During her lifetime it was impossible for writers to speculate about whether she killed her father and stepmother. But after her death, Edmund Pearson lost no time in publishing his opinion that she was the killer. (Even during her lifetime, the local newspaper in Fall River, Massachusetts, printed sarcastic articles on the anniversary of the murder - one of which concluded that the Bordens had not been murdered at all, but had died of the heat.) His *Trial of Lizzie Borden* in the Great American Trial series came out in 1937, and the book is dedicated to the district attorney who built up the case against Lizzie Borden. In 1959, a new piece of evidence turned up. In a book called *Murder and Mutiny,* published in 1959, E. R. Snow tells how he received a letter from an elderly gentleman named Thomas Owens, who had listened to a broadcast about the Borden case by Snow. Owens had a strange story to tell. In 1896, four years after the murder, Lizzie Borden went "into the art gallery and shop of Tilden-Thurber in Providence, Rhode Island, and when she left, the assistant found that two expensive paintings on porcelain were missing. The following February, a lady went into the shop with one of the two paintings, and asked if a crack could be repaired. The manager was told, and he asked the lady where she had obtained the painting. "From Miss Lizzie Borden of Fall River." As a result of this, a headline "Lizzie Again" appeared in the *Providence Journal,* which stated that a warrant for her arrest had been issued for the theft of two paintings. What had happened, said Owens, was that the owners of the gallery had put a proposition to Lizzie: sign a confession to the murders, or we prosecute. Lizzie refused, and the item was published in the newspaper. This caused Lizzie to change her mind. After promises that the confession would not be used, Lizzie typed on a sheet of paper: "Unfair means force my signature here admitting the act of August 4,1892, as mine alone, Lizbeth A Borden." The store decided to have the document photographed in case of accident, and Owens was asked to do it. He did; but he also made a second copy - or, he said, decided that the first copy was indistinct, and made another one for the store, without mentioning that he had the other. As the four principals in the episode died - there were two other men besides the store owners - he expected it to be publicized. And now, Owens was willing to sell the photograph of Lizzie's confessions for one hundred dollars. Snow persuaded him to take fifty, and printed the story in his book.

Another crime writer, Edward Radin, decided to look into the matter, and he soon established that Snow had been the victim of a swindler. It was Lizzie's signature, and the type face was that of a machine of the period, but the signature had been traced from Lizzie's will. It would be interesting to know whether Mr Snow demanded his fifty dollars back.

But obviously, the first part of the story was true. Lizzie *had* stolen the paintings, and the item really appeared in the *Providence Journal* in February 1897. Lizzie was a kleptomaniac. Although she had plenty of money (she left over a million dollars), she was a compulsive stealer. Oddly enough, she was also capable of great generosity.

Radin's book *Lizzie Borden, The Untold Story* asserts that Lizzie was innocent. The killer was Bridget Sullivan, the servant girl. It is known that Bridget was feeling ill on the morning of 4

August; yet Mrs Borden had her cleaning all the outside windows at 7.30 in the morning. Later that morning, Bridget vomited. Certainly, she had a motive of sorts - sheer resentment at her employer. Radin tells how he was completely convinced by Pearson's view of the case until he read the actual trial reports for himself and discovered that Pearson had suppressed many pieces of evidence in Lizzie's favour.

In 1964, Gerald Gross edited a volume of selections from Edmund Pearson's articles on murder, and wrote a postscript to Pearson's "final word" on the Borden case. Gross says, very fairly, that Radin has distorted the evidence for Lizzie's innocence as carefully as Pearson distorted that for her guilt, and he points out that Pearson had to do a great deal of omitting anyway, to pack the trial into one fair-sized volume. But Gross's theory is that Lizzie killed her parents aided and abetted by Bridget. There is a persistent story that Bridget returned to Ireland after the trial, with a great deal of money given to her by Lizzie. Radin points out, quite correctly, that Bridget could certainly not be said to have testified in Lizzie's favour at the trial; on the contrary, most of her evidence told against her employer. If, however, she was an accomplice - or an accessory after the fact - perhaps to helping Lizzie conceal the murder weapon or the bloodstained dress (which Lizzie burnt) - then Lizzie would certainly have a motive for giving her money.

In 1967 there appeared in America, Victoria Lincoln's *A Private Disgrace.* When Foster Damon - another expert on the Borden case - sent me a copy, he enclosed a card which said:

"I think this is the final word on Lizzie." I am inclined to think he is right.

Victoria Lincoln was born in Fall River, so her insight into the town is obviously authentic. She was able to uncover some facts that suddenly make the whole case quite clear. There is only one point in Miss Lincoln's account that might be described as "speculation"; from accounts of the periodic fainting illness that Lizzie suffered from, she arrives at the conclusion that Lizzie suffered from epilepsy of the temporal lobe of the brain. Psychomotor epilepsy is distinguished by seizures of automatic activity. Miss Lincoln cites a case from a medical textbook in which a man woke from a seizure, to find that the boss had raised his salary, impressed by the lucid and forceful way in which the man had asked for a raise. Lizzie undoubtedly had strange attacks about four times a year, always at the time of her menstrual period. The evidence about these attacks points to psychomotor epilepsy. And Lizzie was menstruating at the time of the murders.

But Miss Lincoln's theory is not an attempt to prove that Lizzie committed the murders in a trance-like state. She intended to kill her stepmother - but by poison. She hated her and was violently jealous of her. A year before the murders, her stepmother's room had been broken into and robbed when Lizzie was in the house. The thief was supposed to have flitted in silently, without alerting Lizzie, Emma and the maid Bridget, broken into the room, taken money and jewellery, and flitted out via the cellar door. Andrew Borden soon asked the police to drop the investigation. He had a fairly shrewd idea of the identity of the thief.

Lizzie felt she had reason for hating her stepmother. First of all, it was a quarrel about a house. Mrs Borden's sister had not married so well, and she lived in half a house, the other half of which belonged to her mother. Her mother wanted to sell, but could hardly turn her own daughter out. So Andrew Borden came to the rescue, and quietly bought the whole house, giving half to the sister, and half to his own wife Abby. He did this with great secrecy, knowing the feelings of his children about their stepmother and her family, but the news leaked. Lizzie was furious. She told her father that charity should begin at home. She ceased to call Abby "mother", and from then on, addressed her - when she had to - as Mrs Borden. Andrew Borden tried to restore peace in the home by giving Lizzie and her sister another house, which had belonged to their grandfather. Lizzie was placated; but she never forgave her stepmother, and continued to address her as "Mrs Borden" after twenty-three years of calling her "mother".

The trouble that led directly to the murder was an identical situation, which took place five years later - just before the murder. Uncle John Vinnicum Morse was a mid-westerner, and he decided that he would like to move closer to his brother-in-law's home (he was the brother of Borden's first wife). Borden owned a farm at nearby Swansea, and Morse asked if he could rent it. Borden said yes - and decided to do again what he had already done over the business of his sister-in-law's house - to transfer the farm to his wife's name. Miss Lincoln dug up this curious transaction, the immediate motive of the murder; Pearson and the other writers on the case were unaware of it. Lizzie already disliked Uncle John because he had aided and abetted her father in the previous house transaction. So now he moved into their house again as a guest, she felt distinctly edgy. Miss Lincoln does not produce a convincing explanation why Borden decided to transfer the farm to Abby; perhaps he wanted to give her a present - he had recently bought back the other house from his daughters for two thousand more than its value, thus making them a present of a thousand dollars each. But Borden was seventy; no doubt he wanted to leave his wife well provided for in the event of his death. This was also why Lizzie was so bitterly opposed to these property deals. And it did not take long for the news about the Swansea property to leak back to her. This is when she started trying to buy poison. And although she was unsuccessful in her attempts to buy prussic acid ("for cleaning a fur"), she presumably bought *something,* for that evening Mr and Mrs Borden were very sick indeed. Lizzie said she had been sick too, but we have only her word for this.

There was another factor that has been largely ignored by Pearson and Radin. Lizzie had a deep love of animals, and she owned some pigeons, which lived in the barn roost. Borden kept everything locked up - he was capable of obsessive meanness - and when the barn was broken into twice by youths who wanted pigeon pie for supper, he chopped off the heads of all the pigeons with a hatchet. It was not exactly unkindness; in those days, America was still close to the pioneers, and most people killed their own chickens and butchered their own hogs. But he failed to calculate the effect on Lizzie.

This, in summary, is the new evidence dug up by Victoria Lincoln, and it certainly makes the case in every way more straightforward. The transfer of the deeds on the Swansea property was to take place on the day of the murder. Borden had thought up a stratagem to do this without arousing Lizzie's suspicions - a carriage would be sent to the door, and a note requesting that Mrs Borden visit a sick neighbour. The note arrived - or so Miss Lincoln believes - but by then, Mrs Borden was already dead, or about to die. She was working in the guest room, on all fours, when Lizzie came in behind her with the hatchet, and sliced into her skull with blow after blow. At this point, Miss Lincoln embarks on a speculation that I find difficult to accept. John Morse had left the house much earlier. He had no alibi for the time of the first murder, but an extremely detailed one for the second. Miss Lincoln believes that Morse went along to the house just to make sure that all went according to plan - after all, the affair of the farm was of immediate interest to him. He watched the boy deliver the note, and observed Lizzie's very abrupt manner as she took it, followed by her slamming of the door. Obviously, she was having one of her queer spells. Ever since Morse had been in the Bordens' house, there had been a brooding tension, and Mrs Borden probably suspected Lizzie of wanting to poison her. So Morse listened with more than usual attention to what followed, and rightly interpreted the heavy thud from the upstairs room - its window was wide open on the hot August morning - followed by a succession of squelching noises. Probably Mrs Borden groaned the first time - Bridget was out at the other side of the house cleaning windows, so she would not hear. And Morse, realizing what had happened, knew that an uncle from the mid-west would be a far more likely suspect for a murder than the respectable daughter of the house. So he hurried away and started establishing an alibi.

This *could* have happened, but there is no evidence that it did. All that seems moderately certain is that, with the stifling heat of the August morning, and the irritation of her menstrual period, Lizzie had one of her queer spells, and decided that she could not stand her stepmother a moment longer. Miss Lincoln may well be right; it may have been committed in a dream-like state, and the dream may have involved the headless pigeons. Miss Lincoln could be wrong in her diagnosis of psychomotor epilepsy; but it is hard to doubt that all kinds of factors - the knowledge of another property deal, her hatred of her stepmother and determination to kill her, the heat, menstrual irritation -suddenly decided her to use violence. Earlier writers on the case were not aware of just *how much* violence and tension there was in the air in the Borden house in the weeks before the murder; it was a storm that had to break. Borden broke his usual habit of reticence to tell a business associate that he was having a lot of trouble at home at the moment.

What Lizzie did about her bloodstained dress after this first murder is rather a mystery. Presumably she took it off. At 10.45, Andrew Borden arrived home unexpectedly, no doubt puzzled by his wife's non-appearance at the bank. His daughter was on the point of leaving the house - to establish an alibi. The doors were locked - as usual - and Bridget had to let him in. Lizzie was heard to give a strange laugh as her father came in. She told her father that Mrs Borden had been called away to see a sick neighbour. Possibly Andrew Borden accepted this story; possibly he supposed Mrs Borden and Uncle John were now signing papers that he had already signed. At all events, he went into the sitting room and fell asleep. Bridget Sullivan testified that he was carrying "something like a book". Miss Lincoln is inclined to believe that this "something" wrapped in white paper was the deeds to the Swansea property, and the agreement to transfer it. Lizzie was later seen burning something in the kitchen stove.

What happened next? Miss Lincoln believes that Lizzie genuinely loved her father, but that seeing him asleep was tempted to spare him the horror of seeing his wife's body, and knowing that Lizzie was the killer. (For he *would* have known, just as he knew that Lizzie was the invisible thief of a year earlier.) Undoubtedly, he loved her, and he would cease to do so when the body was discovered. And so, according to Miss Lincoln, she regretfully raised the hatchet. . . .

I find this hard to accept. Andrew Borden was killed with nine blows, one of which sliced through his eye. Lizzie must have gone back upstairs to change her dress before the murder - unless she disposed of two bloodstained dresses - and then gone to get the hatchet from the basement. (It is true that she may have kept the dress in the basement too.) Two days before, her father had suffered from the same serious stomach complaint as her stepmother. She had made up her mind to kill him too. She did it less violently than in the case of her stepmother - nine blows instead of seventeen -but unflinchingly. Then she went to the barn and washed the hatchet, smashed off its bloodstained handle in a vice - which she burnt - and rubbed the blade in ashes. She removed the dress and folded it into a bundle. Or she may have simply hung it in her closet among her other dresses, as Miss Lincoln suggests, simply putting it inside another. By the time Bridget came in from cleaning the windows, and went to her room to lie down for a moment, Lizzie had changed and was ready to give the alarm.

There is some evidence for the epilepsy theory. Lizzie's mother suffered from severe migraines and sudden violent seizures of unmotivated rage. The evening before the murder, Lizzie called on a friend, Alice Russell, and said: "I'm afraid someone will do something. I don't know what but someone will do something." The heat wave had started the day before; she was experiencing the sense of brooding depression that Dostoievsky has described as preceding epileptic fits. "I feel depressed," she told Miss Russell, "I feel as if something was hanging over me that I can't shake off." Only that morning there had been a strange scene; her stepmother had approached a Doctor Bowen who lived opposite, and told him that her husband had received a letter threatening to poison him, and that they had been sick all the previous night. Doctor Bowen finally agreed to come to the house -and was met by a furious Andrew Borden, who told him to mind his own business and go away. And meanwhile the heat was tremendous, oppressive - it was one of the hottest days recorded in Fall River in living memory - and Lizzie's abdomen was aching in a way that indicated the approach of a menstrual period . . . She may well have foreboding.

No, forensic medicine would have made no difference to the Borden case. It might have established blood on the blade of the ash-coated hatchet, and drawn the net of circumstantial evidence a little tighter. And if someone had had Miss Lincoln's shrewdness, the forensic laboratories might have examined the *inside* of all Lizzie Borden's dresses for bloodstains that proved that a bloodstained dress had been hung up inside one of them.

For what Lizzie did with the bloodstained dress between the day of the murder -Thursday - and Sunday morning, when she burnt it, is the chief unsolved mystery of the case. Emma and Alice Russell walked into the kitchen, and interrupted Lizzie, who was holding the Bedford cord dress. "I'm going to burn this old thing," said Lizzie. "It's all covered up with paint." Alice and Emma must have exchanged a horrified glance.

It was their moment of decision. If they snatched it from Lizzie, or casually asked to look at it, it would undoubtedly send Lizzie to the scaffold. But what was the point? The Bordens were dead, and both Emma and her friend Alice knew about Lizzie's "queer spells". Alice merely said: "I wouldn't let anyone see you doing that if I were you," and then conveniently forgot the incident for four months. When Alice was questioned about Lizzie's dresses the next day, she went in to Lizzie and told her she really ought not to have burnt the dress. Lizzie simulated concern, and said: "Why did you let me do it?" Quite.

AMERICAN MYSTERIES

IT would be a mistake to assume that America has had no classic unsolved murders in the Agatha Christie tradition. In fact, the famous Elwell case has been described as one of the classic murder mysteries of the century.

Another remarkable unsolved mystery has found a place in most books on the "Jazz Age"; in fact, the strange death of Starr Faithfull has become one of the recurring symbols of the Prohibition era. Violence, as once remarked by the American senator H. Rap Brown, is as American as cherry pie and this comment is certainly exemplified by some of America's most famous murder mysteries, such as the Axeman of New Orleans (see page 36) and the Evangelista murders. But perhaps the nearest equivalent to London's Jack the Ripper murders is the strange case of Cleveland's "Mad Butcher", where the bodies were violently mutilated by decapitation.

THE MURDER OF JOSEPH ELWELL

JOSEPH Bowne Elwell was found dead by his housekeeper Marie Larsen at 8.25 on the morning of 11 June 1920. He was slumped in an expensive upholstered chair in his living room with a bullet hole in the centre of his forehead, about two inches above the bridge of his nose. Blood flowed down his face and stained an open letter on his knee. Where the bullet had left the back of his head it had blown a roughly cross-shaped hole measuring nine inches across. Much of the contents of his skull were sprayed against the wall behind or lying precariously on his shoulders. Despite the huge loss of brain tissue, Elwell was still alive; his eyelids flickered spasmically as Mrs Larsen watched.

Exactly what happened next, the details of how he reached hospital and died at approximately 10 a.m., is a matter of claim and counter-claim. The reason that many people have differing accounts, and indeed the reason that anyone bothered to find them out, was that Joseph Elwell was a very well-known man in 1920. He frequented the same expensive New York clubs as Scott and Zelda Fitzgerald, relishing being part of that dazzling social set. Some people believe that Fitzgerald's Jay Gatsby was in part based upon Joseph Elwell.

Yet he was born to relatively poor parents. From an early age Joseph showed an incredible skill in bridge, indeed in all card games where skill was an element. He joined the Brooklyn's Irving Republican Club in order to sharpen his talent for bridge with many different partners. Soon he gained such a reputation that he began giving bridge lessons to the daughters of wealthy families. He was not a bridge teacher as such; he managed to give an impression that each paid assignment he received was taken on "as a special favour". He married a plump and reasonably well-off young lady named Helen Hanford, gaining in the process a skilled business manager.

He was approached by a publisher to add to the then growing avalanche of bridge text books. His was easily the most successful. It was in fact written by Helen, using example hands and notes jotted down by the Great Man. Advanced manuals and commentaries upon tournament bridge hands followed, each selling very well.

Bridge was not Elwell's only pre-occupation at this time. Throughout his life Elwell's need to sleep with many women was enormous. Soon after his marriage he began failing to come home. The situation became more extreme when Helen had a child. Soon he began ringing if he *would be* home for dinner. Helen was not entirely the mistreated little woman however - from the outraged and jealous letters that Elwell would fire off occasionally to his wife's male acquaintances it would seem that she managed to adapt to the situation.

The Elwells' public affairs were in contrast rosy. Joseph became bridge tutor to the Vanderbilt family, renowned multi-millionaires. He was a close friend of Walter Lewisohn, the millionaire New York socialite. He even gave bridge lessons to King Edward VII.

His relationship with his wife inevitably grew distant however, with Joseph permanently on the look-out for any grounds for divorce and putting a great deal of his earnings into his parents' names in order to avoid having to pay it to Helen in alimony. When they eventually separated Helen got a meagre payment, and that only on the condition that she renounced any claim to money Joseph was making on real estate deals.

Indeed as Joseph's fortune increased so the range of his business dealings widened. He invested in race horses and Palm Beach luxury property, making money every time. He lost the investments he made in Tsarist Russia in 1917 with the Revolution, and responded by joining and sponsoring the American Protective League, a group whose espoused aim was to root out spies but who in fact just harassed anyone living in America who was not American.

His liaisons with many women continued, made more convenient by the fact that all the servants at his West Seventieth Street apartment lived off premises. All seemed to be ideal for Joseph Bowne Elwell until someone shot him between 7.25 and 8.35 a.m. that hot June morning.

It is possible to be this exact with respect to the time of the shooting due to a strange circumstance. At 6.30 that morning Jost Otten, Elwell's milkman, delivered a pint of milk and some cream. In order to place them against Elwell's door it was necessary to open the large double doors leading to the small hall of the apartment building. This presented no problem, as they were unlocked. Likewise the postman has no difficulty getting to Elwell's postbox on the internal door at 7.25 a.m. However, when Marie Larsen arrives at 8.35 a.m. the double doors are locked. It is clear that Elwell was alive to receive his post - one of the letters was open on his knee. This leads to the conclusion that the killer had a key. All the locks on the apartment had been changed recently due to a burglary attempt - the killer acquired a key soon before the murder. The likelihood seems to be that Elwell knew his killer.

Further evidence for this is presented by what he was *not* wearing when found. Nearly everyone who knew Elwell thought he had even white teeth and attractive shiny hair. In fact he was close to completely bald, and with only three teeth in his head. His expensive wig and tailored dentures remained upstairs in his bedroom. It is unlikely he would have entertained any of his lady friends without them.

The events of the preceding evening are reasonably clear. Elwell was out on the town with Walter Lewisohn and some friends, including Viola Kraus, Lewisohn's sister-in-law, allegedly one of Elwell's mistresses. These friends left Elwell to find his own way home when he declined a taxi ride with them. This was the last certain sighting of him before Marie Larsen found him the next morning.

The word "certain" is used advisedly, as Elwell's notoriety coupled with the detective fiction style of his death led to a hurricane of conflicting stories regarding virtually every aspect of the known facts. As mentioned above, even the manner of his transferral to hospital is hotly debated. The newspapers tried to implicate all Elwell's friends in turn through snide innuendo, while also speculating about Elwell's ties to bootlegging and spying. So many people were intrigued by the case, and so many people took it upon themselves to investigate it that it became clear that the killer's total evasion of justice can be attributed almost entirely to too much speculation and almost no real investigation.

To present the facts without a gloss of idle rumination is thus made quite difficult. The objective details of the crime scene are among the few facts undisputed . . .

In the room where Elwell was discovered two cigarette butts were found. One of them was on the table next to Elwell's chair - a cigarette made especially to order. It had been left to bum completely. It had been lit at the wrong end i.e. the end with the manufacturers logo impressed into the paper. The other cigarette was of an over-the-counter variety. The police felt this to be such a vital clue that they refused to divulge the actual make. This cigarette had been extinguished on the mantelpiece and still showed signs of saliva on the end when Marie Larsen discovered it. For the saliva to remain partially unevaporated in the 70°F heat meant that the smoker must have drooled a great deal. In his book *The Slaying of Joseph Bowne Elwell* Jonathan Goodman asserts that the second butt was in fact left by an investigating officer, explaining their reticence to elucidate on its origins.

Upstairs the police found a great deal of lingerie in the spare bedroom. Although the newspapers got a lot of mileage out of this discovery it seems in retrospect to be quite unimportant.

The autopsy showed that the bullet entered Elwell's forehead at an upwards angle - perhaps meaning that it was fired from the hip. Another, more melodramatic interpretation of this fact has Elwell's head bent slightly back to look into the eyes of his killer. Around the entrance wound were many small gunpowder marks - as distinct from gunpowder burns. This meant that the shot must have been fired from between three feet and five inches from Elwell's head. Any closer and Elwell's face would have been burnt by powder from the gun's barrel. This fact tends to make suicide unlikely, as few suicides shoot themselves at a distance, thus risking a painful but not fatal winging shot. The lack of the weapon tends to further invalidate suicide as an explanation.

Those are the main details - Elwell was shot within the time space of one cigarette from a point lower than his seated head and from less than three feet away. Inevitably however these facts are not enough, the imagination demands some violent and passionate motive. Passion is of course the most proffered explanation, a wronged woman, or a brother or father. Some theories go further - linking this possible motive to possible murderers. For instance Viola Kraus, Walter Lewisohn's sister-in-law and supposed lover of Elwell, met her divorced husband the night before the murders. In fact, the divorce had only just gone through that day. Viola was dancing with Elwell. Did her husband see red and kill Elwell the next morning?

Another theory has Viola herself as killer. Elwell had been belatedly discussing divorce with Helen in the weeks leading up to his death. Did Viola take this as a tacit sign that he wished to marry her when their joint divorces cleared? Did she, when she found he simply wanted more freedom to see many other women, kill him in a fit of jilted rage?

Jonathan Goodman, in *The Slaying of Joseph Bowne Elwell*, puts forward a masterfully imagined theory. Based upon the fact that Walter Lewisohn went mad two years after Elwell's killing, some say for love of a dancer Leonora Hughes, Goodman argues that Lewisohn saw Elwell's (alleged) rejection of Viola as positive proof that he was after Ms Hughes. In order to avoid this situation Lewisohn has Elwell killed by a friend - the owner of the building that Elwell leased. This neatly explains the key problem as the owner would have up-to-date keys for his own building. The theory is supported by the fact that the alleged killer received a sinecure in Lewisohn's establishment after the killing.

Most intriguing of all however is a small point that Goodman raises merely in passing. Marie Larsen was a strict Swedish Lutheran. In her opinion all suicides went to hell. Is it not possible that she removed the gun from the scene in order to save Elwell's loved ones the terrible conclusion that Joseph was in the fire for eternity?

Admittedly all these theories are at best unprovable. It is only natural that many explanations have been presented for a set of circumstances that are, at the end of the day, insoluble.

THE STARR FAITHFULL CASE

IN the early morning sunshine of 8 June 1931, a beachcomber strolling along the sands at Long Beach, on the south shore of Long Island, found the body of a pretty girl. He dragged it clear of the tideline and summoned the police. They quickly identified the girl as Starr Faithfull, the twenty-five-year-old stepdaughter of Stanley Faithfull, a retired manufacturing chemist of Greenwich Village. He had reported Starr missing two days earlier.

An autopsy revealed that the girl had died by drowning about forty-eight hours earlier, and had eaten a large meal not long before she died. There was no alcohol in her system, but traces of the drug veronal. She was clad only in an expensive silk dress, and traces of sand in her lungs indicated that she had been alive as she lay in the water. There were fingertip-shaped bruises on her upper arms, and indications of rape. All this suggested that Starr had been murdered by whoever had shaken her by the arms: that he had raped her - perhaps on the beach - and then held her head under the water. On the other hand, she may have consented to intercourse in a drugged trance, then have collapsed by the edge of the sea and drowned as the tide came in.

Starr was undoubtedly beautiful, and the fact that she was an heiress and the product of a Boston finishing school led the press to devote much breathless attention to the case. As reporters looked into her background, it became still more interesting. Far from being a prim young lady who had had the misfortune to be assaulted, it transpired that Starr had been sexually experienced for more than half of her brief life. At the age of eleven, it seemed, she had been seduced by a middle-aged Boston business man who was the father of schoolfriends; he had drugged her with ether and raped her. This information came from her stepfather, Stanley Faithfull, whom Starr's mother had married some ten years earlier. This relationship had continued down the years.

It also seemed that Starr had been feverishly in love with an English ship's surgeon, Dr George Jameson-Carr, who did not return her feelings. On 29 May, a week before her death, Starr had been attempting to force her drunken attentions on Dr Jameson-Carr, aboard the *Franconia.* He had persuaded her to leave, but she had hidden among the passengers; when found later, she had to be transferred to a tug and taken ashore.

It emerged that Starr had fairly serious mental problems, and had been under psychiatric treatment for years. She was not normally a heavy drinker, but was inclined to get drunk at parties. She had been on two trips to England, where she had mixed with the "bright young things", and she longed to return to Europe; unfortunately, her stepfather was not wealthy - although comfortably-off - and there was no prospect of another trip in the immediate future. So Starr spent a great deal of time hanging around the New York docks, often going aboard liners for farewell parties - which is how she became acquainted with Dr Jameson-Carr. To try to prevent her drinking bootleg gin made of raw alcohol, her stepfather used to pack her a flask of Martini.

Was it possible that Starr had gone aboard a liner and then jumped over the side when it was off Long Island? Otherwise, it was difficult to explain what she was doing on Long Island, twenty miles or so from home. Or had she been pushed overboard? If so, was it by the rapist?

A second autopsy dampened these speculations when the doctor who performed it announced that, in his opinion, she had not been raped, but had submitted voluntarily to sexual intercourse. The missing underclothes certainly suggested that she had been naked at some point.

Starr's diaries increased the lurid speculation, for they revealed that she had had many lovers, one of whom was someone called A.J.P. She seemed to be fond of him but also afraid of him. One entry read: "Spent night A.J.P. Providence. Oh Horror, Horror, Horror!!!" The indications were that, for all her craving for affection, Starr was not overly fond of the physical side of sex. This seemed to be confirmed by a new item of scandal unearthed by the investigators. A year before her death, a policeman had burst into a room of a New York hotel where a girl had been screaming. He found Starr naked and bruised, while a furious young man, dressed only in his undershirt, was glaring at her. She was drunk, and there was half a bottle of gin on the table. The man identified himself as an ex-soldier named Joseph Collins, produced his discharge papers, and was allowed to go. Starr, who was very drunk, was taken to the Bellevue Hospital suffering from "acute alcoholism" and "contusions to face, jaw and upper lip". The implication seemed to be that she had taken Collins to the room for sex, then changed her mind, and the frustrated man had attacked her.

The first "Locked Room Mystery" was Poe's "Murder in the Rue Morgue". The first locked room novel seems to have been John Ratcliffe's Hem Sahib. This inspired a real murder. In 1881, the wife and five children of a Berlin carter named Fritz Conrad were found hanging from hooks in a locked room. It looked as if Frau Conrad, depressed by poverty, had killed her children and committed suicide. Police Commissioner Hollman was suspicious, and when he found out that Conrad was infatuated with a young girl student, he searched the apartment for love letters. He found none, but came upon a copy of Nena Sahib and read Ratcliffe's account of a "perfect murder", in which the killer drilled a tiny hole in the door, passed a thread through it, and used this to draw the bolt after the murder; he then sealed up the hole with wax. Hollman examined Conrad's door, and found a similar hole, filled in with sealing wax, to which threads of horsehair still adhered. Confronted with this evidence, Conrad confessed to murdering his wife and children, and was sentenced to death.

Her mental problems obviously stemmed from her early seduction by the Boston business man. Reporters soon unearthed the fact that, as a child, Starr and her sister Tucker had played with the children of Andrew J. Peters, former Congressman and Mayor of Boston, who was a distant relative of Mrs Faithfull. This could obviously be the "A.J.P." of her diary. If Peters *was* her seducer, he had certainly paid for it, for the investigation revealed that Mrs Faithfull had signed a document aquitting someone of all responsibility for damage done to Starr, in exchange for a large sum of money, probably $80,000. (Stanley Faithfull alleged it was $20,000, but his lawyer indicated that the sum was much greater.)

The story was kept alive by a new sensation at the crematorium. The cremation of the body was interrupted by officials from the District Attorney's office, who announced that it could not go ahead until there was a third inquest. After this inquest, District Attorney Elvin Edwards announced that he knew the identity of the two men who killed Starr Faithfull by holding her head underwater, and that he would be making an arrest within thirty-six hours. When the arrest failed to materialize, he acknowledged that "the lead was false".

At this point, Dr Jameson-Carr returned from Europe and created another sensation by revealing that, in the days between being thrown off the *Franconia* and her death, Starr had written him three letters, and these made it abundantly clear that she had intended to commit suicide. The first declared that she meant to "end my worthless, disorderly bore of an existence - before I ruin anyone else's life as well." "I take dope to forget, and drink to try and like people." The third letter, posted shortly before she left home for the last time, said that she intended to be successful this time (it emerged that she had made an earlier suicide attempt in London), and described how she intended to eat a large final meal, with plenty of alcohol (she was always worried about gaining weight), then kill herself. "I am going to enjoy my last cigarettes. I won't worry because men flirt with me in the streets - I shall encourage them - I don't care who they are. I'm afraid I've always been a rotten 'sleeper'; it's the preliminaries that count with me."

That seemed to settle the matter; Starr *must* have committed suicide. But why at Long Beach? Why wearing only a dress? Why by lying down in the water - as the sand in her lungs suggested - rather than jumping off a bridge or a quay?

In 1948, Morris Markey, a journalist who had worked on the case and become a friend of the Faithfulls, unveiled his own theory on the case. Starr, he believed, *had* left home determined to commit suicide, and had eaten her final meal as planned, although without much alcohol. Then she had picked up a man and gone to the beach with him. As on the previous occasion with the ex-soldier, she had declined sexual intercourse at the last minute, and the man had handled her roughly and raped her. Then, afraid of going to jail, he had drowned her, and walked away through the shallows to avoid leaving footprints.

The theory seems far-fetched - that she was murdered when she set out to commit suicide - yet it covers all the facts, and explains the puzzle of the male semen inside her.

Tucker Faithfull, Starr's chain-smoking younger sister, became a celebrity after Starr's death, with offers of nightclub engagements and movie parts. She loved the limelight, but two weeks after her sister's death, startled reporters with a sudden outburst: "I'm not sorry she's dead. Everybody's happier. She made life miserable." The weekend Starr died, Tucker was spending a dirty weekend with a lover named Jones; she had pawned her fake leopardskin coat to pay her train fare, and had to borrow $5 to get home when Jones declined to give it to her. She married a lawyer in 1937.

A modern criminologist might suggest another solution: that Starr had taken a large dose of veronal and lay down on the beach to wait for the tide to come in; some passing beachcomber had found her - either before or after death - and had intercourse with her. The bruises on her arms could have been caused as her body was pounded by waves - a body will bruise for some time after death. If this theory is correct, then Starr committed suicide as she intended.

On the whole, these theories are probably as close as anyone will ever come to solving the mystery of the death of Starr Faithfull.

THE EVANGELISTA MURDERS

ON the morning of 3 July 1929 Vincent Elias, a dealer in real estate, called at the house of Benjamino Evangelista. Evangelista, or Benny Evangelist as he preferred to be known, was a repair and building contractor who lived in one of the poorer districts of Detroit. Elias arrived at Evangelista's three-storey house at about 10.30, and finding that his knocking brought no reply he decided to enter and investigate. Seeing that the foyer was empty Elias opened the door of Evangelista's office and walked into a scene that resembled an abattoir. Evangelista was slumped in his chair, surrounded and covered with blood. On the floor next to his body was his head, cleanly removed. The visitor fled to summon the police.

Soon patrolmen Costage and Lawrence arrived at the scene, and they continued the grisly investigation. Among the gore in Evangelista's office were two unused swords, a false beard and wig, and a notched staff. Also, on the floor near the severed head were photographs of a child in a coffin. Bloody footprints led to the stairs.

In the upstairs bedroom the shocked patrolmen found Evangelista's wife and youngest child, a baby. The mother had been almost beheaded, and her arm nearly severed, while the baby had been killed by multiple head wounds. In the adjoining room were the elder children's beds, two daughters of four and six, both decapitated, with some attempt to detach the arm of one of them. Finally the eldest daughter, an eight-year-old, was lying in the doorway to the landing, also hacked to death. Unlike Evangelista, who was fully clothed, the upstairs victims were in their night attire. Only the eldest daughter seemed to have had time to react to the murderer, having put on her bathrobe and made for her mother's bedroom.

Another bloody footprint descended the stairs, and a fingerprint of a left thumb, also in blood, was left on the latch of the outer door. What other evidence was left pointing to the identity of the killer will never be known, as the Detroit police failed to properly document or preserve any other physical evidence. Within hours the Evangelista home was packed with police and journalists, attracted not only by the gruesome and terrible aspect of the murders, but also by what the police discovered in the Evangelista cellar.

"Benny Evangelist", apart from being a building contractor, was a local faith healer. People paid high prices to receive cures from the "wise man". Despite this fundamentally unchristian sideline, the whole Evangelista family regularly attended the local Catholic church and seemed at least averagely devout. Both the police and the local people were thus surprised to find that Benny seemed to be the head of a pagan cult. His cellar was decorated like a temple, with the walls and ceiling draped with green cloth and an altar at one end. Above the altar were hung models of hellish demons, made from papier mache with dog hair glued onto them. An outward-facing sign in the basement window read "The Great Celestial Planet Exhibition". Among the papers removed by the police from Evangelista's office was a "Bible" of this cult tided *"The Oldest History of the World, Discovered By Occult Science In Detroit, Michigan"*. It was to run to four volumes, but only the first volume seems to have reached print. The book was a long and bloody story of prehistoric humanity, not unlike the Old Testament in style. There were many episodes of occult magic and royal intrigue. The principal character of the *History* is the Prophet Meil. Possibly Evangelista identified himself with Meil, as the staff found in his office was very similar to the one that the Prophet is described as carrying. The cultists who believed the details of the *History* called themselves The Great Union Federation of America.

The preface describes how the book came to be written: that it took exactly twenty years to write, from 2 February 1906 to 2 February 1926, and that the story came to the author in visions every night between midnight and 3 a.m. It was during this period, the police were later to establish, that the murders took place.

Also found among Evangelista's belongings were many items of female underwear, each labeled with the owner's name. Carried away, perhaps, by the occult atmosphere of the investigation, the police concluded that they were used for psychometry, the art of locating people through psychic impressions gained from their belongings.

Although their crime-scene investigations had been worse than useless, the Detroit police tried hard to find witnesses or dig up connections. The investigation reached the conclusion that the last person to see Evangelista alive was a local called Umberto Tecchio. Together with a friend, Tecchio had visited Evangelista at his house the evening before the murder to deliver the final payment on a house. However there was no mention of a completed sale in any of Evangelista's papers. Suspecting that Tecchio had been cheated by Evangelista and had wreaked bloody revenge, the police searched Tecchio's rooming house. In the barn below the house police found a dull axe, a sharp banana knife and a newly cleaned pair of shoes.

This evidence seemed hopeful, so the police next questioned Tecchio's room mate Angelo Depoli. He was uncommunicative and surly to such an extent that the police bad-temperedly set immigration on him. As it turned out Depoli was an illegal immigrant, and was deported. With him went any hope of establishing Tecchio's movements on the night of the murder.

Umberto Tecchio was certainly a violent man. His first wife had divorced him for knifing her brother to death. When she gained possession of the house and lived there with her new husband, Tecchio threatened to blow them up. Several days later the new husband was shot dead on the steps of his house. The police, apparently for reasons of leniency, ruled it a suicide. Also, just after the murders, police received a tip that a newspaper boy had seen Tecchio standing on the porch of Evangelista's house smoking a cigarette at 5 a.m. on the morning after the murders. Officers sent to find the newspaper boy were told he was dead.

There were other possibilities for violence revealed by police researching Evangelista's background. He had moved from Naples to live with his brother in Pennsylvania. His brother had eventually thrown him out of the house for his occult interests. Before moving to Michigan, Evangelista had lived in York, Pennsylvania, an area renowned for its occult sub-community. While living there he was friendly with Aurelius Angelino, a chief cultist, who was put in a mental asylum for killing two of his family and wounding the others with an axe in an attempt to dispose of them all. Police seemed so taken with this connection that they exhumed Evangelista in order to check his fingerprints. Exactly how he could have beheaded himself after killing his family was never fully explained by the police.

In the absence of any meaningful connections with York cultists, police researched the other possible source of suspects:

Evangelista's reputed connection with the Black Hand, an extortion organization. Local sources reported that Evangelista delivered threats for the Black Hand. A retribution killing had taken place across the street from Evangelista's house early in 1926. At the time the police had known who the gunman was, but despairing of ever convicting him, they allowed him to flee to avoid further violence. The gunman's name was Louis Evangelist. Feeling that Evangelista may have had some connection with this killing police tracked down Evangelist to a railroad track-laying gang near Pittsburgh, but he seemed to know nothing of the subsequent murders.

Evangelista *had* received a death threat from the Black Hand; it was found among his papers dated roughly a year before the killings. There was also an unposted letter by Evangelista saying that a job had been bungled before and that a certain unnamed threat might have to be removed. Intriguing though these things are they provide no real evidence or even solid theory.

The murder investigation foundered, and remained unsolved on the Detroit police files. However information about the murders kept surfacing, a piece at a time.

A Mrs Emmanuel Maiccucci came forward to say that the Evangelistas had owned two machetes that had been missing from the scene. Mrs Maiccucci was the wife of Umberto Tecchio who had divorced him for the murder of her brother. She said that while she had been married to Tecchio he had taken her to Evangelista to cure an illness. She had noticed the machetes during her cure.

A young man came forward to say that he had been the newspaper boy who had seen Tecchio on the Evangelistas' porch. He told police that after he had realized what had gone on that night he had avoided the house for years, never passing it and too afraid to come forward.

Tecchio's fellow guests at the rooming house said that they were not sure whether Tecchio had come home at all on the night of the murders.

The reason for the sudden increase in information was simple: Tecchio had died. Whatever conclusions the police came to it was clear that many people in the local neighbourhood had been too afraid of Tecchio to reveal all that they knew. The existence of the newspaper boy had been hidden by the whole community. Some local people must have thought that Tecchio was the murderer.

However, the murders remain unsolved. There is no doubt that this has a lot to do with the incredible incompetence of the Detroit police. They deported their most valuable witness and when they later came to test the fingerprint on the latch against Tecchio's prints many policemen came to the conclusion that the mark had been made by an investigating officer.

The theories about the motive and murderer are varied and in some cases quite plausible. The photographs of the child in a coffin suggest to some people that Evangelista had failed to cure someone and that, in pagan tradition, he was put to death for the death of his patient. Another theory points out that Aurelius Angelino, the York cultist, had escaped from his asylum at the time of the murders, and that he, like the person who left the thumbprint on the latch, was left-handed. The main police theories, concerning the Black Hand and Umberto Tecchio, are to some degree tenable, but really do not justify such cold-blooded and wholesale violence.

In the end the cult connections are the most gripping if not the most plausible source of explanations. Was Evangelista's cult connected to a more widespread network of believers? The title "The Great Union Federation of America" tends to suggest it was. Did Evangelista somehow compromise or annoy a nationwide group of cultists and was ritualistically punished for it? It seems that the facts are destined to remain unknown.

THE CLEVELAND TORSO KILLER

ON a warm September afternoon in 1935, two boys on their way home from school walked along a dusty, sooty gully called Kingsbury Run, in the heart of Cleveland, Ohio. On a weed-covered slope known as Jackass Hill, one challenged the other to a race, and they hurtled sixty feet down the slope to the bottom. Sixteen-year-old James Wagner was the winner, and as he halted, panting, he noticed something white in the bushes a few yards away. A closer look revealed that it was a naked body, and that it was headless.

The police who arrived soon after found the body of a young white male clad only in black socks; the genitals had also been removed. It lay on its back, with the legs stretched out and the arms placed neatly by the sides, as if laid out for a funeral. Thirty feet away, the policemen found another body, lying in the same position; it was of an older man, and had also been decapitated and emasculated.

Hair sticking out of the ground revealed one of the heads a few yards away, and the second was found nearby. The genitals were also found lying nearby, as if thrown away by the killer.

One curious feature of the case was that there was no blood on the ground or on the bodies, which were quite clean. It looked as if they had been killed and beheaded elsewhere, then carefully washed when they had ceased to bleed.

Medical examination made the case more baffling than ever. The older corpse was badly decomposed, and the skin discoloured; the pathologists discovered that this was due to some chemical substance, as if the killer had tried to preserve the body. The older victim had been dead about two weeks. The younger man had only been dead three days. His fingerprints enabled the police to identify him as twenty-eight-year-old Edward Andrassy, who had a minor police record for carrying concealed weapons. He lived near Kingsbury Run and had a reputation as a drunken brawler.

But the most chilling discovery was that Andrassy had been killed by decapitation. Rope marks on his wrists revealed that he had been tied and had struggled violently. The killer had apparently cut off his head with a knife. The skill with which the operation had been performed suggested a butcher - or possibly a surgeon.

It proved impossible to identify the older man. But the identification of Andrassy led the police to hope that it should not be too difficult to trace his killer. He had spent his nights gambling and drinking in a slum part of town and was known as a pimp. But further investigation also revealed that he had male lovers. Lead after lead looked marvellously promising. The husband of a married woman with whom he had had an affair had sworn to kill him. But the man was able to prove his innocence. So were various shady characters who might have borne a grudge. Lengthy police investigation led to a dead end - as it did in another ten cases of the killer who became known as "the Mad Butcher of Kingsbury Run".

Four months later, on a raw January Sunday, the howling of a dog finally led a black woman resident of East Twentieth Street - not far from Kingsbury Run - to go and investigate. She found the chained animal trying to get at a basket "ear a factory wall. Minutes later, she told a neighbour that the basket contained "hams". But the neighbour soon recognized the "hams" as parts of a human arm. A burlap bag proved to contain the lower half of a female torso. The head was missing, as were the left arm and lower parts of both legs. But fingerprints again enabled the police to trace the victim, who had a record for soliciting. She proved to be a forty-one-year-old prostitute named Florence Polillo, a squat, double-chinned woman who was well known in the bars of the neighbourhood.

Again, there were plenty of leads, and again, all of them petered out. Two weeks later, the left arm and lower legs were found in a vacant lot. The head was never recovered.

The murder of Flo Polillo raised an unwelcome question. The first two murders had convinced the police that they were looking for a homosexual sadist; this latest crime made it look as if this killer was quite simply a sadist - like Peter Kurten, the Dusseldorf killer, executed in 1931; he had killed men, women and children indifferently, and he was not remotely homosexual. And now the pathologist recalled that, a year before the first double murder, the torso of an unknown woman had been found on the edge of Lake Erie. It began to look as if the Mad Butcher was quite simply a sadist.

At least the Cleveland public felt they had one thing in their favour. Since the double killing, the famous Eliot Ness had been appointed Cleveland's Director of Public Safety. Ness and his "Untouchables" had cleared up Chicago's Prohibition rackets, then, in 1934, Ness had moved to Cleveland to fight its gangsters. With Ness in charge, the Head Hunter of

Kingsbury Run - another press sobriquet - would find himself becoming the hunted.

But it was soon clear to Ness that hunting a sadistic pervert is nothing like hunting professional gangsters. The killer struck at random, and unless he was careless enough to leave behind a clue - like a fingerprint - then the only hope of catching him was in the act. And Ness soon became convinced that the Mad Butcher took great pleasure in feeling that he was several steps ahead of the police.

The Head Hunter waited until the summer before killing again, then lived up to his name by leaving the head of a young man, wrapped in a pair of trousers, under a bridge in Kingsbury Run; again, two boys found it on 22 June 1936. The body was found a quarter of a mile away, and it was obvious from the blood that he had died where he lay. And medical evidence showed that he had died from decapitation - it was not clear how the killer had prevented him from struggling while he did it. The victim was about twenty-five, and heavily tattooed. His fingerprints were not in police files. Three weeks later, a young female hiker discovered another decapitated body in a gully; the head lay nearby. The decomposition made it clear that this man had been killed before the previously-discovered victim.

The last "Butchery" of 1936 was of another man of about thirty, found in Kingsbury Run; the body had been amputated in two, and emasculated. A hat found nearby led to a partial identification: a housewife recalled giving it to a young tramp. Not far away there was a "hobo camp" where down-and-outs slept; this was obviously where the Butcher had found his latest victim.

The fact that Cleveland had been the scene of a Republican Convention and was now the site of a "Great Expo", led to even more frantic police activity and much press criticism. The murders were reported all over the world and, in Nazi Germany and Fascist Italy, were cited as proof of the decadence of the New World.

As month after month went by with no further grisly discoveries, Clevelanders hoped they had heard the last of the Mad Butcher. But in February 1937, that hope was dashed when the killer left the body of a young woman in a chopped-up pile on the shores of Lake Erie. She was never identified. The eighth victim, a young negress, *was* identified from her teeth as Mrs Rose Wallace, forty; only the skeleton remained, and it looked as if she may have been killed in the previous year.

Victim No. nine was male and had been dismembered; when he was fished out of the river, the head was missing, and was never found. This time the killer had gone even further in his mutilations - like Jack the Ripper. It was impossible to identify the victim. Two men seen in a boat were thought to be the Butcher with an accomplice, but this suggestion that there might be two Butchers led nowhere.

The Butcher now seems to have taken a rest until nine months later. Then the lower part of a leg was pulled out of the river. Three weeks later, two burlap bags in the river proved to contain more body-fragments, which enabled the pathologist to announce that the victim was female, a brunette of about twenty-five. She was never identified.

The killer was to strike twice more. More than a year after the last discovery, in August 1938, the dismembered torso of a woman was found on a dump on the lakefront, and a search of the area revealed the bones of a second victim, a male. A quilt in which the remains of this twelfth victim were wrapped was identified as having been given to a junk man. Neither body could be identified.

One thing was now obvious: the Butcher was selecting his victims from vagrants and down-and-outs. Ness decided to take the only kind of action that seemed left to him: two days after the last find, police raided the "shantytown" near Kingsbury Run, arrested hundreds of vagrants, and burned it down. Whether or not by coincidence, the murders now ceased.

The suspects. Two of the most efficient of the manhunters, Detectives Merylo and Zalewski, had spent a great deal of time searching for the killer's "laboratory". At one point they thought they had found it - but, like all leads, this one faded away.

Next the investigators discovered that Flo Polillo and Rose Wallace - Victim No. eight - had frequented the same saloon, and that Andrassy - No. two - had been a "regular" there too. They also learned of a middle-aged man called Frank who carried knives and threatened people with them when drunk. When they learned that this man - Frank Dolezal - had also been living with Flo Polillo, they felt they had finally identified the killer. Dolezal was arrested, and police discovered a brown substance like dried blood in the cracks of his bathroom floor. Knives with dried bloodstains on them provided further incriminating evidence. Under intensive questioning, Dolezal - a bleary-eyed, unkempt man - confessed to the murder of Flo Polillo. Newspapers announced the capture of the Butcher. Then things began to go wrong. The "dried blood" in the bathroom proved not to be blood after all. Dolezal's "confession" proved to be full of errors about the corpse and method of disposal. And when, in August 1939, Dolezal hanged himself in jail, the autopsy revealed that he had two cracked ribs, and suggested that his confession had been obtained by force.

Yet Ness himself claimed that he knew the solution to the murders. He reasoned that the killer was a man who had a house of his own in which to dismember the bodies, and a car in which to transport them. So he was not a down-and-out. The skill of the mutilations suggested medical training. The fact that some of the victims had been strong men suggested that the Butcher had to be big and powerful - a conclusion supported by a size twelve footprint near one of the bodies.

Ness set three of his top agents, Virginia Allen, Barney Davis and Jim Manski, to make enquiries among the upper levels of Cleveland society. Virginia was a sophisticated girl with contacts among Cleveland socialites. And it was she who learned about a man who sounded like the ideal suspect. Ness was to call him "Gaylord Sundheim" - a big man from a well-to-do family, who had a history of psychiatric problems. He had also studied medicine. When the three "Untouchables" called on him, he leered sarcastically at Virginia and closed the door in their faces. Ness invited him - pressingly - to lunch, and he came under protest. When Ness finally told him he suspected him of being the Butcher - hoping that shock tactics might trigger a confession - "Sundheim" sneered: "Prove it".

Soon after this, "Sundheim" had himself committed to a mental institution. Ness knew *he* was now "untouchable", for even if Ness could prove his guilt, he could plead insanity.

During the next two years Ness received a series of jeering postcards, some signed "Your paranoid nemesis". They ceased abruptly when "Sundheim" died in the mental institution.

Was "Sundheim" the Butcher? Probably. But not certainly. In Pittsburgh in 1940, three decapitated bodies were found in old boxcars (railway coaches). Members of Ness's team went to investigate, but no clue to the treble murder was ever discovered. The case remains unsolved.

WHO KILLED KENNEDY?

AT 12.30 p.m. on 2 November 1963, President John F. Kennedy was travelling through Dallas, Texas, in the back of an open limousine, with his wife beside him and Governor John B. Connally and Connally's wife in front of them. As the motorcade passed the Texas School Book Depository in Dealey Plaza, shots rang out and the President clutched his neck with both hands and slumped in his seat. A second bullet caused his head to "explode". Connally was also struck by a bullet. Jackie Kennedy cried: "They've killed my husband... I have his brains in my hand!"

The Secret Service ordered the car to drive at top speed to the Parkland Memorial Hospital. But despite all efforts to save him, the President died shortly afterwards. A bullet that later became known as Exhibit 399 was found on the stretcher.

The police had pinpointed the Book Depository as the source of the shots. Near a window on the sixth floor, they found three empty cartridge cases. A few minutes after the shooting, a motorcycle policeman was talking to the superintendent of the building when a man named Lee Harvey Oswald walked out of the elevator on the second floor. The policeman asked the superintendent: "Do you know this man?", and the superintendent said: "Yes, he works here." Oswald was allowed to walk out of the building.

Half an hour or so after the assassination, Oswald was walking down the street when police officer J. D. Tippit, driving a patrol car, called him over. Oswald spoke to him calmly then began to walk away. Tippit jumped from the car and ran after him; Oswald turned, pulled out a revolver, and shot Tippit dead, moving close to him to fire the final shot.

An hour later a ticket seller at the Texas Theater saw Oswald walk in without buying a ticket; she called the police. As they approached Oswald he pointed his gun and pulled the trigger; it misfired. Moments later he was in custody. Soon after, news bulletins announced the arrest of a suspect.

Oswald was an ex-marine who had defected to the USSR and married a Russian girl. Refused a residence permit he had returned to the USA in June 1962. In March 1963 he had purchased a rifle with a telescopic sight from a mail order firm - his original intention was to assassinate a retired army general. He had moved to Dallas after further unsuccessful attempts to emigrate to Russia and Cuba, and had found a job in the Book Depository. It seems that when he learned from newspaper reports that the President would be visiting Dallas, and saw that the route passed below the Book Depository, he made plans to kill Kennedy.

The rifle with the telescopic sight was found on the sixth floor of the Book Depository, and one of Oswald's palm prints was found on it. He denied killing the President and Officer Tippit, and answered questions "arrogantly".

At 11.20 on Saturday, 24 November 1963, Oswald was being taken from the Dallas Police Headquarters to a car waiting outside, and crowds of photographers - including television crews - were taking pictures, when a man stepped forward, jammed a revolver against Oswald's chest, and pulled the trigger. The man was grabbed by a policeman as Oswald collapsed. Newsmen yelled to ask his name, and the man shouted back: "I'm Jack Ruby - you know me."

Oswald was rushed to Parkland Hospital and operated on by the same surgeon who had tried to save Kennedy's life. But by 1.07 he was pronounced dead.

Ruby was a Dallas nightclub owner who had many friends in the police force - as well as gangland connections. Witnesses reported that he had been behaving oddly since Kennedy's assassination, and his charlady mentioned that he had been talking to himself on the morning he killed Oswald. Tried for murder in 1964, Ruby was sentenced to death, but died of cancer in 1967, before the sentence could be carried out.

To large numbers of Americans, it seemed too convenient that Kennedy's assassin had been killed within two days, and that Oswald's killer had had so little trouble in shooting him. There was soon talk of conspiracy. This began when a film taken by a local business man, Abraham Zapruder, was examined frame by frame, and seemed to show that the first shot caused Kennedy's head to jerk *backwards* - although the Book Depository was behind him. This led to the belief that there was a second gunman *ahead* of the President, on a grassy knoll, and that Oswald had, in fact, shot Kennedy, but had probably missed. (In the Marine Corps, Oswald's appalling marksmanship had been a joke.) The Zapruder film seemed to indicate that at least four shots, not three, had been fired. Examination of the wounds suggested that Connally had been hit by the same bullet that passed through Kennedy's neck.

A woman named Julia Mercer testified that she was driving through Dealey Plaza an hour and a half before the assassination when she saw a green truck parked with two tyres on the kerb. A man she later identified as Oswald got out with a rifle and went towards the grassy knoll. She looked back at the driver, and later identified him as Jack Ruby.

Another popular conspiracy theory was that Vice President Lyndon Johnson - who had won Texas for the Democrats by a narrow majority - had planned the assassination in order to become president. A libellous play called *Macbird,* based on this theory, had a long run on Broadway.

FBI Director J. Edgar Hoover was another candidate for the role of paymaster of the assassin. He disliked Kennedy, and disliked his brother Robert - the Attorney General - even more. Robert Kennedy was speaking of an all-out war on the Mafia with his own Justice Department, challenging Hoover's long-established supremacy.

Another conspiracy theory declared that the CIA was responsible - Kennedy's own intelligence agency - because there was a feeling of anger about the incompetence of the Bay of Pigs invasion of Cuba. Many theories include heavy involvement with Cuban anti-Castro exiles - Oswald himself had attempted to join an anti-Castro group in Miami a few months before the assassination. One view holds that he was trying to infiltrate the group for his Communist masters, another that he joined the assassination conspiracy on behalf of Cuban exiles who felt betrayed by Kennedy.

One of the members of an anti-Castro group was an ultra-conservative named David Ferrie, a completely hairless character (he suffered from a disease called alopecia) who glued bits of orange hair to his head and eyebrows. Ferrie called himself "Dr" as well as "Bishop", and had lost his job as an airline pilot because of his sexual preference for boys.

His hatred of Kennedy was almost pathological. He had been a boyhood friend of Oswald, and was seen with him shortly before the assassination.

In the mid-1960s, the New Orleans District Attorney Jim Garrison alleged that Ferrie, Oswald and a business man called Clay Shaw had been behind the assassination. But a few days after Garrison announced his findings to the press, Ferrie's naked body was found in his apartment, together with two suicide notes. Cause of death was listed as a brain haemorrhage, possibly brought on by an unknown poison. The same day, Ferrie's close anti-Castro associate Eladio del Valle was murdered in Miami, shot through the heart - his killer was never found. The only man to go on trial was Clay Shaw, but the evidence against him was negligible, and he was found not guilty.

Perhaps more convincing than any of these theories is the argument that Kennedy was murdered by the Mafia, on whom he - via his brother Robert - had declared war. In the 1950s, Robert Kennedy had served on a senate committee whose aim was to expose Mafia involvement with the Teamsters' Union, headed by Jimmy Hoffa. Kennedy's father Joe Kennedy is alleged to have been in partnership with gangster Frank Costello in the bootleg era. Sam Giancana, the Chicago mob boss, was actually sharing a bedfellow, Judith Exner, with the

President, who was a notorious womanizer. It was alleged that Kennedy was supplied with ladyfriends by Frank Sinatra, a friend of Giancana and other Mafia figures, and that Kennedy's affair with Marilyn Monroe originated in his Sinatra connection. The aim of Giancana may have been to exert pressure on the Kennedy brothers to soften their stance towards the mob. Giancana also believed that he was basically responsible for Kennedy's election as President, since he had "delivered" a vital Chicago vote in the 1960 election - a vote without which Kennedy's bid for the presidency would have been stillborn. Carlos Marcello, a New Orleans Mafia boss who was also being hounded by Robert Kennedy, is reported to have said that Robert Kennedy would be "taken care of" by the killing of his brother the President. "When attacked by a dog, it is no good cutting off the tail. Cut off the head and the dog is out of business."

Significantly, Jack Ruby was born in Chicago, and as a teenager worked for Al Capone as a delivery boy. There is some evidence that it was the Chicago "mob" that placed Ruby in Dallas - his task being to run a restaurant as a front for Syndicate business. A 1956 FBI report mentioned him as a mob contact. Just before the assassination. Ruby was in deep financial trouble, owing the government $60,000 in taxes. Then he suddenly told his lawyer that his problems had been miraculously solved. At about this time, he is known to have had many meetings with old mob acquaintances.

Shortly after Ruby's trial in 1964, Chief Justice Earl Warren, president of the Warren Commission charged with investigating the Kennedy assassination, and Congressman Gerald Ford - the future President - went to Dallas to interview Ruby. Ruby told them that he would have to be taken to Washington before he could answer their questions freely. "I want to tell the truth, and I can't tell it here." He said later: "I have been used as a scapegoat."

When the Warren Report on the assassination was published in 1979, it concluded that all the evidence suggested that Oswald had acted alone in killing Kennedy. It could very well be that this simple solution is indeed the final truth. But, three decades after the assassination, there are certainly very few people who would accept that conclusion.

CRIMINAL TRIALS

THE "Age of Gaslight" sounds almost modern - after all, it is the age before the coming of electricity. But you only have to read any account of trials in the early nineteenth century to realize that life was closer to the Middle Ages than to the twentieth century.

The Bavarian judge Anselm Ritter von Feuerbach, who was active during the first three decades of the nineteenth century, also wrote a vast work consisting of the trials in which he had been concerned. A small part of it was translated into English in 1846 under the title *Narratives of Remarkable Criminal Trials*, and it conveys more clearly than any work of history what it was like to live in Bavaria around the turn of the nineteenth century.

The first case in this chapter is so typical that it is worth describing at length, even though the crime itself is brutal and horrific. Let Feuerbach himself set the scene, in order to give some idea of the flavour of his style.

THE CASE OF JOHN PAUL FORSTER

"Christopher Bäumler, a worthy citizen of Nürnberg, lived in the Königsstrasse, a wide and much-frequented street, where he carried on the trade of a corn-chandler, which there includes the right of selling brandy. He had lately lost his wife, and lived quite alone with only one maid-servant, Anna Catherina

Schütz. He had the reputation of being rich.

Bäumler was in the habit of opening his shop at five o'clock in the morning at latest. But on the 21st of September, 1820, to the surprise of his neighbours it remained closed till past six. Curiosity and alarm drew together a number of people before the house. They rang repeatedly, but no one came to the door. At last some neighbours, with the sanction of the police, entered the first-floor windows by a ladder. Here they found drawers, chests, and closets burst open, and presenting every appearance of a robbery having been committed. They hastened down stairs into the shop, where they discovered in a comer close to the street-door the bloody corpse of the maid; and in the parlour they found Bäumler lying dead beside the stove.

> As soon as the police were informed of the murder, a commission was appointed to visit Bäumler's house. Immediately on entering the shop, to the right of the door in the comer, between two bins of meal and salt, the maid-servant Schütz lay on her back, with her head shattered, and her feet, from which both her shoes had fallen, turned towards the door. Her face and clothes, and the floor, were covered with blood; and the two bins, between which her head lay, as well as the wall, were sprinkled with it. As no other part of the shop showed any marks of blood, it was evident that she had been murdered in this comer. Not far from the body they picked up a small comb, and at a little distance from that a larger one, with several fragments of a second small one. In the very farthest comer of the parlour, between the stove and a small table, upon which stood a jug, they found the body of Bäumler stretched on his back, with his head, which was resting on a small overturned stool, covered with wounds and blood. A pipe and several small coins lay under the body, where they had probably fallen when the murderer ransacked the pocket, which was turned inside out and stained with blood, for money or for keys. The floor, the stove, and the wall were covered with blood, the stool was saturated,

and even the vaulted ceiling, which was nine or ten feet high, was sprinkled with it. These circumstances, especially the stool on which Bäumler's head still rested, and the pipe which lay under his body, showed that the murderer must have suddenly attacked him unawares and felled him to the earth, as he sat drinking his beer and smoking his pipe on that very spot.

On the table, in the parlour, stood a wine-glass with some red brandy at the bottom, and a closed clasp-knife stained with blood on the back and sides. Two newly-baked rolls were found near the entrance-door.

The baker Stierhof stated that Bäumler's maid had fetched these rolls from his shop the evening before, at about a quarter to ten. His wife, who was examined the next day on this point, recognised the rolls as those bought by the unfortunate maid-servant on the evening of the 20th of September.

On examining the body of the maid-servant, a handsome well-shaped girl of twenty-three, the head was found completely shattered; there were also several wounds upon the neck, breast, and hands, and the breast-bone and three of the ribs were fractured. Bäumler's skull was broken into eleven pieces; and although there were no external injuries upon the chest, the sternum and ribs were fractured, as in the maid-servant. There could not be the slightest doubt that the wounds were mortal. The surgeons gave it as their opinion that the wounds on the heads of both victims had been inflicted with a heavy instrument having a flat surface with sharp edges, probably the back of a hatchet. The ribs did not appear to have been broken with the hatchet, but rather by stamping on the bodies.

The evidence of the baker's wife had led to the conclusion that some man who had stayed until late in the evening at Bäumler's house must have been the murderer. Accordingly, all those who had been at

Bäumler's house on that evening were examined, and concurred in saying that a stranger had entered the shop very early, had sat at the farther end of the table, alternately smoking and drinking red brandy out of a wine-glass; and that he had remained there alone at nine o'clock, when the others went away. All agreed in their description of his person; that he was about thirty, of dark complexion, and black hair and beard; that he wore a dark-coloured coat (most of the witnesses said a blue one, which afterwards proved to be a mistake), and that he had on a high beaver hat. With the exception of one witness who had conversed with the stranger about the hop trade and other like matters, and had found him a well-informed, agreeable man, they all stated that he had kept his hat pressed over his face, and his eyes constantly fixed on the ground, and that he had said little or nothing. He stated himself to be a hop-merchant, and said that he was waiting at Bäumler's for his companion, another hop-merchant, who had gone to the play. The witnesses recognised the glass produced in court, as exactly similar to that out of which the stranger had been drinking red clove-brandy."

The first thing that strikes the modern reader about all this is that Bäumler opened his shop at 5 a.m., and that the neighbours wondered what was the matter when he still wasn't open by 6. Elsewhere in the narrative, Feuerbach mentions that the brandy shop stayed open until 11 at night. An eighteen hour day. And it was obviously taken for granted by the rest of the people of Nuremberg, who probably worked roughly the same hours . . .

Feuerbach goes on to say:

"Meanwhile suspicion had fallen upon a certain Paul Forster, who had lately been discharged from the bridewell at Schwabach, and who had been observed for several days before the murder walking about in a suspicious manner before Bäumler's house. His father, a miserably poor day-labourer, lived with two daughters of infamous characters in a cottage belonging to a gardener named Thaler, in the suburb of St John. Forster did not live with his father; but on the morning after the murder he had left the suburb of St John quite early, and had gone to Diesbeck, where he lived with a woman called Margaret Preiss, who had been his mistress for many years. At her house he was arrested by the police on the 23rd of September, the third day after the murder. In her room were found, among other things, two bags of money, the one containing 209 florins 21 kreuzers, the other 152 florins 17 kreuzers. Besides these Preiss's illegitimate daughter, a girl of about fourteen, gave up a small purse containing some medals and a ducat which Forster had given to her when he returned to Diesbeck.

On the following day, when the gens d'armes were escorting Forster and his mistress through Fürth, the waiter of the inn recognised the prisoner as the man who had come to the inn at about eight or nine in the morning of the 21st of September, dressed in a dark grey cloth greatcoat, went away again in about an hour, and then returned dressed in a dark blue coat, and gave him a brown one which he carried under his arm to take care of, requesting him to keep it safe, and to be sure not to show it to any one; adding that in a week he would return and claim it. The waiter now informed the magistrate at Fürth of this circumstance, and produced the greatcoat, which was much stained and in some places soaked with blood.

The description given of the suspicious-looking stranger, who had sat out all the others on the evening of the 20th of September, exactly resembled Forster."

So the murderer was caught easily enough; it could hardly have been easier if he had given himself up.

Now comes one of the oddest parts of the case:

"As soon as the prisoners reached Nürnberg, at about 4 p.m. of the 24th, they were conducted, according to legal practice, to view the bodies lying in Bäumler's house. The corpses were laid in their coffins, with the faces exposed and the bodies covered with their own bloody garments; Bäumler on the right, and the maid-servant on the left hand, thus leaving a passage open between the coffins.

Paul Forster was brought in first: he stepped into the room, and between the two corpses, without the slightest change of countenance. When desired to look at them, he gazed steadfastly and coldly upon them, and replied to the question whether he knew the body on the right, 'No, I know it not; it is quite disfigured: I know it not.' And to the second question, 'Do you know this one to the left?' he answered in the same manner, 'No, she has lain in the grave; I know her not.' When asked how he knew that the body had lain in the grave, he replied, pointing to the face, 'Because she is so disfigured; the face is quite decayed here!' On being desired by the judge to point out the exact spot which he thought so decayed, with a constrained air, but with the coarsest indifference, he grasped the head of the murdered woman, pressed the brow, the broken nose, and the cheeks with his fingers, and said quite coolly, 'Here: you may see it clearly!' He attempted to evade every question addressed to him by the judge, by affecting that the idea of murder was so utterly foreign to him, that in all innocence and simplicity he mistook the deadly wounds for the result of decay.

All the endeavours of the judge to wring some sign of embarrassment or feeling from this man, as he stood between his two victims, were vain: his iron soul was unmoved. Only once, when asked, 'Where, then, is the

> corn-chandler to whom the house belongs?' he appeared staggered, but only for a moment. The judge went so far in his zeal, as to desire him to hold the hands of both corpses, and then to say what he felt. Without a moment's hesitation, Forster grasped the cold hand of Bäumler in his right, and that of Schütz in his left hand; and answered, 'He feels cold - ah, she is cold too;' an answer which clearly contained a sort of contemptuous sneer at the judge's question. During the whole scene, the tone of his voice was as soft and sanctimonious, and his manner as calm, as his feelings were cold and unmoved.
>
> His mistress's behaviour was very different: she was much shaken on entering the room. When desired to look at the dead bodies, she did so, but instantly turned away shuddering, and asked for water. She declared that she knew nothing of these persons, or of the manner of their death. She said that she had learned that she was supposed to be implicated in the horrible deed from the populace, who crowded in thousands round the carriage which brought them from Fürth to Nürnberg, calling her a murderess, striking her with their fists and sticks, and ill-using her in every way. But that God would manifest her innocence, and that she could bring witnesses to prove that she had not left her home at Diesbeck for some weeks. Her evident compassion for the victims, and horror of the crime, spoke more in favour of her innocence than her tears and protestations. An alibi was subsequently most clearly proved."

This method of getting the suspected murderer to view -and even touch - the corpse was common all over Europe at this period. Feuerbach comments that in cases of infanticide, this has never been known to fail. But this murderer was a hardened criminal, and was unaffected.

It was, of course, an open-and-shut case. The police were able to prove that Forster's sister had given him the axe with which he killed Bäumler and the maidservant. Boaster continued to deny knowing anything about the murders until he saw that all these denials would only make things worse. So at this stage he changed his story, and explained that the murders had actually been committed by two men called Schlemmer, who had offered to take him with them to Bohemia, where their rich relations would give him a job. He had met them later in the day, and they had offered to look after his axe while he took a letter to the post. They then vanished with his axe. He met them later at the brandy shop, after all the other guests had gone, and they sent him to go and look out for their cart, which was due to arrive about ten. While he was still waiting for the cart, the Schlemmer's joined him, carrying a trunk and a white parcel. The cart now arrived, and they drove off to the city gate, where the Schlemmer's told him they would not take him to Bohemia after all, but would give him a present . . . This was the white parcel, and when Forster got it home, he found that it contained some bloodstained clothes, and the bags of money that were found in his mistress's house.

It was an absurd story, but the judges had to check it out. They suspected, in any case, that Forster had had accomplices, because Baumler was reputed to be a very rich man, and should have had far more than the 350 or so florins found in Forster's possession. They checked - with German thoroughness -but finally concluded that the Schlemmer's were a figment of Forster's imagination.

Still Forster fought every inch of the way. He had good reason: a man could not be executed unless he confessed. And by 1820, torture had been abolished in Bavaria. (Feuerbach had been responsible for that, in 1806.) Eventually, he was found guilty, and sentenced to life imprisonment in chains, with hard labour. His sister was sentenced to a year in prison as an accomplice.

And that seems to be the end of the case. But in fact, the most interesting part is still to come. Feuerbach goes on to quote at length from an autobiography written by Forster when he was in jail for burglary two years earlier. And this makes it clear that Forster was far from being a brutal and basically stupid killer. He calls it *The Romance of My Life and Loves,* and even Feuerbach is compelled to admit that parts are very well written indeed.

John Paul Forster explains that as a child, he was quiet and thoughtful. A baron came to live in a house in which Forster's father was the gardener, and Forster got to know the baron's two children, and greatly enjoyed acting as a kind of servant to them. The baron liked this so much that he used to invite Forster over every day. His schoolfriends and even his brother began to call him a snob, and refused to play with him. But John Paul had glimpsed a way of life that filled him with longing. And when he left school, the baron offered him a job as a servant. He dressed in grey livery, and accompanied his master and mistress to "balls and assemblies". He was in the seventh heaven, says Feuerbach.

Then came the blow that would eventually turn Forster into a criminal. His father, who was religious, decided that John Paul ought to become a shoemaker. John Paul flatly refused; but he finally agreed to learn the trade of gardening, because that gave him an opportunity of "coming into contact with gentlefolks". And he was apparently an excellent gardener - until he was conscripted into the army (This was about 1805, when all Europe was in arms against Napoleon.)

From then on, things went from bad to worse. He hated army life, with its beatings and semi-starvation. (Again, we have to remember that soldiers were beaten as a matter of course.) He was always in trouble with the NCOs, always being flogged or thrown into jail. One day he stole away to spend the night with a cook named Babetta, with whom he was in love; he returned the next day, but his absence had been noted, and he received twenty lashes.

In 1810 he fell in love again, this time with Margaretha Preiss. He badly wanted to leave the army, but was not allowed to. He began trying to get himself thrown out of the army by thieving. He also deserted several times, and was sentenced each time to "run the gauntlet" (which was as painful as being flogged) and sentenced to serve another six years in the army. Finally, his crimes caused so much trouble that he was drummed out in disgrace.

That, of course, was what he wanted; but ten years of cheating, lying and deserting had undermined his character, and made him bitter. He was soon in jail for three and a half years for burglary. There he wrote the autobiography, intended as a legacy for his beloved Margaretha. Feuerbach sneers that it illustrates how important he thought he was, and quotes with contempt passages about the "soft murmuring of the evening breezes and the melting harmony of the senses." In fact, they reveal that Forster was genuinely a tragic "outsider" figure, a man who had had a glimpse of freedom and then had it snatched from him. The amount of poetry that he quotes reveals that he was highly literate.

The murder, admittedly, was utterly stupid, the act of a man who wanted to get rich quick and marry his Margaretha. Like Raskolnikov in Dostoevsky's *Crime and Punishment,* he was hoping that one single crime would bring him thousands of florins, enough to give him a start in life. Instead, he was to spend the rest of his life in chains. But even the account of his years in jail make us aware that he was no common criminal. Feuerbach says: "For years Forster had borne in dogged silence the hardships of imprisonment, the misery of civil death, the burden of his chains, and the still heavier burden of a troubled conscience." All attempts to make him confess were a failure. His life was totally ruined, yet he told his fellow prisoners:

"Steadfastness of purpose is the chief ornament of a man. He should not easily give up life; however wretched, life is a noble thing. Believe me, comrades, whenever I look upon my ball and chain, I feel proud to think that even on my death bed my last breath shall be drawn with courage." He even polished his chains until they "shone like silver". At first he used to enthrall his fellow prisoners - who all regarded him with the deepest respect - with amazing stories "of enchanted princes and princesses"; then he suddenly decided to speak only in monosyllables, and kept up this resolution "out of pride" for the rest of his life (or what we know of the rest of it.)

His stubbornness was unbending. When given work he considered too hard for him he refused to do it. He was lashed, "receiving the severest blows without moving a muscle or uttering a sound, and returned to his cell just as if nothing had happened." He was beaten again and again, each time he refused to do the work; at last the authorities were forced to give way, and allow him to do the work he preferred.

Feuerbach ends his account by telling us that Forster's face is "vulgar and heavy", the lower part so long that it gives him the look of an animal. Although a humanitarian, he obviously regards John Paul Forster as a contemptible ruffian. For the modern reader, Forster's story is one of tragically wasted powers. He had "ideas above his station", and he had the kind of courage and determination that might have brought him fame and success. Instead, he spent the rest of his life - he was still alive when Feuerbach described the case -mouldering in Lichtenau jail. Life in the year 1820 could be devastatingly cruel.

ANNA ZWANZIGER

THE same point is made by Feuerbach's most remarkable story: his account of the mass poisoner Anna Zwanziger. Again, I quote his account of her crimes:

> "In the year 1807 a widow, nearly fifty years of age, calling herself Nanette Schonleben, lived at Pegnitz in the territory of Baireuth, supporting herself by knitting. Her conduct gained her a reputation which induced Justice Wolfgang Glaser, who was then living at Rosendorf separated from his wife, to take her as his housekeeper, on the 5th March, 1808. On the 22nd of tne following July Glaser was reconciled to his wife, who had been living with her relations at Grieshaber near Augsburg. Soon after her return to her husband's house, though a strong healthy woman, she was suddenly seized with violent vomiting, diarrhoea, &c., and on the 26th August, a month after the reconciliation, she died.
>
> Anna Schönleben now left Glaser's service, and on the 25th September she went to live as housekeeper with

Justice Grohmann at Sanspareil. Her new master, who was unmarried, was thirty-eight years of age, and though a large and powerful man, had suffered from gout for several years, and was often confined to his bed. On these occasions Anna Schonleben always nursed him with the utmost care. In the spring of 1809 he was seized with an illness more violent than any he had had before, and accompanied by entirely new symptoms, - violent vomiting, pains in the stomach, diarrhoea, heat and dryness of the skin, inflammation of the mouth and throat, insatiable thirst, and excessive weakness and pains in the limbs. He died on the 8th May, after an illness of eleven days, and his housekeeper appeared inconsolable for his loss. Every one, the medical men included, took it for granted that Grohmann, who had long been ailing, had died a natural death.

Anna Schonleben was once more out of place, but her reputation for kindness, activity, attention and skill as a sick-nurse soon procured her a new home. At the time of Grohmann's death the wife of the magistrate Gebhard was just expecting to be brought to bed, and asked Anna Schönleben to attend her as nurse and housekeeper during her lying-in. Anna Schönleben, always willing to oblige, readily agreed, and from the day of the confinement she resided in Gebhard's house, dividing her time between the care of the household and of the child. Madame Gebhard was confined on the 13th May, 1809, and both the mother and the child were doing very well until the third day, which the mother fell ill. Her illness became more alarming every day; she was seized with violent vomiting, nervous agitation, distressing heat in the intestines, inflammation in the throat, &c.; and on the 20th May, seven days after her confinement, she died, exclaiming in her agony, 'Merciful Heaven! you have given me poison!' As Madame Gebhard had always been sickly, and moreover had died in childbirth, her death excited no suspicion, and, like Madame Glaser and Grohmann, she was buried without more ado. The widower, embarrassed by his household and the infant which was left upon his hands, thought that he could do nothing better than to keep Anna Schönleben as his housekeeper. Several persons endeavoured to change his resolution. They said that this woman carried death with her wherever she went; that three young persons whom she had served, had died one after the other within a very short time. No one made the smallest accusation against her; their warnings arose from a mere superstitions dread of an unfortunate sympathetic influence exercised by her upon those with whom she lived: her obliging deportment, her piety, and her air of honesty, humility and kindness, protected her from every breath of suspicion. Thus she remained for several months in Gebhard's service unsuspected and unaccused.

During her residence in Gebhard's house various suspicious events occurred, without, however, exciting attention. On the 25th August, 1809, a certain Beck, and the widow Alberti, dined with Gebhard. Soon after dinner they were both seized with violent vomiting, colic, spasms, &c., which lasted until late at night. About the same time she gave the messenger Rosenhauer a glass of white wine, and not long after he had swallowed it he was attacked in precisely the same manner, and was so ill as to be forced to go to bed. On the very same day she took Rosenhauer's porter, a lad of nineteen named Johann Kraus, into the cellar and gave him a glass of brandy. After drinking a small quantity he perceived a sort of white sediment in it, and therefore left the rest, but in a short time he felt very sick. During the last week of August, one of Gebhard's maid-servants, Barbara Waldmann, with whom Anna Schönleben had had several trifling disputes, was taken ill after drinking a cup of coffee, and vomited every half-hour during the whole day. The most remarkable occurrence, however, took place on the 1st September. Gebhard, while playing at skittles with a party of his friends, sent for a few pitchers of beer from his own cellar. He and five other persons drank some of the beer, and were seized soon after with sickness and internal pains; some of the party, among whom was Gebhard, were so ill as to require medical aid.

This first inspired distrust and dislike of Anna Schönleben. On the following day, chiefly at the instigation of one of his fellow-sufferers at the skittle-ground, Gebhard dismissed her from his service, but gave her a written character for honesty and fidelity.

She was to leave Sanspareil for Baireuth on the next day - 3rd September. She expressed her surprise at so sudden a dismissal, but was civil and obliging as usual, and busied herself during the whole evening in various domestic arrangements. Among other things she took the salt-box out of the kitchen (which was no part of her usual duty), and filled it from a barrel of salt which stood in Gebhard's bedroom. When the maid-servant Waldmann commented upon this, Anna Schönleben said, in a jesting manner, that she must do so, for that if those who were going away filled the salt-box, the other servants would keep their places the longer. On the morning of her departure she affected the greatest friendship for the two maid-servants, Hazin and Waldmann, and gave each of them a cup of coffee sweetened with sugar which she took out of a piece of paper. While the carriage was waiting for her at the door she took Gebhard's child, an infant five months old, in her arms, gave it a biscuit soaked in milk to eat, then let it drink the milk, and finally parted from it with the most tender caresses, and got into the carriage which was to convey her to Baireuth, and which Gebhard paid for, besides giving her a crown dollar and some chocolate.

> She had been gone scarce half an hour when the child became alarmingly ill and vomited terribly, and in a few hours more the two maid-servants were attacked in the same manner; and now, for the first time, suspicion was excited. On hearing from his servants how Anna Schönleben had busied herself, Gebhard had the contents of the kitchen salt-box analyzed by a chemist, and a large quantity of arsenic was found among it. The salt-barrel was likewise found at the trial to contain thirty grains of arsenic to every three pounds of salt."

Anna Zwanziger was caught fairly easily. After wandering around for a few months, hoping that Judge Gebhard would send for her - she was obviously slightly insane - she made the mistake of returning to Nuremberg, where she was arrested. Two packets of arsenic were found in her possession. The science of toxicology - detecting poisons - had recently made enormous strides, and when Frau Glaser's body was exhumed, large quantities of arsenic were found. Faced with this evidence, she finally confessed, and was executed by sword in 1811.

Once again, Feuerbach's account of her life throws an entirely new light on the case, and even if we end by feeling no sympathy for the mass murderess, we at least begin to understand why she did it. Born in Nuremberg in August, 1760, the daughter of an innkeeper, Anna was orphaned by the time she was five. After living for five years with various relatives, she was taken at the age of ten into the house of her guardian, a wealthy merchant, and there received a good education. She was more fortunate than John Paul Forster, for she actually lived the kind of life Forster only dreamed about. But when she was fifteen, her guardian decided to marry her to a drunken lawyer named Zwanziger, who was more than twice her age. She objected, but finally had to give way.

Spending most of her days alone, while her husband was out drinking with cronies, she became an avid reader of novels and plays. She was so moved by Goethe's *Sorrows of Young Werther* – which had caused an epidemic of suicide ten years earlier – that she was also tempted to kill herself. She also read Richardson's novel *Pamela,* about a servant girl whose master tries hard to seduce her, but is finally so overcome by her virtue and goodness that he marries her. This also exercised a powerful influence on her. And she was deeply moved by Lessing's tragedy *Emilia Galeotti,* about a girl who is pursued by a wicked prince (who has murdered her fiancee) and ends by persuading her father to kill her to prevent rape.

Her husband soon spent her inheritance - he was capable of drinking ten bottles of wine a day, and was soon a hopeless alcoholic. Anna was now forced to become a high class prostitute to support her husband and two children - although she claimed she only slept with gentlemen. This, at least, was better than starving; she learned to use her physical charms to persuade men to support her. She even thought up a brilliant scheme involving a lottery of watches (we would call it a raffle), which once again made them prosperous; but her husband again spent the money. One lover, a lieutenant, persuaded her to leave her husband, but her husband then persuaded her to return. When she divorced him, he persuaded her to remarry him the next day. Clearly, Anna was not the ruthless bitch Feuerbach represents her as. She admits that she ended by feeling very fond of him.

Finally, Zwanziger died, and after eighteen years, Anna was left on her own. There was no national assistance or social security in Bavaria in 1796. she had to find a way to support herself and her children. She tried to set up a sweetshop in Vienna, but it failed. She became a housekeeper, but had to leave when she had an illegitimate child by a clerk - she put it into a foundling's home, where it died.

James Marsh, the British chemist who invented an incredibly sensitive test for arsenic - so sensitive that it could detect a thousandth of a milligram of arsenic - was a scientific prodigy who was never appreciated. He worked all his life for thirty shillings a week at the Royal Military Academy. For his great discovery he was given the gold medal of the Society of Arts - but would have undoubtedly preferred cash. Frustration turned him into an alcoholic and when he died at 52, he left his wife and children destitute.

Anna was now thirty-eight, still attractive to men. She found a "protector" who installed her in lodgings, and tried to supplement her income with doll making. Tired of being a kept woman, she accepted an excellent job as a housekeeper in the home of a minister, but left after a few months - Feuerbach says because of her dirty habits, but more probably because she gave herself "airs and graces". For, as Feuerbach remarks perceptively, "the insupportable thought of having fallen from her station as mistress of a house and family to the condition of a servant, worked so strongly on her feelings as to cause her to behave like a madwoman." In short, the ups and downs of her life caused her to suffer a mental breakdown. "She laughed, wept and prayed by turns. She received her mistress's orders with a laugh, and went obediently away, but never executed them."

Anna was now definitely insane, and in her misery, she retained one basic obsession: to have a man to look after her and protect her. But her physical charms were fast disappearing. Her old "protector" took her back for a while and got her pregnant again, then left her to chase an actress. She had a miscarriage. After that she attempted suicide by drowning, but was rescued by two fishermen. She was ill with fever for several weeks.

At the age of forty-four, no longer attractive, Anna was forced to take an ill-paid job as a housemaid; now she was at a kind of rock bottom. She stole a diamond ring and absconded. Her master reacted by placing a notice in the newspapers naming her as a thief, which destroyed any remnants of reputation she still possessed. Her son-in-law, with whom she was staying, threw her out.

In the following year, it looked as if fate had finally smiled on her. Working as a needlework teacher, she attracted an old general and became his mistress. Again she dreamed of security and being in charge of her own household. But he walked out on her, and ignored her letters.

And so, in 1807, after more miserable wandering from place to place, she found herself in Pegnitz, near Baireuth, where she was offered a job by Judge Glaser. (To explain her preference for judges, we have to remember that her first husband was a lawyer.) At fifty, the craving for security had given her the cunning of a madwoman. She poisoned the wife of Judge Glaser, hoping he would marry her - an insane hope, since she was now skinny, sallow and ugly. She moved on to the home of Judge Grohmann, who was unmarried and twelve years her junior. Now, surely, she had found the man who was destined to bring security to her old age . . .? Grohmann suffered from gout, and she enjoyed nursing him. She enjoyed nursing him so much that she began slipping small quantities of arsenic and antimony into his food. Eventually, she overdid it - this seems clear, since she can have had no reason to kill her meal ticket - and he died. Feuerbach says she appeared inconsolable, and this is almost certainly because she was.

And so it continued - the tragedy of a madwoman who remembered that she had once been a mistress with servants, an attractive women whom men had once desired, and who was now incapable of facing reality. In our own society, she would have been confined in an asylum after her trial, and so found some kind of security in her final years. As it was, she knelt down at the block, and her head fell into the headsman's basket. Perhaps the woman who had identified with Emilia Galeotti and Pamela felt that it was more appropriate than dying in a workhouse.

ANDREW BICHEL

FEUERBACH records another case of a multiple killer that has the odd distinction of being possibly the first recorded instance of what we would now call the sex murder. This statement must immediately be qualified by saying that there have always been sex crimes, particularly during wars, and that the sixteen century Nuremberg executioner Hans Schmidt records a number of cases in which robbers have also raped their female victims. But the sex crimes of the past were usually committed by drunks, or (as in the case of Schmidt's robbers) with rape as the secondary aim. Bichel's crimes seem to have been motivated by some odd sexual perversion which was certainly not understood at the time.

The case was discussed by Major Arthur Griffiths, one of the best of the late nineteenth century historians of crime, whose *Mysteries of Police and Crime,* published in 1898, is still highly readable. Here is his description of the Bichel case.

> "One of the earliest cases recorded is that of Andrew Bichel, who lived at Regendorf, in Bavaria. His character was strangely contradictory. Until his terrible misdeeds were finally brought home to him, he did not enjoy a bad reputation. He was not a drunkard, nor a gambler, nor quarrelsome; he was married to a wife with whom he lived on good terms, had children, and was esteemed for his piety. But below the surface he was a pilferer and petty thief; suspected of robbing his neighbours' gardens, he was caught by the master he served, an inn-keeper of Regendorf, stealing hay from his loft. His nature really was abjectly and inordinately covetous; he was a coward who persisted in his crimes because he seemed to have secured perfect immunity from detection. They were committed on the defenceless; his victims were helpless, credulous women, who trusted him and made no attempt to defend themselves. Cunning in him was allied to great cruelty, and both were backed by such extraordinary greed that he thought the pettiest plunder worth the greatest crime. 'A man thus constituted will commit no crimes requiring energy or courage,' writes the judge who tried him. 'He will never venture to rob on the highway, or break into a house; but he would commit arson, administer poison, murder a man in his sleep, or, like Bichel, cunningly induce young girls to go to him, and then murder them in cold blood for the sake of their clothes or a few pence.'
>
> No suspicion was roused against Bichel for years. Girls went to Regendorf, and were never heard of again. One, Barbara Reisinger, disappeared in 1807, and another, Catherine Seidel, the year after. In both cases no report was made to the police until a long time had elapsed,

and a first clue to the disappearance of the last-named was obtained by a sister, who found a tailor making up a waistcoat from a piece of dimity which she recognised as having formed part of a petticoat worn by Catherine when she was last seen. The waistcoat was for a certain Andrew Bichel, who lived in the town, and who now followed the curious profession of fortune-teller.

Catherine Seidel had been attracted by his promises to show her fortune in a glass. She was to come to him in her best clothes, the best she had, and with three changes, for this was part of the performance. She went as directed, and was never heard of again. Bichel, when asked, declared she had eloped with a man she met at his house.

Now that suspicion was aroused against Bichel, his house in Regendorf was searched, and a chest full of women's clothes was found in his room. Among them were many garments identified as belonging to the missing Catherine Seidel. One of her handkerchiefs, moreover, was taken out of his pocket when he was apprehended.

Still there was no direct proof of murder. The disappearance of Seidel was undoubted, Reisinger's also, and the presumption of foul play was strong. Some crime had been committed, but whether abduction, manslaughter, or murder was still a hidden mystery. Repeated searchings of Bichel's house were fruitless; no dead bodies were found, no stains of blood, no traces of violence.

The dog of a police sergeant first ran the crime to ground. He pointed so constantly to a wood-shed in the yard, and when called off so persistently returned to the same spot, that the officer determined to explore the shed thoroughly. In one comer lay a great heap of straw and litter, and on digging deep below this they turned up a quantity of human bones. They went a foot deeper, and found more remains. Near at hand, underneath a pile of logs by a chalk pit, a human head was found. Not far off was a second body, which, like the first, had been cut in half. One was believed to be the corpse of Barbara Reisinger, the other was actually identified, through a pair of pinchbeck earrings, as that of Catherine Seidel.

Bichel stood defiant before the searching questions of the judge; he lied continually, and was proved to have lied. Still he would make no avowal. Even when confronted with the corpses of his alleged victims, as was then the custom in Bavaria, he would not yield. Although so greatly agitated that he all but fainted on the spot, he had yet the strength of will to master his emotions, and when again asked if he recognised his handiwork, he protested that he had never seen the corpses before. 'I only trembled,' he protested, when taxed with the weakness, 'I only trembled at the sight. Who would not tremble on such an occasion?' But he could not stand; he sank into a chair. All his muscles quivered; his face was horribly contorted.

Yet a deep impression had been left on his mind, and when relegated to prison 'his imagination,' as Feuerbach says, 'overcame his obstinacy.' He made full confession of these two particular crimes. Reisinger he had killed when she came seeking a situation as maid-servant. He was tempted by her clothes. To murder he had recourse to his trade of fortune-telling, saying he would show her in a magic mirror her future fate, and producing a board and a small magnifying glass, placed them on a table in front of her. She must not touch these sacred objects; her eyes must be bandaged, her hands tied behind her back. No sooner had she consented than he stabbed her in the neck, and it was all over with her.

This success emboldened him to repeat the operation. He sought to entrap other girls, choosing always the best dressed, and putting forward the bait of the magic mirror. But he failed with three, and then caught Catherine Seidel

> in the toils. The process was exactly the same as with Barbara Reisinger, but this victim was not killed so easily. The after part was the same.
>
> Bichel now resolved to adopt murder as a trade, and looked about him for fresh victims. But although the motive was strong and his cunning great, he does not seem to have enticed many more within reach of his knife. The police heard of several cases in which he had used the same lure of the magic glass upon girls who promised to go to him dressed in their best, but who, fortunately for themselves, thought better of it. They escaped, some by want of faith in the mirror, others by a secret aversion to Bichel, a few by mere accident.
>
> Bichel, was found guilty and condemned to be broken on the wheel, but the sentence was commuted to beheading."

Why did Bichel murder girls? Feuerbach seems to accept Bichel's own explanation. "My only reason for murdering Reisinger and Seidel was desire for their clothes." But the next sentence contradicts this. "I must confess I did not want them; but it was exactly as if someone stood at my elbow and whispered: "Do this and buy corn." Which makes it sound as if Bichel's extreme poverty drove him to crime. But if that *was* his motive, then why did he keep the clothes?

A modem psychiatrist would have interviewed Bichel until he understood his motives. Was he, perhaps, fascinated by his sister's clothes as a child, and enjoyed dressing up in them? Did he have some deep resentment of well-dressed women that aroused a kind of sadistic desire to kill? Or is it possible that the motive was simply rape? At this distance in time, we shall never know. And unfortunately, Feuerbach himself has failed to provide us with the biographical clues that he unearthed in the case of Forster and Anna Zwanziger ...

NOTORIOUS AMERICAN CASES

Criminally speaking, America in the early nineteenth century is relatively uninteresting. There were plenty of violent deaths, of course, but they were mostly the work of bandits and common criminals. Soon after World War II, a New York publisher issued a series of volumes on murders in major cities - New York murders, Chicago murders, Denver murders, and so on. But few of them contain any cases before 1850.

The same applies to the best compilation of American crime in the nineteenth century, Thomas S. Duke's Celebrated Criminal Cases of America, published in San Francisco in 1910. The book is full of marvellous accounts of riots and robberies and Indian massacres, of political assassins and murderous thugs. But there are few cases that rate as criminological classics, on the level of Burke and Hare or Lacenaire or Anna Zwanziger.

One of the rare exceptions is the amazing story of the murder in the Harvard Medical School. Thomas Duke was an ex-policeman, and his down-to-earth, factual way of telling the story adds to its impact.

In North Carolina, Lavinia Fisher has become a legend, like Calamity Jane or Bonnie Parker. Lavinia and her husband John Fisher were members of a gang of highwaymen who, in 1818, operated from Six Mile House, north of Charleston, and robbed passing travellers. Cavalry surrounded the house and ordered the gang to leave. They did so quietly, and the cavalry left behind a young man called David Ross to guard the house. The next day the gang came back and threw him out; the beautiful Lavinia attacked him and pushed his head through a pane of glass. The enraged lawmen returned and forced the gang to surrender. Most of them were sentenced to death for highway robbery. But Lavinia persuaded the susceptible prison governor to allow them to occupy a more comfortable - and less secure - part of the jail. In September 1818, they knocked a hole in the wall, and John Fisher and some others escaped down a rope made of sheets. But the rope broke before Lavinia could follow, and John refused to escape without her. Although they received one reprieve, both met the hangman in February 1819, Lavinia fighting and screaming to the last. She seems to have been a bad tempered termagant - but to the people of Charleston she is still the beautiful highway woman who went to her death without flinching.

PROFESSOR WEBSTER

"ON Friday, November 23, 1849, one of the most prominent physicians in Boston, Dr George Parkman, mysteriously disappeared. Being very methodical in his habits, his family immediately suspected foul play.

He was the owner of many tenement houses and was rather exacting in his attitude toward his tenants, many of whom were of the rougher class. As he collected the rents himself, the authorities proceeded on the theory that he had antagonized some of these tenants to such an extent that they murdered him for the double purpose of revenge and robbery, and then concealed his body.

The river was dredged and the doctor's tenements and the buildings adjacent thereto were thoroughly searched, but no trace was found of the missing man, although large rewards were offered.

When the doctor left home, about noon on November 23, he stated that he had an appointment with a person at 2:30 p.m., but did not divulge the name of the person.

About 1:30 p.m. he entered the grocery store conducted by Paul Holland, at Vine and Blossom streets, and after leaving an order, he asked permission to leave a paper bag containing a head of lettuce at the store for a few moments, but he never returned for it. This grocery store was but a short distance from one of the leading medical colleges in Boston, the college being located on Grove street. Elias Fuller, who conducted an iron foundry adjacent to the medical college, and his brother, Albert, saw Dr Parkman in front of the college about 2 p.m. on the date of his disappearance.

Dr John Webster was the professor of chemistry at this college and also at Harvard College. His standing in the social and professional world was equal to that of Dr Parkman, and their families were on terms of considerable intimacy.

Notwithstanding the fact that Dr Parkman called on Dr Webster at the college at 2 p.m. on Friday, the 23rd instant, and his subsequent disappearance was the principal topic of conversation in Boston the next day and for some time afterward, Dr Webster did not inform the almost distracted members of the Parkman family of this visit until the Sunday evening following, although it was proven that he saw an account of the doctor's disappearance in the Boston Transcript on Saturday afternoon.

Dr Webster then stated that Dr Parkman called on him for the purpose of collecting $450 which Webster had previously borrowed, giving as security a mortgage on a piece of real estate.

He claimed that he paid Dr Parkman the full amount due, from the proceeds of the sale of tickets to his course of lectures in the college.

Dr Parkman held a note for this amount, which he had in his possession when he called on Dr Webster and which the latter subsequently produced to prove that he had paid the money. He added that Dr Parkman stated that he would proceed forthwith to Cambridge and cancel the mortgage.

Dr Webster also claimed that he saw Dr Parkman go down stairs and leave the college after this transaction.

Webster made many conflicting statements as to the denomination of the money paid and as to the circumstances under which it was paid, but his standing in the community was such that it was difficult to believe him guilty of any wrong-doing and it would have been considered preposterous at that time to even suspect him of being implicated in the murder of his friend and benefactor.

Merely as a matter of form, the authorities decided to search the medical college, but before proceeding with the formal search an apology was made to Dr Webster for the intrusion.

When Ephraim Littlefield, the janitor of the building, observed the farcical search, he looked on with disapproving eyes, and intimated that a more thorough search would result in sensational discoveries.

The authorities then questioned Littlefield closely, and he made the following statement:

"I have known Dr Parkman for many years. On Monday evening, November 19,1849,1 was assisting Dr Webster when Dr Parkman entered the room. He appeared to be angry at Dr Webster and without any preliminary conversation, abruptly said: 'Dr Webster, are you ready for me tonight?'

"Webster replied, 'No, I am not, doctor.'

"I then moved away, but I heard Dr Parkman reprimand him for selling mortgaged property, and in a final burst of anger said: 'Something must be done to-morrow,' and he then left.

"On the morning of Friday, November 23, I saw a sledge hammer which belonged in the laboratory, behind Dr Webster's door. I had never seen it there before and have been unable to find it since.

"At 2:15 p.m. I was at the front door and saw Dr Parkman approaching the college, but I went inside and did not see him enter the building. About one hour afterward I went to Dr Webster's laboratory to clean up, but found the door bolted from the inside.

"I knocked loudly but received no response, although I heard someone walking inside who, I supposed, was Dr Webster. I then tried all the different doors leading to his laboratory, but they were all locked from the inside - a most unusual occurrence.

"At 4 o'clock I tried the doors again, with the same result. At 5 p.m. I saw Dr Webster leave the building from the back exit.

"I went to a party that night, and at 11 p.m. returned to the college, where my wife and I are domiciled. I again tried Dr Webster's door and again found it locked.

"On the next day, Saturday, Dr Webster was in his laboratory all day, but I did not go near him. That evening I met him on the street, and we discussed the article in the evening paper about the disappearance of Dr Parkman.

"Formerly he would look me in the face when talking, but on this occasion he hung his head and was pale and agitated. On Sunday and Monday the doors to the laboratory were still locked. On Tuesday I found the doctor's room open and mentioned the fact to my wife.

"On this day he was exceptionally friendly toward me and gave me an order for a Thanksgiving turkey. This was remarkable, as I had known him for eight years, and it was the first time I ever knew of him giving anything away.

"On Wednesday, Dr Webster came to the college early and again locked the door.

"The flue from his furnace is between the walls near the stairs leading to the demonstrator's room, and when I passed up the stairs the wall was extremely hot."

The janitor's statement in regard to the door to the laboratory being constantly locked for several days subsequent to the disappearance of Dr Parkman was corroborated by several persons who had called during that period.

These disclosures were made on Thursday, November 29, and the officers proceeded at once to Dr Webster's laboratory, and after vigorous knocking, the door was unbolted from the inside and the officers were admitted by Dr Webster, but nothing was said regarding the janitor's statement.

At this time a bright fire was burning in the furnace. Nothing was found on this date, and the search was resumed on Friday in the absence of Dr Webster.

In the meantime the furnace had become cool enough to permit of an examination, which resulted in the finding of a fractured skull containing a full set of mineral teeth.

By means of a trap door, the officers descended to the cellar, where they found a right leg.

In a tea chest they found the upper part of a man's body and the left leg. The shape of the body corresponded with that of Dr Parkman.

Dr Winslow Lewis and two other reputable surgeons stated that the manner in which the body was separated indicated that it was done by someone having knowledge of anatomy.

The fact that these remains were found concealed in the chemical laboratory where no such subjects were required, made it apparent that they were the remains of some victim of foul play, and Dr Ainsworth, the demonstrator of anatomy at the college, stated that they were not parts of any subject used in the college for dissection.

Dr N. C. Keep, who had made a full set of false teeth for Dr Parkman, inspected the plate and teeth and identified them as work he had done for Dr Parkman, because of a peculiarity of the lower jaw, which caused him much trouble. But to be positive, he produced the model, which fitted the plates exactly.

The result of the police investigations were not

made public until it was proven beyond all doubt that the remains of Dr Parkman had been found. Police Officer Clapp was then sent to Dr Webster's home at Cambridge to arrest him for murder.

When the public learned of the arrest of the eminent professor, it was at once concluded that a grave mistake had been made and that too much credence had been given to the statement of the janitor, who possibly was attempting to shield himself.

At the trial it was proven that notwithstanding his outward show of prosperity, Dr Webster was financially embarrassed. It was proven that he had committed a felony by selling the property upon which Dr Parkman held a mortgage for $450 and that the latter threatened to prosecute him for this offense if he did not immediately pay the principal and interest, amounting to $483.60.

It was proven that it was utterly impossible for Dr Webster, who saw the, state prison and ruin staring him in the face, to raise this small amount of money.

It was proven that he lied when he stated that he paid this amount from the proceeds of the sale of tickets to his course of lectures at the college, as he had received no such amount, and a large portion of what he *did* receive was paid to others.

It was proven that Dr Webster called at Dr Parkman's house and requested the latter to call at the college at 2:30 p.m. on November 23 for the purpose of making a final settlement.

Dr Webster could give no reason for keeping a roaring fire in the furnace for several days after Dr Parkman's disappearance, and during the Thanksgiving holidays, when all of the other professors were enjoying a week of recreation.

While it was the duty of the janitor to build the fires, the latter was barred from Dr Webster's apartments, who personally attended to the building and feeding of the fire.

It was proven that the upper part of the body and left leg found in the tea chest were tied together by a peculiar kind of twine and that Dr Webster had, on November 27, purchased similar twine and several fish hooks which were found in his apartments.

It was proven that when the officers approached the room in which the tea chest containing a greater part of the body was found, Dr Webster endeavored to discourage them from searching that room by stating that highly explosive chemicals were stored there.

A pair of trousers belonging to Dr Webster was found in a closet and subjected to a microscopical examination with the result that human blood was found.

While the search was being made for Dr Parkman, the City Marshal of Boston received three anonymous letters.

One, supposed to have been written by an illiterate person, suggested that a search be made on "brooklynt heights," another stated that Dr Parkman had gone to sea on the ship "Herculian," and a third, signed "Civis," stated positively that the missing doctor had been seen at Cambridge.

Handwriting experts swore positively that all three letters were written by Dr Webster.

The defense produced witnesses to prove the previous good character of Dr Webster and also introduced testimony to the effect that Dr Parkman had been seen after the defendant claimed he left the college. After producing medical experts to contradict the medical testimony introduced by the prosecution, the case was submitted.

Chief Justice Shaw then delivered his charge to the jury, and his instructions regarding circumstantial evidence were so able, comprehensive, and discriminating that they have since been regarded as a model by many of the leading jurists of America. When the cause was finally submitted to the jurors, they almost immediately agreed that the defendant was guilty. As Justice Shaw was also officially connected with Harvard College and had been friendly with Dr Webster for years, he almost collapsed while pronouncing the death penalty on his erstwhile friend.

The date of execution was set for August 30, 1850. Notwithstanding efforts made to obtain executive clemency, Dr Webster went to the gallows on that day, publicly protesting his innocence, although it was claimed that he confessed his guilt to a clergyman."

THE BENDER FAMILY

LONDON'S legendary Sweeney Todd, the Demon Barber of Fleet Street, who precipitated customers into the basement from a swivelling barber's chair, then cut their throats, never existed except in the imagination of his creator, the playwright George Dibdin Pitt. But thirty years after the first production of that famous play in 1842, a real American family, the Benders, achieved a gruesome notoriety that rivals that of the Demon Barber.

The most famous murder in American history took place literally by gaslight. As Abraham Lincoln sat in Ford's Theater in Washington on the night of 14 April, 1865, a 26-year-old actor named John Wilkes Booth walked into Lincoln's box and shot him behind the left ear with a one-shot Derringer pistol. Then, shouting "Sic semper tyrannis" ("Ever thus to tyrants") he leapt on to the stage. Unfortunately, his spur caught in the curtain and he fell, fracturing his left shinbone. The injury slowed his escape back to the south, and twelve days later, he and fellow-conspirator David Herold were surrounded by Union soldiers in a barn in Virginia. When Booth refused to surrender, the barn was set on fire. Then a shot rang out, and Booth fell dead - whether he shot himself, or was killed by one of the soldiers, was never discovered with certainty.

On 9 March, 1873, Dr William York left his brother's house in Fort Scott, Kansas to return home on horseback. Fort Scott marked the border of the Indian territories, but Dr York's journey was through safe, settled prairie and ought to have been uneventful. However Dr York did not arrive back in Independence, his home town. Weeks passed and nothing was heard from him. Something was evidently wrong. Colonel York, the doctor's brother, organized groups to search the area between Independence and Fort Scott. It was Colonel

York himself who stopped at the Wayside Inn near Cherryvale to ask after his brother.

The inn was actually a tiny log cabin, roughly sixteen by twenty feet, surrounded by some farmland and an orchard. It was owned by European immigrants, the Bender family. The local people did not know exactly where they came from, only noticing that they spoke in thick guttural accents. The household consisted of Ma and Pa Bender, fifty and sixty respectively, and two grown-up children, both born in America. Kate Bender, the daughter, was a spiritualist and gave lectures on the subject as Professor Miss Kate Bender. She also advertised in the local paper as a faith healer who could not only cure disease, but also blindness and deafness. Their son was less gifted, only helping his father around the farm and inn. The whole family was heavily built and florid.

Colonel York knew that his brother had planned to stay at the Wayside Inn and thus made it one of the first places at which he enquired. Old Man Bender denied any knowledge of Dr York, pointing out that the Indians where still a real danger and that there were bandits everywhere. He and his son offered to help dredge the nearby river for Dr York's body. The Colonel was convinced and left to search elsewhere.

Soon another of the organized search parties called at the Benders' inn and asked after Dr York. Again they denied all, but after the party had left, they packed possessions into their covered wagon and fled.

No-one noticed they had gone for some while; guests were infrequent. Then on 9 May yet another search party noticed that the Wayside Inn seemed deserted, and that the cattle were making distressed noises. On entering, they found that the house stank of decomposition. At the back the cattle and sheep had been left penned for some time, and many were dead of thirst or hunger. Then someone noticed that the dry half-acre of orchard to the right of the house looked strange. The topsoil had been ploughed between the trees, and due to heavy rain some of the ploughed ground seemed to have subsided. The subsidence was in the shape of a grave.

Digging soon revealed the body of Dr York. His skull was crushed and his throat had been cut. Before nightfall seven other bodies had been recovered from the orchard's soil. All had been killed in the same way, except one small child who had been asphyxiated. From her position it seemed clear that she had been thrown into the grave alive, her murdered father thrown in on top of her, and both then covered over.

The next day another body of a child was unearthed. This one was so badly decomposed that only its sex and approximate age could be ascertained. It was an eight-year-old girl. Unlike the other adult victims this girl seemed to have been deliberately mutilated, her right knee disconnected and her breastbone driven in.

Upon searching the inn, officers discovered that the smell was not only coming from the neglected animals. A trapdoor in the floor led down to a cellar - in fact a roughly-dug pit -coated in rancid blood.

The story behind the bodies soon emerged through deduction. The Bender family murdered guests who looked like they had some money. They would do this in an ingenious way. The dining area of the tiny cabin was divided from the sleeping area by a thick curtain suspended from the ceiling. The dining table was positioned within the small space in such a way as to make the diner sit with his back directly against the curtain. If the guest seemed worth the risk, either Old Man Bender or his son would wait in the sleeping area for a clear outline of the victim's head against the curtain and then smash the skull with a heavy stone-breaker's hammer. After searching the corpse for money, they would cut its throat in order to be certain that no life remained and then throw them down through the trapdoor in to the cellar to await nightfall and burial. The orchard turf was kept constantly ploughed in order to hide any signs of grave-digging.

Naturally the community of Cherryvale and its surroundings was horrified. Local farmers were quick to form a vigilante group and scour the area for signs of the Bender's flight. Four groups set out north, south, east and west to find their tracks. Another group "arrested" a Mr Brockman, an acquaintance of the Benders and an accomplice in the eyes of the local townsfolk because he had once been Bender's business partner. The vigilantes hanged him from a tree until he was almost dead in an attempt to force information from him.

Other local people began remembering strange events that at the time were ignored. A Mr Wetzell remembered answering Kate Bender's advert in the newspaper. He suffered from acute facial neuralgia, and decided to try Kate's mystic powers as a cure. He and a friend visited the inn, where Kate greeted them in a friendly and charming manner, telling him that she could easily cure his neuralgia, but would he not prefer some dinner first? The two guests sat down, whereupon Old Man Bender and his son, who had been watching them closely, disappeared behind the curtain. For a reason neither of them could adequately explain, the two guests decided to stand up and eat their dinner at the bar. At this Kate became angry and abusive, and the rest of the family looked on threateningly. Sensing that something strange was going on the two men quickly left.

Apart from this first-hand account of the Bender's methods, another piece of evidence was unearthed by officers. Some time before the discovery of the Bender's secret the body of a man had been found deliberately concealed under the ice of a frozen creek. The skull had been smashed and the throat so severely cut that the head was almost detached. A hole had been cut in the ice and the body pushed through it. Tracks in the snow of the river bank showed that the murderer's cart had a severely skewed wheel; one of the ruts had a decidedly zig-zag appearance. When tested the Bender's farm cart left the same tracks. It would seem that during the winter the ground in the Bender's orchard was too frozen to dig.

Officially the Bender's were never found. The search continued sporadically for the next fifty years, with many pairs of unhappy travelling ladies identified as Ma and Kate Bender.

However it seems possible that the Benders did meet justice. In his book *Celebrated Criminal Cases of America* (1910), Thomas Duke prints two letters from local police chiefs in response to his question: what happened to the Benders? One reports, "There was a vigilance committee organized to locate the Benders, and shortly afterwards Old Man Bender's wagon was found by the roadside riddled with bullets. You will have to guess the rest." The other states, "A vigilance committee was formed, and some of them are still here, but they will not talk except to say that it would be useless to look for them, and they smile at reports of some of the family having been recently located."

It is possible that the vigilantes killed the Benders and kept it a secret. However it is also possible that living so close to the scene of such gruesome and heartless murder, the locals had to create a happy ending.

THE KIDNAPPING OF CHARLEY ROSS

THE word kidnap, meaning to "nap" (or nab) a child, came into use in the late seventeenth century, when homeless children were nabbed and sold to the plantations in North America. But the first case of kidnapping, in our modem sense of the word (to seize someone for ransom) occurred in Philadelphia in 1874.

Charley and Walter Ross, four and six years old respectively, disappeared from their suburban Philadelphia home on 1 July, 1874. Walter was soon home again, recovered by a Mr Henry Peacock who had found him crying loudly in front of a downtown sweet shop. Walter's story was, for the period, a strange one. For the past four days two men had been driving past the front lawn of the Ross's stone mansion and offering the children sweets. On the fourth day Walter had suggested that they go into Philadelphia to buy some fireworks for the approaching Independence Day celebrations. The two men readily agreed, and took the children to "Aunt Susie's", a sweet shop on the corner of Palmer and Richmond street. Walter was given twenty-five cents to spend and gleefully ran into the shop. When he came out the carriage had gone.

The idea that Charley had been kidnapped did not at the time seem plausible. In fact the crime was not really established as existing; Pennsylvania had no specific law against it. The other reason why extortion seemed unlikely was that despite owning a large stone house, Christian Ross, the boy's father was only moderately wealthy. He had made his money in selling groceries but had recently gone bankrupt. At the time of the abduction he was only just beginning to break even again.

Then, on 3 July, a note from the kidnappers arrived. It was hand-written and only semi-literate. Despite the uneducated appearance of the spelling and grammar, the style was florid: ". . . if any aproch is made to his hidin place that is the signil for his instant anihilation. if you regard his lif puts no one to search for him yu money can fetch him out alive an no other existin powers . . ." The note demanded money without stating an amount, or specifying a method of payment. It was obvious that the kidnappers wished to bargain.

Ross gave the letter to the police and they made the contents public. The community was outraged in a way that perhaps is no longer imaginable. When the police decided to closely search the whole local area, the inhabitants voluntarily allowed officers to search their homes, something that the police would have had legal difficulty in compelling them to do. Anyone who refused the police entry was looked upon with suspicion. Although the child was not found, a great deal of stolen property was, and prosecutions followed.

Three days after the last another note arrived, demanding $20,000 and threatening to kill the child if any detectives were set on their trail. Ross was directed to enter a personal ad in *The Philadelphia Ledger* when he was ready to negotiate. It was decided that the longer an exchange of notes could be maintained the better the chance of forcing the kidnappers into a blunder. Therefore the ad read: "Ross will come to terms to the best of his ability."

A reply soon arrived, saying that the abductors were getting very impatient, and that the reason for the evasive reply was obvious to them. Despite this Ross continued to publish ambiguous answers. In fact, he had made up his mind not to compound a felony by paying the criminals, and went as far as to announce the fact publicly. This in effect severed the link of communication with the kidnappers and put Charley Ross' life in a great deal of danger.

Seeing that the worry of this situation was driving his wife into an early grave, Ross relented. Through the small ads he signalled his willingness to hand over the money. Shortly another note arrived, remonstrating with Ross for behaving so recklessly and postponing any deal. The reason given was that the phase of the moon was not propitious for business transactions.

On 30 July the instructions arrived at last. Ross was to put the money in a white painted suitcase and board the night train to New York with it. For the entire journey he was to stand on the rear platform of the last carriage, looking back down the track. He was to throw the suitcase off the train at the signal of a torch. It was clear that the kidnappers had been waiting for a moonless night, in order to avoid being followed.

Ross complied, and waited for the whole journey without receiving a signal. On his return a note awaited him, chiding him for failing to keep the deal. It seemed that the kidnappers had read a newpaper report "revealing" that Ross intended to go with the police to follow up a clue somewhere entirely different. Consequently they themselves had not taken the trouble to rum up. Even if the kidnappers had got hold of the case, they would have found that it contained only a letter demanding a simultaneous exchange of money for child. Ross now communicated this demand to the kidnappers. They replied that simultaneous transfer was impossible, and again threatened to kill the child.

Meanwhile the New York police had found an informer capable of identifying the handwriting of the ransom notes. According to this man the writing belonged to a William Mosher. The informant said that a few years previously Mosher and a man named Joseph Douglas had approached him to be an accomplice in abduction of a millionaire's child. The information seemed promising, and the police traced Mosher to 235 Monroe Street, Philadelphia where he lived with his family. Douglas lived in the same house. Unfortunately, by the time police searched the building the Moshers and Douglas had moved to New York.

At about the same time a final communication reached Ross. It instructed him to place an ad in *The New York Herald* reading "Saul of Tarsus: Fifth Avenue Hotel" followed by the date that he would be there with the money. Ross did as he was told, sat in the hotel all of 15 November, but there was no visitation. The kidnappers remained silent.

On 14 December the summer home of a Mr Van Brunt situated on the Upper East Side of New York was burgled. Mr Van Brunt was in residence, and heard the intruders climbing down into his cellar over the sounds of a storm. By the time that the burglars re-emerged from the cellar, there were five armed men waiting for them. Mr Van Brunt shouted "Halt!" The burglars fired two shots, both of which missed, and tried to escape out of the window. Van Brunt shot the nearest man with his shotgun, nearly blowing him in half, while his son jumped on the other burglar and accidentally shot him through the chest with a handgun. It was clear that both men were dying. Although in terrible pain, the burglar with the chest wound refused to be moved, and asked for an umbrella to keep himself dry during his last moments. In between fits of pain the man spoke: "Men, I won't lie to you. My name is Joseph Douglas and the man over there is William Mosher. He lives in New York, and I have no home. I am a single man and have no relatives except for a brother and a sister whom I have not seen for twenty years. Mosher is married and has four children" (here pain for a moment overcame his speech) "I have forty dollars in my pocket that I made honestly. Bury me with that." After another fit he continued: "Men, I am dying now and it's no use lying. Mosher and I stole Charley Ross." Van Brunt asked him why they had done it. "To make money." was the simple reply. When asked where the boy was Douglas told them to ask Mosher. He was told that Mosher was already dead, and his blasted body was dragged over in order to prove it. Douglas said that they had known that the police had them cornered. All he would say about Charley was that: "the child will be returned home safe and sound in a few days." Douglas survived over an hour of agony in the rain. Eventually he lapsed into unconsciousness and died.

The bodies were taken to the morgue, where a terrified Walter Ross identified them as the men who had taken Charley. Despite Douglas' dying assurances, and a reward of $5,000 and no questions asked for anyone who returned the child, Charley was never seen again.

Mr Ross carried on searching for his child, heartened by a statement made by William Westervelt, Mosher's brother-in-law and the man with whom Mosher and Douglas had lived in New York. He had told Ross that the day before he died, Mosher had said that he would arrange a simultaneous transfer if that was the only way to get the money. This presupposes that the boy was still alive.

Westervelt was tried as an accomplice in New York, and despite a lack of any firm evidence he was sentenced to seven years in solitary confinement.

It has to be assumed, despite Westervelt's statement, that Charley Ross was dead long before Mosher and Douglas were shot. Perhaps he was killed when Christian Ross announced publicly that he had no intention of aiding a felon. An unconfirmed story reports that Charley Ross was delivered into Westervelt's hands almost immediately after his kidnap, Mosher and Douglas remaining in Philadelphia to arrange ransom notes and payment. Westervelt, according to the story, became nervous and drowned the child in the East River. This was impossible to confirm however, as Westervelt disappeared after serving his sentence.

Christian Ross spent the rest of his life and his money checking up reports of Charley, travelling as far afield as Europe.

On 25 February, 1875 Pennsylvania Legislature officially recognized kidnapping as a crime.

THE SCIENCE OF DETECTION

THE most remarkable achievement of the Age of Gaslight was undoubtedly its development of the science of detection. Scientific crime detection had been taking slow, hesitant steps since the last quarter of the eighteenth century, when a number of brilliant chemists - Scheele, Hahnemann, Metzger, Rose - learned how to detect arsenic, even after it had been absorbed by the human body - it was this new knowledge that convicted Anna Zwanziger.

By 1820, the great Mathieu Orfila had created the science of toxicology, which meant that poison was no longer the murderer's most reliable weapon.

The art of photography also came to play an important part in crime detection. By the 1870s, most police forces in Europe added a photograph of a criminal to his file. Their main problem was the popularity of beards - a photograph of one bearded, scowling face looked very much like another.

Moreover, an archive of a hundred thousand photographs is useless unless they are classified in a way that enables the police to decide where to start looking.

When parts of a woman's body - including her head - were found In the river Seine in 1887, photographs of the head were sold at newsagents in an attempt to identify her. Hundreds were bought. This led to her identification as the wife of an old soldier called Billoir. His defense was that he had kicked her in the course of a drunken quarrel and that she had collapsed and died. But medical examination showed that her heart had still been beating when she was dismembered. Billoir was sentenced to death, remarking gloomily: "The doctors have done for me."

ALPHONSE BERTILLON

WHEN the twenty-five-year-old Alphonse Bertillon became a clerk at the Sûreté in 1879, most of the old identification procedures were practically useless. Bertillon was a dreary, pedantic young man whom most people found rather repellent; but he came from a cultured and scientific family, and the chaos irritated him. He was certain there *ought* to be some simple way of arranging the hundred thousand photographs and descriptions.

Bertillon's story would be ideal for Hollywood. He compared photographs of criminals to see if there was some way of classifying noses and faces. Then he thought it might be a good idea to take measurements of criminals when they were arrested - height, reach, circumference of head, height sitting down, length of left hand, left foot, left leg - Bertillon chose the left-hand side because it was unlikely to be affected by work. He was subject to constipation, stomach upsets, headaches and nosebleeds; but he had a certain stubbornness that made him ignore the knowing smiles of colleagues. A doctor named Adolphe Quetelet had asserted that the chances of two people being exactly the same height are four to one. If that was so, and the same thing applied to the other statistics, then you needed only two or three measurements of each criminal to raise the odds to a hundred to one. When the prefect of police ignored Bertillon's letter about this method, Bertillon bought himself a set of filing cards, and started to work on his own, staying in the office until late at night. His boss Gustave Mace revealed a lack of insight when he read Bertillon's report, and said it was too theoretical. The prefect, Andrieux, told Bertillon to stop making a nuisance of himself. And three years went by before Bertillon could persuade a new prefect, Jean Camecasse, to give him an interview. Camecasse was as sceptical as his predecessor, but he was impressed by the clerk's persistence. He told Bertillon that they would introduce his method experimentally for three months. This was obviously absurd; it would take more than three months to build up a file, and a method like Bertillon's depended on accumulation. But with Mace himself opposed to the whole idea, he knew his only chance lay in working on and praying for luck. His card index swelled at the rate of a few hundred a month. But with more than twenty thousand criminals in Paris alone, the chances of identifying one of them was low. Towards the end of the third month, Bertillon had towards two thousand cards. Theoretically, his chance of identification was one in ten - fairly high. But it must be remembered that a large number of his criminals were sent to jail, often for years, so most of his file was lying fallow, so to speak.

On 20 February 1883, luck was with him. His system led him to identify a petty criminal who had been measured three months earlier. It was a very small triumph, but it was enough to make Camecasse decide to allow the experiment to continue. This was not far-sightedness. The post of prefect was a political appointment; Camecasse was hoping for fame. Unfortunately, a new prefect had been appointed by the time Bertillon became a celebrity; but history allows Camecasse the credit. As the file swelled, identification became more frequent. Before long, it averaged one a day. But what Bertillon needed was a really sensational case.

He had to wait until 1892 for it, but when it came, it spread his name all over the world. And the reason for the notoriety of the case was more or less accidental.

Since the early 1880s, a terrifying group of people known as the Anarchists became steadily more well known. People were not all that interested in their idealistic doctrine of the inherent goodness of human nature - which means that man does not need Authority to keep him virtuous. In 1881, Russian anarchists - they called themselves Narodniki - blew up Tsar Alexander II with a bomb; in Chicago, in May 1884, someone hurled a home-made bomb into a crowd of policemen who were about to break up a meeting of strikers, killing seven of them. Eight anarchists were condemned to death; one of them blew himself up with a bomb, and wrote in his own blood: "Long live Anarchy!" Four of the anarchists were eventually hanged. In France, anarchists like Malatesta, Grave and Reclus spoke darkly of the "propaganda of the deed", and the bourgeoisie shuddered. On May Day 1891, three anarchists were arrested for taking part in demonstrations at Clichy, and badly beaten-up by the police. At their trial, the prosecuting attorney Bulot demanded the death penalty for all three - although no one had been killed in the riots. The judge, Benoist, acquitted one of them and gave the other two prison sentences of three and five years. In March the following year - 1892 - a tremendous explosion shook the house in which Judge Benoist lived, destroying the stairway. Two weeks later, another explosion blew up Bulot's house in the Rue de Clichy. Luckily, no one was killed in either explosion. But the panic was tremendous. Large quantities of dynamite had been stolen from quarries at Soiry, and the Parisians wondered where the next explosion would occur. A Left-Wing professor was arrested for the first explosion, and he agreed that he had planned it; however, a man named Ravachol had carried it out. Ravachol was known to the police - not as an anarchist, but as a burglar who was suspected of murder; he had killed an old miser and his housekeeper, two women who kept a hardware store, and an old miser who lived in a forest hut. He was also believed to have robbed the tomb of a countess to steal her jewellery. The alias of this forty-year-old criminal seemed to be Konigstein.

On the day of the Rue de Clichy dynamiting, Ravachol dined in the Restaurant Very in the Boulevard Magenta, and tried to convert a waiter named Lhérot to anarchism. Two days later, he returned, and Lhérot noticed a scar on his thumb, which had been mentioned in descriptions of Ravachol. He notified the police, and the man was arrested.

Here was Bertillon's chance to prove his system to the world. Luckily, "Konigstein" had been briefly under arrest at St Etienne as a suspect in the murder of the old man, and the police there had taken his measurements before he managed to escape. Bertillon himself measured Ravachol, and the measurements corresponded exactly. The idealistic anarchist Ravachol was the murderous criminal Konigstein, and for the time being, at least, the anarchist movement was discredited. On the evening before Ravachol's trial, the Restaurant Very was blown up by a bomb, which killed the proprietor and a customer - it was obviously retaliation for the arrest of Ravachol, and an attempt to intimidate the judges. It succeeded; Ravachol was only condemned to prison. But the judges of St Etienne were less scared of anarchist bombs; with Bertillon's proof in their hands, they were able to bring home the five murders to Ravachol, and he was executed on 10 July 1892. For the next few years Paris rocked with bombs - there was even one in the Chamber of Deputies - and President Carnot himself was assassinated. Bertillon luckily escaped the wrath of the anarchists.

THE METHOD OF FINGERPRINTING

BUT, absurdly enough the method known as "Bertillonage", which had revolutionized almost every police force in the world, was already out of date by this time. In India in the 1860s, a civil servant named William Herschel had observed that no two fingerprints are ever alike. He put it to use in his job of paying off pensioned Indian soldiers. These men could seldom write, and they all looked alike to English eyes. And when they realized this, the pensioners began collecting their pensions twice, or returned and collected other people's pensions. When Herschel noticed that fingerprints were always different, he made them sign for their pensions by placing the index finger on an inked pad, and pressing it gently at the side of his name on the list. The swindling ceased. Some years later, a Scot named Henry Faulds made the same discovery, and wrote a letter to *Nature,* declaring that this might be a means of identifying criminals. The year was 1880, two years before Bertillon was allowed to start making his experiments in measurement. Faulds and Herschel were later to be involved in bitter disputes about priority, but these do not concern us here.

A disciple of Darwin, Sir Francis Galton, became interested in Bertillonage because he thought it would help in the study of problems of heredity. He became friendly with Bertillon, and this interest in police work led him to write to Herschel about his methods of fingerprinting; he had read the exchange of letters between Herschel and Faulds in *Nature.* Galton settled down to the study of fingerprints, and soon decided that there were only four basic classifications; the core of his method was the triangle, or "delta", in the centre of a fingerprint. In 1892, Gallon's book *fingerprints* came out. So in the year of his greatest triumph, Bertillon had become redundant. He refused to acknowledge it - for years he fought grimly for his system, betraying an unfortunate lack of the truly scientific spirit. But fingerprinting was bound to prevail in the end; it was so much simpler than Bertillonage.

The first murder ever to be solved by a fingerprint took place in Necochea, Argentina. A twenty-six-year-old woman named Francesca Rojas ran into the hut of a neighbour saying that her children had been murdered. The two children, aged four and six, lay dead in bed, their heads beaten in. She accused a man named Velasquez, who was in love with her. She wanted to marry another man, and she claimed that Velasquez had threatened to kill "what she loved most". She had returned from work to find the children dead . . .

Velasquez was arrested and badly beaten, but he denied the murders, while agreeing to the threat. The police methods in Necochea were primitive; they tortured Velasquez for a week, without result; then the police chief tried making moaning noises outside the woman's hut, hoping to frighten her into confession by pretending to be a ghost.

A police inspector named Alvarez went out to investigate from La Plata. And he knew something about the work of a Dalmatian named Juan Vucetich, head of the Statistical Bureau of Police in Buenos Aires, who had developed his own fingerprint system after reading an article by Galton. Alvarez went into the woman's hut and searched for clues. All he could find was a bloody thumb-print on a door. Alvarez sawed off the portion of the door and took it back to headquarters. Then he sent for Francesca Rojas, and made her give her thumb-print. Alvarez knew very little about classification, but it was quite obvious that the two prints were identical. When he showed the woman the two prints through a magnifying glass, she broke down and confessed - she had murdered her own two children because she wanted to marry a young lover who objected to them. This Argentine Lady Macbeth, who tried to rid herself of illegitimate children and an unwanted lover with one blow, obviously deserves to stand very high on a list of the world's worst women.

THE STRATTON BROTHERS

THE first English murder case involving fingerprints took place in Deptford in 1905. At 7.15 a.m., on 27 March of that year, a passing milkman saw two men emerge from a shop at 34 High Street, Deptford, and slam the door behind them. It was a paint shop, and the manager, an elderly man called Farrow, ran the shop with his wife.

At half past eight, the shop boy arrived and found the place closed up; he went to fetch the shop's owner, and they forced a kitchen window. Farrow was found dead on the ground floor, his head battered in; his wife was found dead in bed. What had happened was clear enough. The two men had broken into the shop, and Mr Farrow had heard the noise and hurried downstairs - where he was beaten over the head with jemmies and left for dead. The men went upstairs, and killed his wife in the same way. They found the cash box under her husband's pillow and emptied it. Farrow was not dead; after the men left the shop he staggered to the door and looked outside, where he was seen by a little girl who thought nothing of a bloodstained man; then he locked the shop door, and died.

The police were on the scene by 9.30, and soon found a thumb-print inside the cash box. It was photographed and enlarged. The police now checked on local criminals, and discovered that two brothers named Stratton were missing from their usual haunts. They were known as a violent and brutal pair, who had been in the hands of the police several times. They were picked up later in the week and fingerprinted. The thumb-print in the cash box was identical with that of the elder brother, Alfred. The police had no other evidence against them, since the milkman had been unable to identify them. Sergeant Collins, the fingerprint expert, would be the most important prosecution witness.

It was obviously an important case, and the future of fingerprinting might stand or fall by it - for a few years at least. Neither the judge - an elderly gentleman named Channell - nor the jury knew anything about fingerprints. The defence decided to take no chances, and called two of their own fingerprint experts. One of these was none other than Henry Faulds, the Scot who had discovered fingerprinting and declared that it should be used for police work. Through an unfortunate accident, he had never received the credit that was his due. When Sir Francis Galton had written to ask *Nature* for the addresses of the two men who had been conducting a correspondence about fingerprinting, the editor accidentally sent him only the address of Herschel. Herschel, like Galton, was a generous and disinterested sort of person, who immediately handed Galton all his results - with the consequence that Galton never had reason to consult Faulds. But Faulds, unfortunately, was an obsessive egoist who wanted credit for his discovery. (It will be remembered that Herschel actually discovered fingerprinting first, but Faulds was the first to publish the discovery.) For years, Faulds fought a violent battle to gain recognition; the British felt this was rather unsporting, and ignored him. So now Faulds decided to make himself felt by opposing the Crown case. The other "expert" was yet another disappointed egoist, Dr Garson, who had first sneered at fingerprinting (he was a champion of Bertillonage), then decided to change horses, and invented his own system. And it was Garson's appetite for recognition that swung the case against the Strattons. Sergeant Collins gave a lecture on fingerprints and drew sketches on a blackboard. Garson and

Faulds made no attempt to deny that no two fingerprints are ever alike, but they *did* assert that the print on the cash box was not identical with the print of Alfred Stratton's thumb. To the judge and jury, all fingerprints looked alike, and they were inclined to credit the assertion that the two prints were not really identical. Collins replied that the discrepancies were the kind that are bound to occur when fingerprints are taken, because lines will look thicker or thinner according to the pressure applied and the angle at which the finger is pressed on to the paper. He demonstrated this convincingly by taking fingerprints of the jury on spot, and showing exactly the same discrepancies. But the seeds of doubt had been sown. The prosecutor now played his trump card. Garson was called back to the stand, and was asked whether it was not true that he had written a letter offering to testify for the prosecution? Yet he was now testifying for the defence. Clearly, this was a man who would change his opinions for the sake of being an important witness in an important trial. The judge remarked that he was obviously untrustworthy. And the last hope of the Stratton brothers vanished. They were found guilty, and both of them proceeded to shout abuse at the court, dissipating the impression of wronged innocence they had been aiming for. The judge sentenced them to death. England's first fingerprint murder had established that a fingerprint alone is enough to hang a man.

In Mysteries of Police and Crime, Major Arthur Griffiths tells the story of a robber who was detected by means of a finger he left behind. The thief was climbing over a factory gate with iron spikes on top when a policeman saw him and shouted. The thief ran away; it was only in the next days that his finger was found on one of the spikes. It had stuck into it as he tried to escape, and his own weight had pulled it off. The fingerprint proved to be in Scotland Yard's collection, and the thief was captured and sentenced to jail.

THE MURDER OF PC COLE

ANOTHER new science was aiding the law in its battle against crime; it was called ballistics - the study of guns and bullets. When Louis Bertrand used a one-shot pistol to kill Henry Kinder in 1865, such weapons were already becoming obsolete. By 1840, a young man named Samuel Colt had invented the colt revolver. By 1870, mass produced revolvers were producing a crime epidemic like the poisoning epidemic of the seventeenth century. The revolver seemed a boon for criminals, since every bullet apparently looked alike. Yet even before scientists learned to study the "rifle marks" on bullets under a microscope, the police were learning that a bullet could convict a criminal just as surely as a fingerprint. Major Arthur Griffiths rites the classic case that has become known as "Orrock's chisel."

On 1 December 1882, the cobbled, gaslit streets of east London were wrapped in choking fog as a young constable set out from Dalston police station on a beat that took him down a narrow thoroughfare called Ashwin Street. As he turned the comer, he came to a sudden halt as he saw a man placing a lantern on top of the wall outside the Baptist chapel, and beginning to scramble over. PC Cole took a swift step forward, laid his hand on the man's shoulder, and asked: "What do you think you're doing?" For a moment, the man - who seemed little more than a youth - looked as if he was going to resist; then he changed his mind and agreed to "go quietly". But PC Cole and his captive had only gone as far as the pub on the comer when the man broke loose and ran. Cole ran after him and grabbed him by the left arm; as he did so, the man reached into his pocket, pulled out a revolver, and fired three shots. A woman who was walking towards them screamed and fled; as she ran, she heard another shot. Moments later, she encountered two policeman in Dalston

Lane, and led them back to the scene of the shooting. PC Cole was lying on the pavement outside the Baptist chapel, his head in the gutter; a trickle of blood ran from the bullet hole behind his left ear. He died five minutes after being admitted to the local German Hospital.

Inspector Glass, who took charge of the case, ordered a search of the area where the policeman had been found; on the wall of the Baptist chapel, the burglar had left his dark lantern; behind the railings, a chisel, a jemmy, and a wooden wedge had been left on the ground. The only other clue was a black billycock hat, which the burglar had lost in the course of the struggle. The woman who had seen him running away described him as short and slightly built; another witness gave the same description.

There was one man in the Dalston police station who believed he knew the identity of the murderer. Only minutes before Cole had arrested the burglar, Police Sergeant Cobb had been walking along Ashwin Street with another sergeant, Branwell, when they had noticed a man standing under a streetlamp. Cobb recognized him as a young cabinetmaker named Tom Orrock, and when he saw the policeman, he looked furtive and uncomfortable. Orrock had no criminal record, but he kept bad company - thugs and professional criminals - and it seemed a reasonable assumption that he would one day try his hand at crime. As they passed Orrock that night, Cobb had been tempted to arrest him for loitering. But standing under a streetlamp was no crime, and Cobb had derided against it. Now he regretted it, and was inclined to blame himself for the death of PC Cole, who was a young married man with children.

Informed of Sergeant Cobb's suspicions, Inspector Glass was inclined to be dismissive - to begin with, he disliked Cobb, regarding him as too unimaginative and too conscientious. But he ordered Tom Orrock - who was nineteen - to be brought in for an identity parade. When the witnesses who had glimpsed Cole's captive failed to identify him, Orrock was released. Soon after that, he disappeared from his usual haunts.

Months after the murder, the investigation was at a standstill. The clues seemed to lead nowhere. The hat bore no marks of identification, and the chisels and the large wooden wedge might have belonged to anybody. But the bullets looked more promising. All four had been recovered - two from the policeman's skull, one from his truncheon, another from the truncheon case. They were unusual in that they had been fired from a revolver that was little more than a toy - the kind of thing ladies sometimes carried in their handbags. The science of ballistics was unknown in 1882, but the rarity of a gun suggested that it might one day provide a valuable piece of evidence.

When studied through a magnifying glass, one of the chisels also yielded an interesting clue. A series of scratches near the handle looked like an attempt at writing, probably with a sharp nail. And when the chisel was photographed for the case file, the letters could be seen more clearly, and they resolved themselves into a capital R, followed by what looked like an o, a c, and a k. Rock. Could it be short for Orrock? Cobb began calling in every tool shop in the Hackney and Dalston area, asking if they recognized the chisels, but met with no success.

Cobb refused to give up. A year after the murder, he was talking with an acquaintance of the missing cabinetmaker named Henry Mortimer, who occasionally acted as a police informer. And Mortimer's rambling discourse suddenly arrested the sergeant's attention when he mentioned that Tom Orrock had possessed a revolver - a nickel-plated, pin-fire miniature affair. Orrock had seen it advertised in the *Exchange and Mart,* and he and Mortimer had gone to Tottenham to purchase it from the owner for the sum of half a guinea. They had also been accompanied by two men named Miles and Evans, both professional - if unsuccessful - criminals. On the way home, the four men had stopped on Tottenham Marshes and used a tree for target practice. At Cobb's request, Mortimer accompanied him to Tottenham and showed him the tree. The following day, Cobb returned alone, and dug some bullets out of the tree with his penknife. One of them was relatively undamaged, and was obviously of the same calibre as the bullets that had been fired at PC Cole.

Now Cobb was sure he had his man, and that view was confirmed when Mortimer admitted that Orrock had virtually confessed to killing PC Cole. When Mortimer had expressed disbelief, Orrock had replied: "If they can prove it against me, I'm willing to take the consequences." This is precisely what Cobb now set out to do.

The first step was to lay the new evidence before his immediate superior. Inspector Glass was still inclined to be indifferent, but he agreed to ask for help from New Scotland Yard in trying to trace the shop that had sold the chisel. And it was the Scotland Yard team that finally located a woman named Preston, a widow who carried on her husband's tool-sharpening business. She recognized the chisel because she always made a practice of scratching the name of the owner near the handle; she remembered the young man who brought in the chisel for grinding had given the name Orrock, which she had shortened to "Rock".

Now at last, they had the kind of evidence that might impress a jury. All that remained was to locate Tom Orrock. Scotland Yard was asked to circulate his description to every police station in the country. This would normally have brought prompt results, for in those days before the population explosion, most police stations were aware of any strangers who had moved into their district. So when another year failed to bring news of the wanted man, Glass was inclined to assume either that he was dead or that he had gone abroad. Cobb refused to believe it. And one day he had an inspiration. One place where a man could "lie low" with reasonable chance of escaping recognition was prison. Once again, Cobb began painstaking enquiries -enquiries that entitle him to be ranked with Canler and Mace as a distinguished practitioner of the needle-in-the-haystack method. And he soon learned that a man answering Orrock's description had been serving a term for burglary in Coldbath Fields for the past two years. Coldbath Fields, in Farringdon Road, was one of London's newer prisons, and had a reputation for severity. The name under which the prisoner was serving his sentence was not Tom Orrock, and when he was summoned to the governor's office, the man denied that he was called Orrock or had ever been in Dalston. Sergeant Cobb attended an identity parade, and had to admit reluctantly that he was unable to recognize Orrock among the seven uniformed convicts who now faced him. But as the men filed out again, they passed under a light, and Cobb suddenly recognized the profile of the man he had last seen standing under a gaslamp in Dalston more that two years earlier. He stepped forward and laid his hand on the shoulder of Thomas Henry Orrock.

Now it was a question of building up the web of circumstantial evidence. Orrock's sister, Mrs Bere, was questioned, and admitted that on the night of the murder her brother had returned home with a torn trouser leg, and without his hat, claiming that he had been involved in a street brawl. Orrock's two friends Miles and Evans were questioned separately. They admitted that they had spent the day of the murder drinking with Tom Orrock in various pubs, and that soon after 10 o'clock in the evening, the three had been in the Railway Tavern in Ashwin Street when Orrock boasted that he intended to embark on a criminal career by "cracking a crib" - stealing the silver plate of the Baptist church, which he attended regularly, and taking it to his brother-in-law to be melted down. Orrock had then left the pub. Not long after, Miles and Evans heard the sound of revolver shots, but claimed they had taken them for fog signals. All the same, they had left the pub and been among the crowd that gathered around the wounded policeman. Three weeks later, when a reward of £200 had been offered for information leading to the capture of the murderer, Orrock went to Evans and begged him not to inform on him; Evans swore that he would not "ruck" on a comrade even for a thousand pounds.

But all this was merely hearsay evidence. The vital link between Tom Orrock and the murder of PC Cole was the revolver. This had disappeared - one witness said that Orrock admitted throwing it into the River Lea. But the police were able to track down the man who had sold Orrock the revolver - his name was McLellan - and he unhesitatingly identified bullets and cartridge cases as being the calibre of those he had sold to a young man in the last week of November 1882, one week before the murder. McLellan's description of the purchaser fitted Thomas Henry Orrock.

A few decades later, all this corroborative evidence would have been unnecessary. Examination of the bullets under a comparison microscope would have proved that the bullet found in the tree at Tottenham was identical with the bullet that killed PC Cole. But in the year 1884, no one had yet thought of studying the pattern of rifle marks on the side of a bullet; it would be another five years before Professor Alexandre Lacassagne would provide the evidence to convict a murderer by studying bullet grooves under a microscope. Nevertheless, when Tom Orrock came to trial in September 1884, it was the bullet evidence that carried most weight with the jury. The bullet found in the tree at Tottenham was "precisely similar to the one found in the brain of the dead constable", said the prosecution. "If the prisoner purchased the revolver, where was it? A man did not throw away a revolver that cost him 10 shillings without good cause." The jury was convinced. On Saturday 20 September 1884, Thomas Orrock was convicted of the murder of PC Cole and sentenced to be hanged. The jury added a special recommendation to Sergeant Cobb for his persistence in tracking down the killer. But the chronicler relates that, in after years, Inspector Glass liked to claim credit for capturing Orrock, and "has often remarked that the man who in reality put the police in possession of their information to this day is ignorant that he disclosed to them this knowledge" - from which it would appear that Glass continued to resent the success of his subordinate and to deny him any of the credit.

THE MYSTERY OF JACK THE RIPPER

By the 1880s, the Age of Gaslight was drawing to a close. In 1881, Edison developed the first electric power plant in the world. In 1890, electric lights were switched on in the Chamber of Horrors at Madame Tussaud's waxworks in London - they had to be shaded in green to produce the same "creepy" effect as the flickering gaslamps.

But the most sensational British crime of the century occurred in the final years of the gaslamp. The nature of the crimes was so horrific that the soubriquet of the unknown murderer was soon famous around the world.

JACK THE RIPPER

IN view or our complete ignorance of the identity of Jack the Ripper, it is strange that the case has continued to exercise such fascination for over half a century. Many people suppose that the Ripper crimes took place over many years and that his victims ran into dozens; whereas, in actual fact, the murders took place over a few months in 1888 and the victims were certainly not more than seven in number - quite possibly only four. The present writer has read an article in a spiritualist newspaper called *Two Worlds,* in which it is alleged that a medium, Mr Lees, helped to catch the Ripper; the article speaks of the murders as extending over several years and running into hundreds. Similarly, an article in the surrealist magazine of the 1920's, *Minotaur,* by Maurice Heine, speaks casually of "the eleventh victim", and includes a dubious photograph of the "eleventh victim".

The facts, briefly, are these: between 31 August 1888 and 8 November 1888 five murders took place within an area of half a mile in Whitechapel in the East End of London. All the women were mutilated with a knife and on several occasions some of the internal organs were taken away. After 8 November the murders ceased abruptly.

During the early part of 1888 there were two murders of women in Whitechapel that may possibly have been the work of the Ripper. The first was of an unfortunate woman named Emma Elizabeth Smith, aged forty-five, who was returning home in the early hours of the day following Easter Monday (3 April) when she was attacked. Twenty-four hours later she died in hospital of peritonitis, some sharp instrument like a spike having penetrated her abdomen. She claimed she was attacked by four men in Osborn Street at about four in the morning as she was returning home from a public house; they took her money (only a few coppers) and mistreated her. Her account of the four men seems circumstantial enough; she described one of them as being only nineteen.

The murder which is often regarded as the Ripper's first crime took place in Gunthorpe Street (then known as "George Yard") in the early hours of the day following Bank Holiday Monday, 7 August. A prostitute named Martha Turner (or Tabram) was picked up by a soldier on Bank Holiday night and seen in The Angel and Crown drinking with him. Several hours later (at about 5 a.m.) her body was found on the first landing of George Yard Buildings. She had been stabbed thirty-nine times; the murderer had used two weapons, one a bayonet or long-bladed knife, the other some kind of surgical instrument. He was also ambidextrous. The soldier who had been seen with her was traced, but had an alibi; all the soldiers in the Tower were paraded, but no arrest was made. It is impossible to state with any certainty whether this was the Ripper's first crime in Whitechapel, but most writers on the case are inclined to believe that it is the work of the Ripper. The present writer is inclined to doubt it.

At 2.30 a.m. on Friday 31 August, a woman friend saw a prostitute named Mary Anne Nicholls (known as "Polly") at the comer of Osborn Street; she admitted to having had "no luck". Three-quarters of an hour later, her body was found by a carter named Cross in Bucks Row (now called Durward Street), lying in the entrance to the Old Stable Yard at the west end of the street. In the mortuary of the Old Montague Street Workhouse it was discovered that she had been disembowelled. Death was due to severing of the windpipe. She was identified by her husband, a printer's machinist, from whom she had been separated for seven years. She was forty-two years of age, and known as a habitual drunk. When her husband saw her body, he was heard to say, "I forgive you for everything now I see you like this." It was revealed that she had been staying at a dosshouse in Thrawl Street, where a bed could be had for fourpence a night. On the previous evening she had been turned away from the dosshouse because she had no money. She commented, "Don't worry, I'll soon get the money. Look what a fine bonnet I've got."

A bruise on her face indicated that the murderer clamped his hand over her mouth before cutting her throat. A woman sleeping in a bedroom only a few yards from the murder heard no sound.

The next murder took place on 8 September. Annie Chapman, aged forty-seven was turned away from a lodging house in Dorset Street, having no money to pay for a bed. It seems probable that the murderer accosted Chapman outside the yard where the murder took place - at 29 Hanbury Street. She accompanied him down a passageway at the side of the house some time after 5 a.m. The body was found shortly after 6 a.m. The head had been almost severed from the body, and then tied in place with a handkerchief. The body was cut open, as in the case of Mary Nicholls, and the kidney and the ovaries had been removed. Two front teeth were missing (repeating a curious feature of the Nicholls murder) and two brass rings and some coppers were laid at her feet. In another comer of the yard was the torn comer of a bloodstained envelope, containing the crest of the Sussex regiment. Under a tap was a leather apron. It seems possible that these last two items were intended to mislead the police. A soldier had been suspected in the Tabram case, and Whitechapel gossip named a man called "Leather Apron" as the murderer. (He was actually a Polish Jew named Pizer, a shoemaker, who was arrested and then released.) Again the murderer had carried out the crime with extreme coolness and had made no sound. There were sixteen people living at 29 Hanbury Street and a scream would have quickly brought help to the victim.

On 28 September a letter was sent to the Central News Agency signed "Jack the Ripper" and threatening more murders. "I am down on whores and shant quit ripping them till I do get buckled." Whether or not it was by a practical joker, the name caught the public imagination when it first appeared in the newspapers (after 30 September).

The murders caused a universal panic. Meetings were held in the streets, criticizing the police and the Home Secretary. Bloodhounds were suggested, but they promptly lost themselves in Tooting. The newspapers of the time gave extremely full reports of the murders and inquests, and were tireless in offering theories.

A description of the murderer offered by someone who saw Annie Chapman talking to a man outside 29 Hanbury Street included a large moustache and a "foreign appearance".

On the morning of 30 September two murders were committed in Whitechapel. The first was of a Swedish woman called Elizabeth Stride. A hawker named Louis Deimschutz drove his horse and cart into the back yard of the International Workers Educational Club in Berner Street. (A council school now stands on the site.) He saw a woman's body on the ground and rushed into the club to give the alarm. The woman's throat had been cut and she had been killed very recently - so recently that it is possible that "Jack the Ripper" was interrupted and made his escape as Deimschutz entered the club. This was at 1 a.m.

At this time a forty-three-year-old prostitute named Catherine Eddowes was released from Bishopsgate police station, where she had been in charge for drunkenness. She was picked up by the Ripper and taken into a narrow alleyway that extends between Mitre Square and Duke Street, known as Church Passage (now St James Passage). Police Constable Watkins passed through the passage on his beat at one-thirty. A quarter of an hour later he again passed through the square, and found the body of Catherine Eddowes in the comer of the square near Church Passage. Her face had been badly mutilated - perhaps to delay identification - and the body cut open in the usual way; the left kidney and entrails had been removed and taken away. It was some time before she was identified, and in the meantime, one of the newspapers published a report that she was thought to be a certain "Mary Anne Kelly". This is a remarkable co-incidence, since the name of the final victim was Mary Jeanette Kelly.

A householder who lived in Berner Street (off the Commercial Road and the farthest afield of the Ripper's murders) testified that she saw a young man carrying a shiny black bag away from the scene of the crime. (Men carrying black bags were sometimes attacked in the street in Whitechapel at this time, and the Ripper murders made this type of bag go quite conclusively out of fashion.)

After the murder the Central News Agency received another letter signed "Jack the Ripper", regretting that he had been interrupted with his victims, and had not been able to send the ears to the police. (There had been an attempt to cut off the ear of Catherine Eddowes.) He also mentioned that "number one squealed a bit", which is borne out by a witness in Bemer Street who heard the cry. The letter was posted only a few hours after the murders, and was written in red ink.

The murders had caused unprecedented excitement, and bands of vigilantes patrolled the streets of Whitechapel at night. But as weeks passed without further crimes, the panic died down. (One theory suggests that the Ripper was incarcerated in a mental home during these weeks.) On 9 November the last of the murders took place at a house in Millers Court, which ran off Dorset Street (now Duval Street), probably between Dorset Street and Whites Row to the south. Mary Jeanette Kelly was younger than the other victims, but of the same class. She was twenty-four. On the morning of 9 November at 10.45 a.m. a man knocked on the door of Mary Kelly to collect the rent. Getting no reply, he peered in at the broken window. What remained of Mary Kelly lay on the bed. The head had been almost severed from the body; the heart had been placed on the pillow. The entrails had been draped over a picture frame. The murderer had apparently worked by the light of a pile of rags, the ashes of which were burnt in the grate. Neighbours testified to hearing a cry of "Murder" at about 3.30 a.m. The inquest revealed that no parts of the body had been taken away this time.

The panic caused by the murder led to the resignation of Sir Charles Warren, the unpopular Chief of Police.

There were three other crimes that some writers on the case believe may have been committed by the Ripper. In June 1889, parts of a female body were found in the Thames. The head was not found, but a scar on the wrists enabled the police to identify the victim as Elizabeth Jackson, a prostitute who lived in a lodging house in Turks Row, Chelsea.

On 17 July the body of Alice McKenzie, known as "Clay Pipe Alice", was found in Castle Alley, Whitechapel; her throat was cut and there were gashes across her abdomen. In his introduction to *The Trial of George Chapman*, H. L. Adam quotes the McKenzie case as one of the Ripper murders.

The final words of Or Neil Cream - poisoner of four London prostitutes in 1891 - were: "I am Jack the . . ."; then the trap dropped. Could Cream have been Jack the Ripper? Apparently not: he was in Joliet Penitentiary, in Chicago, serving a life sentence for poisoning a patient, at the time of the murders.

But a Canadian professor has noted that Joliet was a notoriously corrupt prison, where a rich prisoner could buy his freedom. And in 1897, the year before the Ripper murders, Cream's father died, and left him £5,000 . . .

So it is just possible that Cream's last words were true after all.

Finally, on 13 February 1891, the body of Frances Coles, a prostitute of about twenty-five, was found under a railway arch at Swallow Gardens in Whitechapel; her throat had been cut and there were injuries to her abdomen. She was still alive when found, but died soon afterwards.

There have been many theories about the Ripper's identity. One of the earliest was put forward in 1929 in *The Mystery of Jack the Ripper* by Leonard Matters, a Member of Parliament. He claimed that the Ripper was a certain Dr Stanley, who had confessed to the crimes on his deathbed in Buenos Aires. According to Matters, Stanley's son had contracted syphilis from Mary Kelly - the last victim - and Stanley set out to track her down. Whenever he questioned a prostitute about her, he killed her so she could not warn Mary Kelly. And eventually he found Mary, and slaughtered her with vengeful ferocity . .

Unfortunately, Dr Stanley is not to be found in the Medical Register for 1888, and was almost certainly a figment of Matters' imagination. Moreover, if Mary Kelly had been syphilitic, it would certainly have been recorded in the post mortem report.

What *was* noted in that report is that Mary Kelly was three months pregnant. And this led an artist named William Stewart to the conclusion that Jack the Ripper was a woman - a sadistic midwife, who had gone to Miller's Court to perform an abortion. To demonstrate that a woman would be capable of sadistic violence, he cites the case of Mrs Eleanor Pearcey, who killed the wife and baby of her lover Frank Hogg in October 1890, almost decapitating Phoebe Hogg. A bloodstained axe established her guilt and she was hanged on 23 December, 1890. But Mrs Pearcey's crime was committed out of jealousy. The notion of a female Jack the Ripper, killing out of pure sadism, is psychologically unrealistic.

A writer named William Le Queux had claimed in 1923, in *Things I Know,* that the Ripper was a mad Russian called Alexander Pedachenko, sent to London by the Tsar's secret police to embarrass the British police. He explained that he had unearthed this information in a manuscript on great Russian criminals written in French by the "mad monk" Rasputin, and discovered in the cellar of his house after his assassination in 1917. But Rasputin spoke no French, and his house did not have a cellar - he lived in a flat. In 1959, a journalist named Donald McCormick revived the Pedachenko theory, with "new evidence" from a manuscript called *Chronicles of Crime* by a Dr Thomas Dutton. But although Dutton certainly existed, his manuscript has vanished. And in 1988, the year of the Ripper centenary, McCormick declined to appear on television to defend his theory, which would seem to suggest that he has abandoned it.

One of the most interesting theories was first publicized by the television interviewer Dan Farson in 1959. Farson had tracked down the manuscript notes for *Days of My Years,* the autobiography of Sir Melville Macnaghten, the CID chief who joined Scotland Yard soon after the murders. Macnaghten mentioned that there were three major suspects, against two of whom "the case was weak". The third, who had committed suicide in the Thames soon after the last murder, was almost certainly - according to Macnaghten - Jack the Ripper. Macnaghten did not mention the actual names in his book.

Macnaghtens's original notes contained the three names; the two "weak suspects" were called Ostrog and Kosminksi, while the leading suspect was one "M. J. Druitt", "a doctor who lived with his family, and who drowned himself immediately after the murder of Mary Kelly."

Farson looked into the history of Montague John Druitt, and discovered that he was a barrister who committed suicide late in 1888. His career as a barrister had been a failure; he had taught in a private school in Blackheath, but had been dismissed for unknown reasons just before his suicide.

Both Farson and a journalist named Tom Cullen wrote books naming Druitt as the Ripper. But the objections against this are overwhelming. To begin with, it is obvious that Macnaghten is writing from mere hearsay. Druitt was not a doctor, he did not live with his family (he had rooms in the Temple), he did not commit suicide immediately after the Kelly murder, but a month later. We also know that he committed suicide because his mother had become insane, and he was afraid that the same thing was happening to him.

But perhaps the strongest objection to the Druitt theory is that Druitt was a member of the upper middle class. The study of "serial murder", which has received much attention in recent years, has revealed the interesting fact that all serial killers have been working class, and often suffered traumatic poverty and abuse in childhood. So far, at any rate, there has been no middle or upper class serial killer.

That observation also seems to dispose of an interesting theory held by a doctor named Thomas E.A. Stowell, who contacted the present writer in 1960. For various reasons, Stowell was convinced that Jack the Ripper was Queen Victoria's grandson, the Duke of Clarence, (known as Eddie), who would have become king of England if he had not died in the 'flu epidemic of 1892. Stowell had unearthed information that seemed to indicate that the Queen's physician, Sir William Gull, suspected Eddie of being the Ripper. He told me that Gull's private papers - which he had seen - revealed that Eddie had not died of 'flu, but of softening of the brain due to syphilis.

Stowell swore me to silence - in case it "upset her majesty" - but in 1970, finally published his theory in a magazine called *The Criminologist.* He called his suspect *"S"*, but dropped enough hints to make it clear that he had Eddie in mind. The tremendous public furore that resulted - the story appeared in newspapers all around the world - killed him soon after the article appeared.

Another expert on the Victorian period, Michael Harrison, studied Stowell's article and decided that Stowell had misread Sir William Gull's papers, and that "S" was not the Duke of Clarence. It was probably Gull himself who referred to the suspect as "S"; but why call Clarence "S" when his name was Eddie? Harrison concluded that "S" was, in fact, Eddie's close friend (and tutor) James Kenneth Stephen, who died insane after a blow on the head from the vane of a windmill. Harrison unearthed some fascinating information about Stephen (the cousin of novelist Virginia Woolf, who also had mental problems and committed suicide), including some oddly sadistic poetry about women. But Jim Stephen sounds nothing like the descriptions of the Ripper given by woman who saw him. And if the observation that serial killers tend to be working class is correct, then his upper class origins make him a highly unlikely candidate.

Clarence was involved in a complicated theory put forward by journalist Stephen Knight in *Jack the Ripper: The Final Solution*, in 1976. According to Knight - who based his theory on the statements of a man called Joseph "Hobo" Sickert, son of the painter Walter Sickert - Clarence had secretly married an artist's model named Annie Crook. When the Palace found out, the model was kidnapped and confined in a mental home, and Sir William Gull was entrusted with the task of murdering Mary Kelly and a number of other prostitutes who knew the secret and were trying to blackmail the Palace. He did this in association with a coachman called John Netley, killing the women in the coach, and leaving deliberate clues associated with Freemasonry.

There is, in fact, some evidence that Clarence was the father of an illegitimate child, who in turn became the mother of "Hobo" Sickert. But Sickert himself admitted that the rest of his story - about Jack the Ripper - was a hoax. This should have been clear all along from the fact that Gull suffered a stroke in the year before the murders.

In the year of the Ripper centenary, a television production company, David Wickes Productions, announced that it had gained access to "secret Ripper files" and had established his identity beyond all possible doubt; this would be revealed in a fictional "documentary" in which Michael Caine would play Inspector Abblerline, the officer in charge of the case. The production company was later forced to acknowledge that their claims were "less than truthful", and to make a shamefaced climb-down. When the "documentary" finally appeared, it proved to be a well scripted but almost totally fictional account of the murders, in which Jack the Ripper proved to be Sir William Gull, in association with John Netley. All reference to the Annie Crook theory of "Hobo" Sickert were dropped;

Gull's motive was reduced to insanity. As entertainment it was excellent; as a serious study of the murders, it must be dismissed as spurious and exploitatory.

Another Ripper expert, Robin Odell, advanced the theory that the killer was a Jewish slaughterman, a *shochetz,* who used ritualistic slaughter techniques on his victims; he defended this notion in *Jack the Ripper: Summing Up and Verdict,* (1988) co-authored with myself. The problem with Odell's interesting theory is that his evidence is purely circumstantial; all Whitechapel records that might have proved the existence of his hypothetical *shochetz* have been destroyed.

In *The Crimes, Detection and Death of Jack the Ripper,* Martin Fido, has argued that "Kosminski", another of Macnaghten's three suspects, was "Jack the Ripper, on the evidence of remarks made by Sir Robert Anderson, Assistant Commissioner of Police, who is recorded as saying that Jack the Ripper was a Polish Jew. Fido tracked down information about a man named Aaron Kozminski, who was committed to an asylum in 1891, and speculated that he might have been identical with a violent madman named David Cohen and a syphilitic named Nathan Kaminsky. Once again, the problem is simply lack of any concrete evidence to connect the suspects with the murders.

In *The Ripper Legacy,* Martin Howells and Keith Skinner return to Farson's theory that Druitt was Jack the Ripper, and add the speculation that he was murdered by former Cambridge friends to prevent the scandal from becoming known. Their research is excellent, but does not overcome the objections to the Druitt theory stated above.

Equally well researched is Melvin Harris's book *Jack the Ripper: The Bloody Truth.* He takes up a theory first advanced by the "magician" Aleister Crowley, and later elaborated by Richard Whittington Egan, to the effect that the Ripper was a doctor and adventurer named Roslyn D'Onston Stevenson, who committed the murders as part of a ritual to obtain "supreme magical power". Stevenson actually existed, but is on record as believing that the Ripper was a doctor named Morgan Da vies. There is no real evidence to identify D'Onston (as he preferred to call himself) as the Ripper, and if the "working class" theory is correct, then it is virtually impossible, since he was from a wealthy middle class background. The same objection applies to a theory put forward by Jean Overton Fuller to the effect that the painter Walter Sickert was himself Jack the Ripper.

Other candidates for "Ripperhood" include John Netley himself (Tim Wright), Mary Kelly's common law husband Joseph Barnett (Bruce Paley) and Oscar Wilde's artist friend Frank Miles (Thomas Toughill). In all three cases, the evidence offered is once again purely circumstantial, without the kind of concrete facts that might support it. In the opinion of the present writer, the likeliest candidate is the father of a seventy-seven year old man who wrote to Dan Farson from Melbourne, Australia, and signed himself G.W.B. The letter reads:

"When I was a nipper about 1889 I was playing in the streets about 9 p.m. when my mother called, 'Come in Georgie or JTR will get you'. That night a man patted me on the head and said, 'Don't worry Georgie. You would be the last person JTR would touch'." (This man was apparently the writer's own father.) "I could not remember the incident but it was brought to my mind many years later. My father was a terrible drunkard and night after night he would come home and kick my mother and us kids about something cruelly. About the year 1902 I was taught boxing and after feeling proficient to hold my own I threatened my father that if he laid a hand on my mother or brothers I would thrash him. He never did after that, but we lived in the same house and never spoke to each other. Later, I emigrated to Australia. I was booked to depart with three days' notice and my mother asked me to say goodbye to my father. It was then he told me his history and why he did these terrible murders, and advised me to change my name because he would confess before he died. Once settled in Melbourne I assumed another name. However my father died in 1912 and I was watching the papers carefully expecting a sensational announcement". But this never came; his father died without confessing.

In Melbourne, "Georgie" changed his name, but after the death of his father, changed it back again.

"Now to explain the cause of it all. He was born 1850 and married 1876 and his greatest wish was his first-born to be a girl, which came to pass. She turned out to be an imbecile. This made my father take to drink more heavily, and in the following years all boys arrived. During the confession of those awful murders, he explained he did not know what he was doing but his ambition was to get drunk and an urge to kill every prostitute that accosted him."

> Georgie's father seems to have been a collector of horse manure. On one occasion, after killing a woman, he was wearing two pairs of trousers. He removed the bloodstained outer pair and buried them in the manure. Later, when he and his mate stopped at the Elephant and Castle, where they usually ate sausage and mash, his father told his mate he was not hungry, and would bury himself in the manure to keep warm. While he was hidden there he heard a policeman asking questions about Jack the Ripper, and was "scared to death".

This letter certainly sounds authentic, and it is hard to imagine why a seventy-seven-year-old man in Melbourne should take the trouble to write a long anonymous letter if it was not true - it could hardly be a craving for attention. (Presumably, in spite of the anonymity, it should not be too difficult to discover G.W.B's name by studying sailing lists of ships to Melbourne in 1902.) Assuming, then, that "Georgie" believed every word he wrote, is it not conceivable that his father invented the story about being Jack the Ripper simply to get a kind of revenge on his son after years of ignoring one another? This is obviously a possibility. Yet in all other ways, Georgie's father sounds like the kind of suspect who *could* be Jack the Ripper - a highly dominant type, a heavy drinker, a bully where his family was concerned, and capable (as Charlotte MacLeod suggested) of holding down a job. Many serial killers and sadists have been heavy drinkers and have committed their acts of violence when drunk. If Georgie's father was not Jack the Ripper, then it is at least possible to state that he was the type of person who easily *could* have been. That is probably as far as we shall ever be able to go in solving the problem of the identity of the most notorious killer of all time.

Perhaps the most sensible comment on the identity of Jack the Ripper was made by London policeman Donald Rumbelow, author of The Complete Jack the Ripper. He remarked that if, on the Day of Judgement, the Archangel Gabriel says: "Stand forth, Jack the Ripper, and tell us your name", everybody in the audience will say: "Who?"

THE ETERNAL TRIANGLE

MOST famous crimes of passion involve an "eternal triangle" -husband, wife and lover (or mistress) - and in the majority of these, the murderer and the lover are partners in crime. But there is another type of eternal triangle in which the lover - or mistress -remains innocent, a mere catalyst who happens to inspire the crime. The most celebrated example of the "catalyst" effect occurred in the Crippen case, which we shall examine in the next chapter. But an earlier case, that of Dr Cross, provides an equally interesting example.

DR CROSS AND THE CATALYST EFFECT

A RETIRED army surgeon, sixty-two years of age, Dr Philip Cross lived comfortably with his wife and six children at Shandy Hall, near Dripsey, County Cork. His wife was twenty-two years his junior; they had been married eighteen years, and it had been, on the whole, a satisfactory marriage. In October 1886, Mrs Laura Cross engaged a new governess for the children, a twenty-year-old girl named Effie Skinner. Effie, like Ethel Le Neve, was the catalyst type: not particularly pretty, but with something soft and yielding about her.

As soon as he saw her, the military, rather forbidding Dr Cross felt like a hawk eyeing a sparrow. For the first time, he realized that his marriage had been merely satisfactory, never ecstatic. It had never provided him with any real outlet for his male dominance.

One day. as Effie stood talking to him about the children, he bent and kissed her. He was afraid she would tell his wife or leave immediately. But she stayed, and his desire to possess her increased. His wife noticed it, and she took what seemed to her the sensible course: she sacked Effie. The girl was shattered, she went to Dublin, and when Dr Cross visited her there, she finally gave herself to him. Possession did not cool his desire; he wanted to be married to her, living in comfort in Shandy Hall.

Early in May, 1887, Mrs Cross began to suffer attacks of vomiting. Her husband told her she had a weak heart. She died on 1 June, and was buried three days later. Less than two weeks after this, he married Effie Skinner in London. At first, he decided that they had better keep the marriage a secret and live separately, but when he got back to Dripsey, he discovered the news had preceded him.

There seemed no point keeping Effie in London, so he moved her to Shandy Hall. Inevitably, there was gossip, and the police finally decided to act. Laura Cross was exhumed, and the coroner found 3.2 grains of arsenic in her body, as well as strychnine. There was no trace of heart disease.

The police were also able to trace the firm from whom Dr Cross had bought arsenic "for sheep dipping". Tried at the Munster Assizes in Cork, he was found guilty on 18 December, 1887, and hanged in the following January. Effie was so shocked by the realization that she had been the cause of the murder that she refused to see him in the condemned cell, and Cross's hair turned white overnight.

ADELAIDE BARTLETT

AT the time Dr Cross was engaged in seducing Effie Skinner, another celebrated crime of passion was exciting the usual fever of morbid interest among British newspaper readers - in fact, moreso than usual, since the third member of the triangle was a clergyman who showed a regrettable lack of chivalry towards the woman with whom he may or may not have committed adultery.

The classic murder case on which Theodore Dreiser based his famous novel An American Tragedy took place on 11 July, 1906. Chester Gillette, a twenty-two-year-old labourer with aspirations to rise in the world, worked in his uncle's skirt factory in Courtland, New York. There he had an affair with eighteen-year-old secretary Billie Brown and made her pregnant. By this time, Gillette had met an attractive young socialite at a dance and become engaged to her. When Billie threatened to disclose her condition to his uncle, Chester invited her out for a day's boating on Big Moose Lake. Later that day, he was seen walking in the woods, his clothes dripping wet. Checking into another hotel he asked the clerk "Has there been a drowning reported?" The clerk said no.

Billie's body, her face battered, came to the surface the following day, and an inquest found that she had been murdered. Gillette's replies to police questions were evasive. Charged with murder, his defence was that Billie had committed suicide. But he then changed his story and claimed that the boat had capsized accidentally. The tennis racket with which he had beaten her was found buried near the lake, and proved crucial in contributing to the guilty verdict. Gillette was electrocuted in March 1908. Seventeen years later, he was immortalized by Theodore Dreiser, whose American Tragedy became a best-seller.

Theodore Edwin Bartlett was a hard-working and highly ambitious grocer. By the time he was twenty-nine, he and his business partner owned a chain of small shops in south London. This explains why, although he was a good-looking man, fond of the open air, he had never married; life was too busy for romance. Then, one day in the early 1870s, he went to call on his brother Charles, who lived in Kingston, and was introduced to a dazzlingly attractive eighteen-year-old girl named Adelaide Blanche de la Tremoile. She had dark curly hair, large appealing eyes, and a sensual mouth. Edwin found her fascinating. But it seems likely that, at this stage, marriage did not enter his head.

Adelaide was definitely a "lady", and therefore far above him socially. Then he learned that there was some odd secret in her background. Adelaide's mother had borne her out of wedlock: Her father was a wealthy Englishman who preferred to keep his identity secret - it has been suggested that he was a member of Queen Victoria's entourage when she visited France in 1855, and was therefore probably titled.

Now Adelaide lived with a guardian in a house in Richmond - she was staying in the Kingston house as a guest of Charles's sixteen-year-old daughter. So it seemed that, although she was a "lady", her chances of being accepted into English society were minimal. Edwin saw his chance, and pursued it with single-minded vigour. He called on her when she returned to Richmond, and seems to have persuaded her guardian, or her father, that a virtuous and successful grocer would make a desirable husband.

To Adelaide he explained solemnly that his intentions were more than pure - there was no element of carnal desire in his feeling for her, and when they were married, their relationship would be wholly platonic. And by way of proving his good faith, Edwin Bartlett packed off his newly-wedded bride to a ladies' finishing school in Stoke Newington. She came to stay with her husband during the school holidays but, according to Adelaide, their relationship was like that of father and daughter. And when she had finished at the Stoke Newington school, Edwin sent her off to a convent in Brussels.

She stayed there until 1877, two years after their marriage, when she returned home to a newly furnished flat above Edwin's largest shop in Herne Hill. And for just one month, life was pleasant and peaceful, and Adelaide no doubt enjoyed being a young married woman in charge of her first home. Then Edwin's mother died, and the dutiful son invited his father to come and live with them.

It was a mistake. The old man was a bad-tempered old sponger, and he had never liked Adelaide. He made himself so unpleasant that Adelaide ran away from home - there is evidence that she went to stay in the house in Kingston where Edwin had first met her. And this seems to have led to further trouble. Edwin's younger brother Frederick also lived in the house, and the old man suspected a love affair. One writer on the case states that she became Frederick's mistress, but there is no evidence whatsoever for this assertion. All we know is that the old man accused Adelaide of having an affair with Frederick, and that Edwin was so incensed that he made his father sign an apology, which was drawn up by a solicitor. Then an uneasy peace reigned in the household.

Four years later, in 1881, two things broke the monotony of their lower middle class lives: Edwin had a nervous breakdown (brought on, according to his father, by laying a floor), and Adelaide had a stillborn baby. The latter accident was Edwin's fault; the nurse he engaged to look after his wife had sensed that this might be a difficult birth, and begged Edwin to call in a doctor. But the Victorian Edwin was rather shocked at the idea of another man "interfering with her", and refused. By the time a doctor was finally called in, the baby was dead.

Soon after this, perhaps to distract her, they moved to the village of Merton, near Wimbledon. Edwin's motive may also have been to get rid of his father - he selected a house that had no spare bedroom. So the old man was forced to find a home elsewhere.

Early in 1885 - the Bartletts had now been married ten years - the couple decided to try another place of worship one Sunday morning. They attended the Wesleyan chapel in Merton. The preacher that day was a young man named George Dyson.

He had a black moustache, a receding hairline, and was of slight build. Dyson made a pastoral call soon after that. And when he told Edwin Bartlett that he was about to go to Trinity College, Dublin, to take his degree, Bartlett was deeply impressed. He had an almost pathetic admiration for anyone with education - he himself was an avid but disorganized reader. He cross-questioned Dyson about his studies, and pressed the young man to come and visit them again as soon as he returned from Dublin. Slightly overwhelmed - for he was modest and not very clever - Dyson agreed. And a warm, if rather peculiar friendship, began between these three rather lonely people.

There have been spectacular lonely hearts cases - but perhaps the most extraordinary of them involved the death of a mother and daughter, who may both have been mistresses of the killer. The daughter, Maria Domenech, was a pretty 28-year-old social worker from New York; her body, clad only in black panties, was found at the bottom of the cliffs of Moher, on the west coast of Ireland, on May 24,1967.

It took more than a week for the Irish police to identify her, with the aid of Interpol, and by that time her mother, 51-year- old widow, Mrs. Virginia Domenech, had also vanished from her New York home. The trail led the police to Orly Airport, Paris, where Maria had prepared to fly to Ireland on the afternoon of May 22, in company with a man. Careful detective work revealed that they had arrived in Dublin hours later, hired a car, driven across Ireland, and arrived at the cliffs at five in the morning.

There he had knocked her unconscious, taken a large sum in traveller's checks from her pocketbook, and thrown her to the beach below. He then caught a plane from Shannon back to Paris a few hours later. He thought the alibi was perfect; but when the police established his identity as Patrick D'Arcy, an Irish-American who had been having a tempestuous affair with Maria before she left America - as well as showing marked attention to her mother - he realized the gamble had failed. D'Arcy committed suicide in a motel room in Florida a few weeks after the murders. Virginia Domenech's body has never been found.

Dyson found Edwin Bartlett "exceedingly odd". He seemed to have eccentric ideas on all kinds of subjects. For example, he was a devotee of a work called *Esoteric Anthropology* by Thomas Low Nichols, whose long sub-title declared it to be a "confidential" treatise on the passionate attractions and perversions of the most intimate relations between men and women.

It was not, as the judge later assumed, disguised pornography, but an early "women's lib" discourse on the unfairness of using women as sexual objects. It recommended birth control, and suggested that sexual intercourse should only be practised for the purpose of begetting children. Another of Edwin's rather peculiar beliefs was that men should have two wives, one for "use" and one for intellectual companionship.

He was also, like many Victorians, interested in hypnotism, and in the doctrines of Anton Mesmer, according to which human beings possess a "vital magnetic fluid" that can be passed from one to another.

Soon, Edwin Bartlett was professing the warmest affection for the Reverend Dyson. In fact, he proposed that Dyson should continue Adelaide's education, teaching her geography, history, Latin and mathematics. Dyson, who was making a mere hundred pounds a year, agreed. He would arrive in the morning while Edwin was out at business, and often stay all day. During most of this time, he was alone with Adelaide. Whether she became his mistress depends on one's final view of her guilt or innocence, but certainly she often sat at his feet, with her head on his knee, and he often kissed her, alone and in her husband's presence.

And, oddly enough, Edwin seemed delighted with the whole arrangement. His wife was lonely - she had only one close female friend, a Mrs Alice Matthews - and now he had found her a male friend and teacher who could be trusted implicitly. Edwin had unlimited faith in clergymen. If he found Edwin still in the house when he came in for supper, he warmly pressed him to stay for the evening. When the Bartletts went to Dover for a month, Edwin tried to persuade Dyson to come too, and offered him a first class season ticket so he could rush down every time he was free. Dyson refused, but Edwin still found time to travel to Putney (where Dyson lived) and whisk him off to Dover as an overnight guest. And he asked Dyson to be an executor of his will, in which, naturally, he left everything to Adelaide.

That September, the Bartletts moved into a new lodging - it was to be their last - in Victoria. Edwin told their new landlady, Mrs Doggett, that they would be having a regular visitor, a clergyman, as a dinner guest. And George Dyson continued to call as regularly as ever, travelling from Putney, where he was now in charge of his own church, on a season ticket presented by Edwin Bartlett. They even kept a special jacket and slippers for him to change into. Dyson was finding this close friendship with a young married woman disturbing, and he confessed openly to Edwin that he was growing attracted to Adelaide and that it was upsetting his work; he felt he ought to stop seeing them. Edwin dismissed the idea, assuring Dyson that Adelaide had become a better and nobler woman since she had known him. He seemed to be trying to throw them into one another's arms. And Mrs Doggett noticed one day, after Dyson had left, that the window curtains were not merely drawn, but pinned together. It is hard to imagine why they should do this unless, at the very least, they had been engaging in some heavy petting.

And now, suddenly, Edwin became ill. One day he felt so exhausted at work that he hurried home. The next morning, he and Adelaide and Dyson went to a dog show - dogs were one of Edwin's main interests - but he felt so ill that they had to return home. Adelaide went out to fetch a doctor. She found a young man called Alfred Leach, whom she had never met before, but who immediately accompanied her back home. Edwin was suffering from sickness, diarrhoea and bleeding of the bowels; he had also had toothache. When Dr Leach looked into his mouth, he observed a blue line round the gums, a symptom of mercury poisoning. When he asked Edwin if he had taken mercury, Edwin denied it, but admitted that he had swallowed a pill he had found in a drawer - he had no idea what it was for. Leach arrived at another explanation. Edwin's teeth were in an appalling condition and his breath smelt foul. Apparently the dentist who made his false teeth had failed to draw the stumps; for some reason, he had sawed off the teeth at the gums. When these had rotted, the dentist merely made more false teeth, and the condition of his mouth made it impossible for Edwin to dean his remaining teeth. Leach's theory was that Edwin had, at some time, got a dose of mercury into his system, and that the sulphides produced by his rotting teeth had combined with it to form mercuric sulphide, hence the blue line. A dentist who was called in verified that Edwin was suffering from mercury poisoning, and extracted fifteen roots and stumps.

So throughout December the patient remained in bed. On Christmas Day, 1885, he received an unpleasant shock when he went to the lavatory and passed a round worm. He was naturally something of a hypochondriac, and this gave him "the horrors". He swore that he could feel worms wriggling in his throat, and became deeply depressed.

On the last day of December, and the last day of Edwin's life, he went to the dentist for yet another tooth extraction. Young Dr Leach, who had become a devotee of Adelaide, went with them. On the way, Adelaide remarked that they had just been saying that they sometimes wished they were unmarried, so they could have the pleasure of getting married again. Later, when Edwin got home, his appetite had improved, and he ate a large meal of oysters, jugged hare and cake, with a helping of chutney. He told Mrs Doggett that he would have a haddock for his breakfast, Obviously, he was at last on the road to recovery.

Just before 4 a.m. on New Year's Day, Adelaide knocked on the Doggett's bedroom door. "Go and fetch Dr Leach. I think Mr Bartlett is dead." She explained that she had fallen asleep, holding Edwin's foot, which apparently soothed him, as she sat beside his bed. She had awakened and felt that he was cold. She had tried to revive him with brandy, but without success. Dr Leach observed a glass of brandy on the shelf, with a smell of chloroform.

The moment old Mr Bartlett heard of his son's death, he concluded he had been murdered. He sniffed his son's lips, then turned to Dr Leach and said, "We must have a post mortem".

The post mortem revealed a baffling and astonishing fact: that Edwin Bartlett had died of chloroform poisoning. This was so astonishing because chloroform is an unpleasant-tasting substance that would be almost impossible to swallow; moreover, it causes vomiting. If chloroform was poured down someone's throat when he was unconscious, for example, from the fumes of chloroform, it would get into the lungs. And there was no chloroform in Edwin Bartlett's lungs. Which seemed to point to the completely mystifying conclusion that Edwin Bartlett had drunk the chloroform voluntarily. Yet his cheerfulness before he went to sleep, and the fact that he had even ordered his breakfast, made it unlikely that he intended suicide.

And where had the chloroform come from? This was soon revealed. The Reverend Dyson had bought it, at Adelaide's request. He had even gone to three separate chemists to get a fairly large quantity, claiming that he wanted to use it as cleaning fluid. Adelaide had told him she wanted it to make her husband sleep. And now, when he heard that chloroform had been found in Edwin's stomach, Dyson was panic stricken. He saw it as the end of his career. He rushed along to see Adelaide, and when Mrs Matthews came unexpectedly into the room, she heard Dyston saying: "You did tell me Edwin was going to die soon." And when Adelaide denied it, he bowed his head on the piano and groaned: "Oh, my God!" Later that day, he saw Adelaide alone, and she asked him to say nothing about the chloroform. Dyson refused, and said he was going to make a dean breast of it.

And so he did. And the result was that Adelaide Bartlett found herself on trial for murder. When, in the spring of 1886, it became known that she was to be tried for poisoning her husband, and that the Reverend George Dyson would probably stand in the dock beside her, public excitement was intense. It had all the signs of being a thoroughly scandalous murder case, complete with revelations of secret adultery and a plot by the lovers to kill the husband. And when it was known that the great advocate Edward Clarke would defend Adelaide, people nodded significantly. Clarke was not one of those barristers who depended on verbal fireworks and bullying to win his cases; he was known for a certain quiet sincerity. Yet for all that, he had a formidable reputation. It was obvious that no suburban grocer's wife could afford his services, which could only mean that her mysterious father had intervened.

In the event, Adelaide finally stood alone in the dock; Dyson had managed to clear his own name by shamelessly doing his best to hand her over to the hangman. Edward Clarke had an apparently impossible task: to convince a Victorian jury that this pretty Frenchwoman, quite probably an adulteress, was innocent of her husband's murder. He had only one thing on his side: the total mystery of how even the most cunning murderess could have got the chloroform into Edwin Bartlett's stomach.

Clarke's defence was brilliant. His line of argument was that Edwin was a highly eccentric man who had almost thrown his wife into the arms of the clergyman, and who had actually told them that he expected them to get married when he was dead. He had insisted that his marriage to Adelaide should be purely platonic, and they had only had sexual intercourse once, as a result of which a baby had been born. But in the last days of his illness, Edwin had suddenly shown a desire for sexual intercourse. Adelaide felt this was wrong, since she now regarded herself as affianced to Dyson. So she asked Dyson to get her chloroform, so she might wave it in his face if he made sexual demands. However, she had been unable to go through with it. She had never been able to keep a secret from Edwin, and on that last evening of his life, had confessed her intention and showed him the bottle of chloroform. Edwin had been rather sulky about it, and had placed the bottle on the mantelpiece. And somehow, while Adelaide dozed by his side, holding his foot to comfort him, some of that chloroform had got into Edwin's stomach. (She admitted she had disposed of the rest by throwing it from the window of a train.) The main point of the defence was that Edwin was eccentric to the point of insanity, and that such an unpredictable man might easily have swallowed chloroform, perhaps simply to upset his wife and gain attention.

Amazingly enough, the jury swallowed this unlikely story of a wife too virtuous even to permit her own husband sexual intercourse, even when it was revealed that Edwin had rubber contraceptives in his pocket and undoubtedly used them in making love to Adelaide. But the central point of the defence, of course, was that baffling mystery of the chloroform: if Adelaide poisoned her husband, how did she get it into his stomach? To that question the prosecution had no answer. After that, there could only be one verdict. "Although we think there is the gravest suspicion attaching to the prisoner, we do not think there is sufficient evidence to show how or by whom the chloroform was administered." So the verdict had to be not guilty. The judge had to reprove the court sternly as it burst into cheers.

The question of Adelaide's guilt or innocence has been argued by criminologists ever since. Some, like Nigel Morland, have no doubt that she was innocent, and that Edwin took the chloroform himself in a spirit of resentment or mischief. The majority are inclined to believe that Adelaide was poisoning Edwin from the beginning with some mercury compound, and only decided on the dangerous expedient of ether when he looked like recovering. And one, Yseult Bridges, believes that Adelaide somehow used hypnosis to induce Edwin to swallow the chloroform. None, as far as I know, have hit upon what seems to be the simplest and most obvious solution.

In 1972, Francisco Pineda, a car mechanic of Guadalajar, Mexico, walked into the bedroom of his employer, Fernand Ortega, a 32-year-old hunchback. His employer lay stretched of the floor in his pyjamas, dead. Francisco's pretty step-daughter Maria Pineda, lay dead on the bed, her skirt around her thighs Police discovered that both had died of cyanide pdisoning Ortega had forced her to drink cyanide at knife point, then drank it himself.

Ortega was suffering from tuberculosis; Maria had been acting as his nurse, administering injections. Ortega fell violently in love with her, but she was not attracted to the hunchback. She may have thought that the drink he forced on her containec knockout drops, and that his intention was simply to rape her

In fact, in spite of the position of her dress, Maria had no been sexually molested. Onega could have raped her before he killed himself; but that was not what he wanted. He loved her and wanted to join her in death.

Let us try to reconstruct a hypothetical scenario. When Edwin Bartlett meets the beautiful Adelaide, he is too shy to hope that she will become his mistress as well as his wife, and so he assures her that their relationship will be a purely platonic one. But after two years of marriage, he is less humble and self-effacing, and insists on his marital rights. As a result, Adelaide becomes pregnant, but due to her husband's peculiar ideas about doctors, she loses the baby.

Edwin's curious attitude, his feeling that a doctor who examined his wife would be "interfering with her", indicates a powerful physical jealousy. It is surely the attitude of a man who has the utmost difficulty in persuading his wife to permit him the use of her body, so the idea of another man examining her intimately arouses intense jealousy. Adelaide, for her part, finds sex with her husband rather unpleasant, perhaps because his rotten teeth cause permanent halitosis, and she does her best to persuade him to abide by their "platonic" contract by petting him, fussing over him, showing him a great deal of affection, in fact, everything but allowing him into her bed. (At the trial, it was emphasized that they seemed to be an extremely happily married couple.) She makes use of the standard excuse, that she is afraid of becoming pregnant again, but Edwin counters that by buying contraceptives.

For Edwin, life becomes a permanent siege on his wife's virtue, with very infrequent successes. In his efforts to soften her, he deliberately introduces the Reverend George Dyson into their household, and encourages a flirtation. In effect, he is asking the clergyman, whom he trusts implicitly, to "warm her up". While she is feeling kindly and grateful to her husband, she can hardly refuse him the occasional embrace.

Edwin falls ill; we do not know whether, as Yseult Bridges believes, she has been administering small doses of lead acetate or some mercuric poison. But it gives her a flash of hope, she sees the end of her martyrdom in sight. Then he begins to recover and to indicate that his sexual appetites are returning to normal. Perhaps she finds the contraceptives in his pocket.

And it is at this point that she asks Dyson to buy the chloroform. Presumably the idea of killing Edwin is at the back of her mind - it is hard to believe that she intends to soak a hankerchief in the drug and try and press it over his nose whenever he becomes amorous. But she also knows Edwin well enough to know that, as a hypochondriacal invalid, he quite enjoys taking "medicines". He is in a state of neurotic depression about his "worms". Dr Leach has given him all kinds of medicines for them, without effect - Edwin is convinced he is still swarming with worms. All Adelaide needs to do is to produce the chloroform, and tell Edwin that Dr Leach has recommended this to get rid of worms. Perhaps only the lightest of hints is needed. Perhaps she offers him a little chloroform mixed with brandy, but he finds it unpleasant. Then, as she sits beside him, holding his foot and breathing deeply, he decides that he will win her approval by taking his medicine, and he cautiously reaches out for the bottle.

Sir James Paget, a well-known doctor, made the famous comment: "Now the case is over, she should tell us in the interests of science how she did it". The answer is surely that she did not do it, Edwin did. Whether it was at Adelaide's suggestion we shall never know.

MRS MAYBRICK

BECAUSE she was suspected of adultery, Adelaide Bartlett was fortunate to avoid meeting the hangman. Because she undoubtedly *had* committed adultery, her younger contemporary Florence Maybrick came an uncomfortable shade closer to the gallows. Both women were married to drug-taking hypochondriacs, but Mrs Maybrick's defence failed to convince the judge or jury at her trial for murder.

Florence Chandler, born in Mobile, Alabama in 1862, was a "southern belle" in the tradition of Scarlett O'Hara; her father was a wealthy banker, and her main aim in life was to secure a rich husband. He appeared on the scene when she was eighteen - an overweight, forty-one-year-old English cotton broker named James Maybrick, whom she met on a ship crossing the Atlantic. When she accepted his proposal, Florence may have suspected that he was not a virgin, but she was certainly unaware that he had an American mistress named Mary Hogwood, by whom he had sired three children. For a while the newlyweds lived in Norfolk, Virginia, where Maybrick spent his days at the cotton exchange. A male child was born there. When they moved back to Liverpool two years later, another child, this time a girl, arrived. It was soon after this that Florence learned that her husband had a mistress named Mary Hogwood, and that Mary had given birth to two more children since James Maybrick's marriage. She was upset, but accepted the "double standard" that was current in the late Victorian age. And for another four years, life continued uneventfully at Battlecrease House, their home in the Liverpool suburb of Aigburth.

The great American cause célèbre of 1904 was the trial of Floradora girl Nan Patterson for the murder of her lover Caesar Young in a hansom cats. The shot that killed gambler Caesar Young was fired at about 8 o'clock on the morning of 4 June, 1904; he was dead by the time he reached hospital. Nan Patterson claimed he committed suicide but the police disbelieved her - to begin with, the revolver was in Young's pocket, and it seemed unlikely he would have placed it there after shooting himself.

Young, who was married, had met Nan Patterson on a train to California two years earlier. It was a passionate affair, but by 1904, Young wanted to terminate it; to that end he booked passage for Europe for himself and his wife on the Germanic. He and Nan spent a last evening quarrelling violently. He nevertheless met her for a breakfast of brandy and whiskey, after which they called the hansom, and Young was shot soon after. Under the circumstances, Nan's story that he killed himself because he was upset about leaving her seemed unlikely - the bullet had entered at the wrong angle. At her first trial, a juror became ill, so a mistrial was declared. Her second trial ended with a hung jury. When the third trial also ended in deadlock, all charges against her were dropped. In retrospect it seems clear that Nan was acquitted, not because she was innocent, but because the men on the jury felt she was too pretty to hang.

Nan cashed in her notoriety by accepting leading roles in various musicals, but proved to lack talent, and soon vanished into obscurity.

The Maybricks often gave dinner parties, and it was at one of these in December 1888 that Florence met a tall, good-looking man named Alfred Brierley, a thirty-eight-year-old bachelor who was, like her husband, a successful cotton broker. She saw him a great many times that winter, and when the spring came, Brierley accompanied the Maybricks on a tour of the spring race meetings. Brierley's obvious admiration was welcome; her husband was frequently bad tempered, and had ceased to treat her with the courtliness a southern belle expected. Brierley, on the other hand, behaved like a medieval knight.

So when her husband went to London alone on 12 March, 1889, and Brierley took the opportunity to tell Florence he loved her, she admitted shyly that she returned the feeling. Brierley went on to press her to go away with him - but he was not thinking of an elopement, only of a dirty weekend. By this time, Florence was as eager to commit adultery as he was, and agreed.

It happened a week later. Telling her husband that she was going to stay with an aunt who was about to have an operation, Florence checked into a small hotel in London. Brierley's took another suite. That night, Mrs Maybrick spent the night in Brierley's suite; the following night, he slept in hers. But although both suites had been reserved for a week, they checked out after only three days. This may have been because, having satisfied their curiosity, they were tired of one another, or possibly because Florence wished to establish an alibi. She went to stay with her cousin Margaret Baillie.

The day after she returned home, she and her husband attended the Grand National at Aintree. Brierley was also there, and he offered to take Florence to take a look at the Prince of Wales in the grandstand. By this time, Maybrick seems to have begun to develop belated suspicions; when his wife returned, he told her angrily that she had been away too long.

That evening, the Maybricks had a noisy quarrel, and he ordered her to leave the house, sending for a cab. In fact, the cab was finally dismissed, and Florence spent the night in a room next to the nursery. The next morning, she had a black eye. That day, Mrs Maybrick told a female confidant that she wanted a divorce. The family doctor intervened, and the

Maybricks apparently made up their quarrel - even when Mrs Maybrick revealed that she was heavily in debt to money lenders. But harsh words were exchanged again the next day. After sounds of a noisy altercation, the servants found Florence in a faint. She spent a week in bed.

On 8 April, Florence went to see Alfred Brierley to display her black eye; she was evidently hoping that he would propose an elopement. Instead he looked embarrassed and got rid of her as soon as possible.

In mid-April, James Maybrick went to London to pay off another of his wife's creditors. He also took the opportunity to see a doctor about pains in the head and numbness in the limbs. The doctor prescribed various medicines for indigestion and constipation. He does not seem to have been aware that Maybrick made a habit of dosing himself with arsenic and strychnine, both of which are stimulants when taken in small quantities, and which can produce the symptoms Maybrick complained about. He seems to have been concerend enough to re-draft his will - although he now left most of his estate to the children.

Soon after this, Florence bought no less than two dozen fly papers from the local chemist - the old fashioned type consisting of a sheet of paper soaked in a solution of arsenic. A servant noticed that the fly papers were soaking in water in a sink. A week later, Mrs Maybrick ordered yet another two dozen. Three days later, on 27 April, 1889, James Maybrick had a severe attack of vomiting. He attended the Wirral races, but his hand was so shaky that he spilt his wine when dining with friends.

As the attacks of indigestion continued on into May, the servants - who were inclined to be hostile to Florence - informed some of Maybrick's friends that they suspected his wife of poisoning him. Maybrick's brother Michael arrived from London, and ordered that no one but a nurse was to attend the sick man. When he caught Florence pouring medicine from one bottle to another, he shouted at her and took charge of the medicine, refusing to accept her explanation that it had so much sediment that a bigger bottle was more convenient for shaking. Michael took the medicine for analysis, but it proved to contain no poison. Neither did some food that Michael confiscated and took to the same doctor.

Nevertheless, on 11 May, James Maybrick died. A post mortem showed stomach inflammation due to "some irritant substance". On 14 May, Florence was arrested and charged with his murder.

One thing was quite clear: that Maybrick had been for years in the habit of taking various dangerous substances as stimulants, including arsenic and strychnine. In any modem court of law, this would have been sufficient to ensure his wife's acquittal. Moreover, even the Home Office expert, Dr Thomas Stevenson, admitted that arsenic is a cumulative poison that will be stored up in the system; this in itself should have been enough to acquit Florence Maybrick.

Unfortunately, her three nights in London with Alfred Brierley had become known. Three days before her husband's death, she had written him a letter describing her husband as "sick unto death", and telling Brierley that there was "no fear of discovery". A servant intercepted it and handed it to Michael Maybrick.

And although the letter contained no evidence that Florence was poisoning her husband it virtually condemned her. Before a hostile jury, and an audience that hissed her, Mrs Maybrick heard Mr Justice Fitzjames Stephen read the sentence of death on Wednesday 7 August, 1889. The date of execution was fixed for 26 August.

The verdict caused nationwide indignation. But in those days there was no court of appeal. Thousands of people signed a petition for mercy. Even Maybrick's ex-mistress, Mary Hogwood, wrote from Virginia to say that he took arsenic all the time, and that she had fully expected him to die of it. Three days before she was due to hang, Florence Maybrick's sentence was commuted to life imprisonment.

She was released in 1904, and returned to America, where she wrote a book called *My Fifteen Lost Years,* and became a popular lecturer, never failing to move her audience with her simple statement: "I swear to you I am innocent." She spent the later years of her life as a recluse, surrounded by cats, dying in 1939. Her son Jim, convinced that she had murdered his father, forbade her to see her daughter Gladys; he carried a photograph of his father with him to the day of his death. Oddly enough, he also died of poison. Working in a laboratory in British Columbia, Canada, in 1911, he accidentally picked up a beaker containing cyanide - instead of water - to wash down a sandwich, and died soon after.

America differed from England in never having had a "Victorian age". Nineteenth century America was noisy, vulgar and almost painfully alive.

Mrs Fanny Trollope - mother of the novelist - and Charles Dickens took one look at the United States, and hurried back to England to write highly critical travel sketches. But American crudeness was counterbalanced by sheer inventiveness and an endless capacity for innovation. This was as apparent in its crimes of passion as in its railroads and dime stores.

In 1895, a Sunday school teacher named Theodore Durrant lured two virtuous girls - separately - into the Baptist church on Bartlett Street in San Francisco, where he killed and raped them. The first, Blanche Lamont, was placed in the belfry; the second, Minnie Williams, was left in the library where she had been stabbed to death.

Durrant had been seen with both girls just before they vanished, and was found guilty and sentenced to death. In the days when sex crime was virtually unknown, the Durrant case made headlines all round the world.

In 1897, a Chicago sausage maker named Adolph Luetgart, who had more than one mistress, decided to dispose of his wife in such a way that her body would never be found; he boiled her in one of his sausage vats, turning her into soft soap with a solution of caustic potash.

He overlooked one small detail: his wife's rings. These were found in the bottom of the vat, together with a false tooth and a sesamoid bone from the human foot. Nevertheless, Luetgart's ingenuity was not entirely wasted, because he was convicted on purely medical evidence, he escaped the death penalty and was sentenced to life imprisonment.

In France, the most sensational murder trial of 1890 was that of a pimp named Michel Eyraud and his attractive but unscrupulous mistress Gabrielle Bompard. She lured a wealthy businessman named Gouffé to her room, where Eyraud strangled him. The corpse was then placed in a trunk and dumped in a wood near Lyon. By the time the trunk was found, the body was so decomposed as to be unrecognisable. But brilliant forensic work by the great pathologist Alexandre Lacassagne revealed a legbone malformation that proved the body to be that of the missing Gouffé. Eyaraud fled to America, was recognised in Cuba through a newspaper photograph, and was taken back to Paris to face the guillotine; his mistress received life imprisonment.

THE GULDENSUPPE CASE

IT was also in 1897 - on 26 June - that two teenagers who were swimming in the East River near the foot of 11th Street discovered a floating parcel that proved to contain human remains. The headless torso was wrapped in a red and gold oilcloth with a cabbage rose pattern, and the hairy chest had a patch of skin missing, suggesting that a tattoo had been removed; the mutilations seemed to indicate surgical skill. The next day, the lower half of the body, minus the legs, was found in woods near 176th Street - the legs were later found by another two boys swimming off the Brooklyn shore.

The newspaper magnate William Randolph Hearst, virtually the inventor of the "Yellow Press", saw an opportunity to sell more of his newspapers, and assigned a "murder squad" of reporters to the case. One of these, George Arnold, was inspecting the remains (now complete except for the head) in the city morgue when he observed that the hands and the fingers were heavily calloused. Arnold was a devotee of the Turkish baths, and he knew that masseurs develop the same kind of callouses. Since the big man on the slab looked vaguely familiar, he hurried down to his favourite establishment in

Murray Hill and asked if any of the masseurs had failed to report for duty. The answer was that a man called Willie Guldensuppe had not been in for two days. And he had a tattoo on his chest. Guldensuppe had lived at a boarding-house at 439 Ninth Avenue, which was run by an unlicensed midwife called Augusta Nack.

Hearst's "murder squad" now set out to trace the distinctive oilcloth in which the remains had been wrapped, and the newspaper, the *Journal*, published appeals for information, and a coloured reproduction of the oilcloth. It was a Hearst reporter who was making a round of dry goods stores on Long Island who found the dealer who had sold the oilcloth; the man's name was Max Riger, and he described the woman who had purchased it as a well-built but not unattractive lady. Since this description fitted Augusta Nack - who had the dimensions of an opera singer -Hearst reporters galloped off to the Ninth Street boarding-house, narrowly forestalling those of a rival newspaper, the *World*, and persuaded Augusta Nack to accompany them to the police headquarters. To keep rival reporters away, Hearst rented the whole boarding-house and placed guards on the door; they even severed the telephone wires.

The police decided on shock tactics, and took Mrs Nack to view the remains. Pointing to the legs, the detective asked: "Are those Willie's?"

Mrs Nack looked at him haughtily. "I would not know, as I never saw the gentleman naked."

But the *Journal* reporters had heard another story from the inhabitants of the boarding-house and from neighbours. They asserted that Mrs Nack and Willie Guldensuppe had been lovers for years. But they had quarrelled recently, the cause apparently being a fellow lodger, a young barber named Martin Thorn.

The police managed to forestall the *Journal* reporters at the barber shop where Thorn worked. There another barber named John Gotha told them that Thorn had confessed the murder of Willie Guldensuppe to him. Thorn's story was that Mrs Nack had seduced him when her regular lover, Guldensuppe, was away. But when Guldensuppe had found them in bed together, the brawny masseur had beaten Thorn so badly that the barber had to go into hospital. And when he reported for work with two black eyes, he was dismissed. Thorn decided to change his lodgings. But Mrs Nack had continued to visit him there. And Thorn had purchased a stiletto and a pistol, determined to revenge himself . . .

Martin Thorn was arrested, and the *Journal* headline declared: MURDER MYSTERY SOLVED BY JOURNAL. By now, both the *Journal* and the police had located the spot where the murder took place. It was in a pleasantly rural area on Long Island called Woodside, not far from the store where the oilcloth had been purchased. A farm stood next to the cottage, and on the day Willie Guldensuppe's torso had been recovered from the river, the farmer had been puzzled to see that his ducks had turned a pink colour. The reason, he soon discovered, was that they had been bathing in a large pool of pink-coloured water, which had issued from the bathroom drainage pipe of the cottage next door. But it was not until the farmer read of the arrest of Martin Thorn and Augusta Nack that he connected this event with a couple who had rented the cottage two weeks earlier. They had called themselves Mr and Mrs Braun, and had paid $15 rent in advance. But they had only visited the cottage on two occasions, the second on the day of the disappearance of Willie Guldensuppe . . . Belatedly, the farmer decided to pass on his suspicions to the police.

A revolver, a carving knife and a saw were found in the cottage; but, advised by their respective lawyers, the two declined to confess. Thorn succeeded in escaping to Canada and was brought back; yet even when shown the "confession" he had allegedly made to John Gotha, he continued to insist on his total innocence.

The difference between the Nack-Thorn trial and that of Eyraud and Bompard is a measure of the difference between Paris and New York in the *fin de siècle* period; the French would have been horrified by the carelessness and levity of the American courtroom. Thorn was represented by a brilliant but not over-scrupulous lawyer named Howe, whose line of defence was simply that the two defendants were unacquainted with one another, and that neither of them knew the victim anyway. What evidence was there, asked Howe, that the assorted arms and legs belonged to Willie Goldensoup? (On other occasions he pronounced it Gludensop, Gildersleeve, Goldylocks and Silverslipper.) They might belong to any corpse. What evidence was there that the victim had ever existed?

This audacious line of defence might well have succeeded - New York jurors liked to be amused, and Howe had talked innumerable clients out of the electric chair - except that Mrs Nack decided to confess. Hearst had sent a Presbyterian minister to see her in prison every day, and one day he had brought his son, a curly-haired child of four, who climbed on to her lap and begged her to clear her conscience; Hearst naturally printed the story a day ahead of his rivals. And on the second day of the trial, Mrs Nack declared that she had seen the light, and gave a gruesomely detailed account of the crime. On the day before the murder, she and Martin Thorn had rented the cottage on Long Island. She then told Willie Guldensuppe that she had decided to run it as a baby farm, and asked him to come and give his opinion.

When Willie entered the building, Thorn was waiting behind a door, and shot him in the back of the head. Then they threw him into the empty bathtub and, while he still breathed stertorously. Thorn sawed off his head. While Mrs Nack went out to buy oilcloth, Thorn dismembered the body - he had once been a medical student, which explained the surgical skill noticed by the police surgeon. He left the taps running, under the impression that the water would run down a drain and into the sewers; in fact, there was no drain, and it formed a pool in the farmyard, where the ducks were delighted at the opportunity of a midsummer bathe. Thorn then encased the head in plaster of Paris, and threw it in the river . . .

The narrative so upset one of the jurors that he fainted and had to be carried out of court. This caused a mis-trial, and when the case was resumed, Thorn had changed his story. He now declared that the cottage had been rented only as a love nest, and that on the day of the murder, he had arrived to find Mrs Nack already there. "Willie's upstairs. I've just killed him." Once again, Howe rested his defence upon the assertion that there was no proof that the corpse was that of Willie Guldensuppe, and for a while it looked as if the absence of an American Lacassagne might sway the issue in favour of the accused. But the jury chose to be convinced by the negative evidence of the missing tattoo, and found them both guilty. Martin Thorn went to the electric chair; Mrs Nack was sentenced to twenty years. The *Journal* was jubilant, but the *World* took the view that Thorn was the victim of a scheming woman.

Mrs Nack was apparently an exemplary prisoner, and was paroled after ten years; she returned to her old neighbourhood on Ninth Avenue and opened a delicatessen shop; but for some reason, the neighbours found her cooked meats unattractive, and she retired into obscurity.

In 1914,138 articles and cartoons appeared in the Paris newspaper Le Figaro deriding the finance minister Joseph Caillaux. On 13 March, 1914, Mme Henriette Caillaux, his wife, strode into the office of Le Figaro and shot dead its leading columnist - and the man largely responsible for the lampoons - Gaston Calmette. Tried the following July, Mme Caillaux pleaded great provocation, and that the gun had gone off accidentally. She was acquitted.

SEXUAL DEVIANTS

IN 1902, Queen Victoria had been dead for only a year, and Britain was still governed by Victorian morality. This meant inevitably that any crime that involved an element of sex scandal aroused far more excitement than a crime that merely involved violence against the person. Which in turn explains the widespread press coverage given to "the Peasenhall mystery" - although in the age of the serial killer, its details seem commonplace enough.

THE PEASENHALL MYSTERY

1 JUNE, 1902, was a bright, sunny morning after a night of storm. William Harsent, a carter, walked through the peaceful Suffolk village of Peasenhall, on his way to take clean linen to his daughter Rose. He walked through the wet garden of Providence House, where the girl was in service, and pushed open the back door. What he saw made him drop the linen. Rose Harsent lay, half naked, at the foot of the stairs. Her throat was cut from ear to ear, and deep gashes covered her bare shoulders. She had been wearing a nightdress, but this had been partly torn from her, and partly burnt away. A broken medicine bottle lay on the floor beside the body.

The local policeman arrived, followed by the doctor. The policeman discovered that the broken medicine bottle had contained paraffin - which had apparently been used in the attempt to burn her. The girl's bed had not been slept in, but there were three letters in the room, one of which made an appointment to come and see her at midnight.

The signature made it clear that the author was William Gardiner, a young foreman carpenter who lived nearby; he had a wife and six children, and was known as a devout Methodist. Medical examination revealed that Rose Harsent had been dead at least four hours, and that she had been pregnant.

No one had any doubt that the father of the unborn child was William Gardiner, for in the previous year he and Rose had been the subject of scandal in Peasenhall. Two youths had seen them walking towards an empty cottage known as the "Doctor's Chapel", which stood alone in a field. The youths had hidden behind a hedge until the two had gone inside, then crept closer. They were unable to see what was happening, but the sounds made it clear. There was a rustling of clothes, then the girl gasped "Oh, oh."

The silence that followed seemed to suggest a state of mutual satisfaction. Gardiner was heard to ask her what she was thinking. She answered: "What you were reading last Sunday." He asked her what he had been reading, and she replied: "About what we are doing now." She then went on to quote the verses from Genesis, chapter 38, about how Onan "spilled his seed on the ground".

When the story was repeated in Peasenhall, the villagers, who knew their Bible, had no doubt that Gardiner and Rose Harsent had either been engaged in extremely intimate "petting", or that the youths had overheard an act of *coitus interruptus*. Gardiner was a Sunday School teacher; Rose Harsent was one of his choir girls.

The scandal was so great that an enquiry had been conducted by the Reverend John Grey; Gardiner had denied the story, saying that he had been in the "chapel" with the girl only to help her move a stiff door. Gardiner had been told "Let this be a warning to you for life", and had appeared to be suitably chastened. Yet although he promised to have nothing further to do with the girl, it was plain to people who observed them closely that they were still on intimate terms.

The day after Rose Harsent's body was found, a superintendent of police called on Gardiner, and asked him if the handwriting on one of the letters was his; Gardiner denied it. The policeman asked if the envelope in which a certain letter was contained was not identical with those used by Gardiner's building firm; again he denied it. But the next day, he was arrested and charged with Rose's murder.

Certainly, the case against him looked black. His clasp knife was found to be stained with blood, although he claimed he had been cutting up rabbits: in 1902, there was no way of testing whether a bloodstain was from a human being or an animal; Paul Uhlenhuth *had* discovered the basic principle in 1900, but it had never been used outside Germany.

Various witnesses said that they saw a large fire burning at the back of Gardiner's house on the morning after the murder; the prosecution argued that this explained why no bloodstained clothing was found in the house; Gardiner's wife testified that there had been a fire, but that it was only the usual fire they lit on Sundays; but she did not explain why they needed a fire on a hot June morning.

Gardiner's defence was an alibi, supported by his wife; he said he had been at home all evening, and been in bed beside his wife all night. Gardiner was lucky. In those days the jury's verdict in a murder trial had to be unanimous, and one member of the jury stubbornly refused to be convinced of his guilt. The judge had to order a retrial, and once again the jury failed to agree.

Gardiner should have been tried a third time; but the authorities decided he had been through enough, and entered a *nolle prosequi* - which meant no further prosecution would take place. It was equivalent to the Scottish verdict of "not proven". Gardiner and his wife moved to a London suburb, where they opened a shop. Whether they prospered or not has never been recorded.

Was Gardiner guilty? We can never know. Certainly, Gardiner was not the only man who might have made Rose pregnant. Highly indecent verses were found in her room, and proved to have been written by the youth next door, who was in love with her. She was no blushing wallflower, but a forthright country girl who had no objection to keeping obscene verses. She may well have had other lovers beside Gardiner - a solution adopted by Brian Cooper in *Genesis 38* his novel about the murder, which suggests that the dissenting jury man who saved Gardiner's neck at the first trial knew the identity of the real murderer.

Only one thing is clear: Gardiner came close to the gallows, not because the evidence against him was particularly strong, but because the jury found it hard to forget that this Sunday School teacher had misbehaved himself on the floor of a disused cottage with one of his choir girls.

THE CRIPPEN CASE

IN the year 1908, a young medical assistant succeeded his superior, Dr Pepper, as pathologist at St Mary's Hospital, London. Bernard Spilsbury was recently married, and had been receiving a salary of only £200 a year. Two years later, Spilsbury achieved sudden fame as a result of the most sensational murder trial of the decade.

Dr Harvey Hawley Crippen was an American whose medical degrees, if they existed, would not have allowed him to practise in England; his diploma came from a college of homoeopathy, still regarded by many members of the medical profession as a crank aberration. He was a thirty-year-old widower when, in 1892, he met a nineteen-year-old Polish girl who had anglicized her name to Cora Turner.

She was the mistress of a stove manufacturer, who had set her up in a flat and was paying for her singing lessons - Cora was convinced she would become a great singer. The notion of being a doctor's wife appealed to her, and she induced Crippen to propose by telling him that her lover wanted her to run away with him. The great depression of 1893 made life difficult; when they were forced to move in with Cora's parents, she told him it was time to forget general practice and become a quack. Crippen remained, basically, a quack and a confidence man for the rest of his life.

The Seddon poisoning case (1912) and the Brides in the Bath case certainly deserve a place in any collection of twentieth-century crime. Seddon was a miser, who killed his lodger - another miser named Eliza Barrow - with arsenic for the sake of some India stock. Seddon's defence argued that be was already well-off and did not need the money, but Seddon's performance in the witness box made it obvious that he was an obsessional miser who would probably have killed for a five pound note. When, after his appeal against the death sentence had been dismissed, he heard the poor price that his property had fetched, he exploded: "Well, that finishes it".

George Joseph Smith was a confidence man who married lonely spinsters, relieved them of their cash, then deserted them. When one lady, Bessie Munday, refused to part with her money, he persuaded her to make a will in his favour, and drowned her in a zinc bath tub in July 1912. In December 1912, his next wife, a nurse named Alice Burnham, was also found drowned in her bath. In December 1914, the third and last victim, Margaret Lofty, was found drowned. And when a relative of Alice Burnham read the report, she went to the police. Inspector Arthur Neil decided to experiment to see how a woman could be drowned in her bath; they found that it was remarkably simple - the killer simply had to grab her knees and raise them. The experiment almost cost the life of a "volunteer" in a bathing suit. But the jury were convinced; in any case, it was impossible to believe that the deaths of three wives in zinc bathtubs could be coincidence, and Smith was hanged, still tearfully protesting his innocence.

He worked as a salesman for a patent medicine company, and in 1897, became manager of its London office. His employer called himself Professor Munyon, and his care for piles, advertised by a picture of himself with an upraised finger, gave rise to many ribald jokes. But Munyon fired Crippen when he found he was the "manager" of a music-hall singer - Cora was now calling herself Belle Elmore and was on the stage -

and from then on, Crippen was forced to struggle on as a low-grade quack selling worthless nostrums. He became a consultant to a firm of dubious ear specialists, Drovet's, and a magazine editor who called on Crippen had his ears examined with a filthy speculum which he made no attempt to disinfect. He was also startled by Crippen's flamboyant dress - the loud shirt and yellow bow tie, the enormous diamond stick-pin. For a quiet, unassuming little man, Crippen had an odd taste in clothes. He also had a reputation for meanness - he made a habit of offering to buy a drink, then discovering he had left his money at home, and borrowing half a crown. The editor commented on Crippen's "flabby gills and shifty eyes".

The "ear specialist" Drovet went bankrupt when the firm was convicted of gross negligence in the death of a locksmith and other examples of what amounted to medical homicide. But it was there that Crippen met a seventeen-year-old typist named Ethel LeNeve (whose real name was Neave). She was a moaning hypochondriac whose endless complaints of headache and catarrh had earned her the nickname "Not very well thank you". She had been a miserable child, painfully conscious of a deformed foot, and hating her father because he insisted that it would cure itself if she walked properly. (He proved to be right.)

She was also jealous of her vivacious younger sister. Yet underneath these unpleasant traits, she had a highly dominant character, and this is undoubtedly what attracted Crippen to her. Crippen was something of a masochist in his relations with women. This is presumably why he did not divorce Cora when he found she had taken an ex-prize-fighter as a lover, and why he put up with a series of lodgers who shared his wife's bed. With bankrupt stock purchased from Drovet's, Crippen set up his own business, with Ethel as his bookkeeper.

As Belle Elmore, Mrs Crippen became a moderate success in the London music-halls. The British liked the American act, and Belle seems to have been the sort of person that everyone liked anyway - immensely vital, good natured, embarrassingly frank. She earned the enduring friendship of Marie Lloyd and many other music-hall artists. But at home, she became inclined to bouts of screaming temper. And most of her friends detested her husband, regarding him as a sponger.

Ethel was in love with her employer, and in some ways they were well suited. Crippen was a crook, although as a result of weakness rather than moral delinquency, and Ethel was a pathological liar, whose biographer Tom Cullen writes that she "lied from sheer perversity - in fact she seemed incapable of telling the truth". But she was also determined not to yield her virginity until they were legally married. It was not until Crippen discovered his wife in bed with the German lodger - and Ethel, presumably, had reason to feel that his marriage was at an end - that she consented to become his wife in the physical sense of the term; the date was 6 December 1906, seven years after their first meeting. It seems to have happened in a hired hotel room during the day, as did their subsequent intimacies - Crippen continued to return home at night.

Crippen became a dentist, and Ethel his assistant. At one point, Ethel became pregnant; she was determined to have the baby, and for a while it looked as if it might transform their lives, and bring about the inevitable break with Belle. Then she had a miscarriage. And to make things worse, Belle went around telling the Music Hall Ladies' Guild members that no one was sure which of Ethel's many lovers was responsible. This may well have been the last straw. Instead of leaving her, which would have been the obviously sensible course, Crippen decided to murder her.

If the Christine Keeler affair was the great British political scandal of the 1960s, the Max Garvie affair was its equivalent among crimes of passion. Game, a wealthy farmer, lived with his wife Sheila and their three children at West Cairnbeg in east Scotland. But when Garvie began to develop an interest in nudism - he founded a local club - pornography, homosexuality and abnormal sex, the marriage began to founder. In 1967, Garvie connived at an affair between his thirty-three-year-old wife and a twenty-two-year-old school teacher, Brian Tevendale (to whom he was also attracted). Tevendale in turn introduced Garvie to his married sister, Trudy Birse, who became his mistress, her policeman husband apparently accepting the situation. (At a party, Garvie provided him with a girl, "so the foursome turned into a sextet".) On one occasion Game and Tevendale tossed up to decide who would make love to Sheila first.

When Sheila Game and Brian Tevendale ran away together, Game was upset and finally persuaded her to return. He paid to have Tevendale beaten-up twice.

On 14 May, 1968, Garvie disappeared after a Scottish National Party meeting. Eventually, Sheila Garvie admitted to her mother that her husband was dead and, after a struggle with her conscience, Mrs Watson went to the police. Game's body was discovered in an underground tunnel at Lauriston Castle. Sheila Garvie, Brian Tevendale and Tevendale's friend Alan Peters were charged with murdering him by striking him with a rifle butt or an iron bar.

Mrs Game's defence centred on her husband's sexual perversions, and the newspapers made the most of the affair, with its "sixsome" and wife-swopping. The defence did her no good; a puritanical Scottish jury found Sheila Garvie and Brian Tevendale guilty, and they were sentenced to life imprisonment (in practice, about ten years). Alan Peters was released on a verdict of "not proven". An outraged crowd chased Trudy Birse and her husband down the street, and they had to take refuge in a newspaper office.

On 17 January 1910, he bought no fewer than seventeen grains of hyoscine, a vegetable poison that he had seen administered to calm the violently insane at London's Royal Bethlehem Hospital. There is a strong probability that Ethel knew that her lover intended to kill his wife - she may even have planned it. On the evening of 31 January 1910, two of Belle's music-hall friends came to dinner at the Crippens' house at 39 Hilldrop Crescent, Camden Town. They said goodbye to Belle at 1.30 the next morning; it was the last time Belle was seen alive. The following day, Crippen pawned Belle's diamond ring and ear-rings, and Ethel slept at Hilldrop Crescent. The following day, letters were received by the Secretary of the Music Hall Guild, signed Belle Elmore and resigning her membership; they explained she was leaving for America to nurse a sick relative. Just before Easter, in the third week of March, Crippen told his friends that Belle was dangerously ill in Los Angeles; soon after, he announced her death.

Belle's friends were suspicious. Someone checked with the shipping lines, and discovered that no one of that name had sailed for America in February. A music-hall performer called Lil Hawthorne paid a visit to New York with her husband John Nash, and they also made enquiries, which achieved no positive result. Back in London, they talked to Crippen, who sobbed convincingly, but told contradictory stories about precisely where Belle had died. The Nashes decided to go to Scotland Yard. There they spoke to Chief Inspector Walter Dew of the CID, who agreed to go and talk to Crippen. And Crippen smoothly admitted that his wife was still alive. She had simply walked out on him and gone to join her former prize-fighter lover in Chicago. Dew was completely taken in. A thorough search of the house convinced him that there were no suspicious circumstances. When Dew left the house, he was more than half convinced that Belle was alive.

Then Crippen made his greatest mistake; he decided to flee. He and Ethel left for Antwerp, and took a ship for Canada. Ethel was dressed as a boy. When Dew returned two days later, and found the house deserted, he called in his team of diggers. Beneath the coal cellar floor, buried in quicklime, he found the remains of Mrs Crippen.

On board the SS *Montrose,* Crippen's secret had already been discovered by Captain Henry Kendal, who quickly realized that "Mr Robinson's" son was a girl in disguise. In a copy of the *Daily Mail* which he had taken on board, the captain found a picture of the wanted "cellar murderer" Crippen. He handed his radio operator a message that began: "Have strong suspicion that Crippen London cellar murderer and accomplice are among saloon passengers." So it came about that Crippen was the first murderer to be caught by means of wireless telegraphy, for which Marconi had received the Nobel prize in the previous year. On the morning of 31 July 1910, as the ship lay off the mouth of the St Lawrence river, Crippen went on deck, and was greeted by Dew, who greeted him with "Good morning, Dr Crippen."

On the morning Cora Crippen's remains were found, Bernard Spilsbury was preparing to leave for a holiday in Minehead with his wife and child. Then he received a summons from his eminent colleagues Drs Pepper, Willcox, and Luff, to go and view the body. Richard Muir, who had prosecuted the Stratton brothers, was in charge of the prosecution. (When

Crippen heard this, he remarked dolefully, "I fear the worst.")

Crippen was defended by the brilliant but unscrupulous Arthur Newton, who would later go to prison for forging Crippen's "Confession" and selling it to a newspaper. As a defendant, Crippen was certainly his own worst enemy. His only chance of escaping the rope was to admit everything except intent to kill. But if Crippen pleaded guilty, the whole sordid story about Belle and Ethel would emerge. Crippen chose to protect Ethel and enter a plea of innocence. His defence was that Belle had left him, just as he said, so the body in the cellar must be that of some other woman, buried by some previous tenant, or hidden there during his tenancy. It was obviously an absurd story, and it amounted to suicide. And, of course, it left to the prosecution the fairly light task of proving that the corpse *was* that of Cora Crippen. So the forensic evidence lay at the heart of the case. On one side was the formidable team of Pepper, Willcox, Luff, and Spilsbury, on the other, Drs Turnbull, Wall, and Blyth. Turnbull had been accosted by the defence at a bridge party, and had casually agreed to give his opinion as to whether a piece of skin was from the stomach, and contained an operation scar; he decided it was from a thigh, and that the scar was merely a fold. Since the operation scar was almost enough in itself to identify Mrs Crippen, the defence was delighted. When Arthur Newton broke his promise not to call Turnbull as a witness, the doctor was horrified and tried to change his mind. But unless he was willing to make a public confession of error, it was too late.

The ideal solution to the murderer's problem would be to make the body disappear into thin air; next on the list, to hide it where it could never be found. Putting it in a trunk, where it is sure to be discovered, is no way to conceal a murder. This was the view held by the Chief Constable of Brighton when, on June 17, 1934, he was called to the Brighton left- luggage office to examine the nude torso of a woman that had been found in a plywood trunk. Railway clerks could recall nothing about the man who had deposited the trunk there on Derby Day - June 6th - the busiest day of the year. But there seemed to be an abundance of clues. Sir Bernard Spilsbury examined the remains. They were of a young

woman in her early twenties. The head, arms and legs had been removed; but the torso suggested that the girl belonged to the middle or upper classes. She had a good figure, with no slack flesh, and the muscles were well developed, suggesting plenty of exercise. The golden brown of the skin also indicated that she spent much of her time in a warmer climate than England. At the time of death, she had been four months pregnant.

An alert sent out to all other cloak-rooms in England led to the discovery of the legs in a case at King's Cross station in London. Each had been severed at the thigh and the knee, and they confirmed the view that the girl had been athletic and well-proportioned. The conclusion that the trunk had been left by a man was reached by weighing it; only a strong man could have lifted it without help.

There were two important clues. On a sheet of brown paper - in which the body had been wrapped - there as the word 'ford'. It looked as if it was the second half of a place name, like Guilford or Watford. In the trunk, there were two newspapers. The copies of the Daily Mail dated May 31st and June 2nd were of an edition that was circulated only within fifty miles of London.~ When a porter recalled helping a man to carry the trunk on Derby Day, it began to look as though a solution was near but this mystery has never yet been solved.

Willcox had found hyoscine in the remains, and Crippen was proved to have bought seventeen grains of the drug not long before his wife's disappearance. Spilsbury, an expert on scar tissues, had no doubt whatsoever that the fragment of skin was from a stomach, not a thigh. And when they found part of a rectus muscle of the abdominal wall attached to the skin, the identification was proved beyond doubt. In court, Turnbull identified the skin as coming from the thigh, and the scar as a fold. Spilsbury, with the calm, grave manner that later led juries to think him infallible, pointed out the older man's errors with a pair of forceps, and the harassed Turnbull left the box with an embarrassed flush. He was followed by Dr Wall, who admitted that he had changed his mind about the piece of skin, and that it came from the abdomen. Dr Blyth disputed the presence of hyoscine in the body, but made a poor showing. It was Pepper's team that carried the day, and it was the junior member of that team who made the most powerful impression in court.

Crippen's downfall was not due entirely to this medical team. Part of the body had been wrapped in a piece of pyjamas jacket, and it contained the maker's name. One pair of Crippen's pyjamas had a missing jacket, but Crippen insisted that these had been purchased years before, in 1905 or 1906 - the intervening years would explain why the jacket was now missing. But Muir was able to establish that the pyjamas to which the jacket belonged had been purchased in 1909. Crippen was caught out in a direct lie, and this did as much as anything to convince the jury of his guilt. It took them only 27 minutes to reach their verdict. Crippen was hanged on 23 November 1910. Ethel was tried separately, but acquitted.

Ethel LeNeve emigrated to Canada, but she returned to England in 1916, took a job in a furniture store in Trafalgar Square, and married an accountant there. Her husband is said to have borne a strong resemblance to Crippen. They lived in East Croydon, and in 1954, she revealed her identity to the novelist Ursula Bloom, who had written a novel called *The Girl Who Loved Crippen.* Miss Bloom became a close friend, and it was to her that Ethel LeNeve remarked one day that she had never ceased to love Crippen. She died in 1967, at the age of eighty-four.

Many writers have pointed out that the great mystery remains: why did Crippen kill his wife when he could simply have walked out of her life? In his novel, *Dr Crippen's Diary,* Emlyn Williams settles for the explanation that Crippen gave her hyoscine tablets in mistake for aspirin. Dr Ingleby Oddie, who worked with Muir for the prosecution, had a more plausible theory. It was his belief that Crippen intended to kill his wife with hyoscine, convinced that her death would be ascribed to a heart attack - which is highly likely. What Crippen did not realize is that a large dose of hyoscine does not invariably act as a sedative, but can have the opposite effect. Witnesses claim to have heard screams coming from 39 Hilldrop Crescent on the morning of the murder, and another neighbour heard a loud bang. Crippen possessed a pistol and ammunition. Oddie speculates that the dose of hyoscine, given in a "night cap", caused her to become hysterical and start screaming. If neighbours rushed in, all Crippen's plans would collapse; there would be an inquest, and hyoscine would be discovered. Crippen salvaged what he could of the murder plan, and shot her through the head - the skull was never found. Then he had no alternative but to dismember the body and seek a place to hide it...

BYWATERS AND THOMPSON

AFTER the trial of Crippen, the next crime to arouse a comparable sensation was the case of Thompson and Bywaters - in fact, it is arguably the widely publicized *crime passionel* of the period between the two wars.

A little after midnight on 4 October, 1922, a couple were returning to their suburban home in Ilford, Essex, after an evening at the theatre. Suddenly, a man sprang out of the shadows and attacked the husband. The woman was heard to scream: "Oh don't! Oh don't!", but it was too late. Her husband lay on the pavement, and the man ran off into the darkness.

Passers-by helped her and called a doctor; he discovered that the man was already dead. The woman, twenty-eight-year-old Edith Thompson, was escorted home by the police; she was in shock, and told them she had no idea what had happened. Her husband had simply collapsed, she said; she thought he had had one of his heart attacks.

The next morning, the police informed her that her husband, Percy Thompson, had died of number of stab wounds; she still maintained that she had no clear memory of what had happened. But eventually she was able to recall that her husband had been "attacked by a strange man".

By now, the police had heard a name that interested them: Frederick Bywaters, a young man who had once lodged with the Thompsons, but had left after a quarrel with the husband. Percy Thompson's brother Richard believed that Bywaters - a laundry steward on a P & O liner – was at present at sea. But

Superintendent Frederick Wensley, the detective in charge of the case, soon ascertained this was not true. In fact, Bywaters, a young man of twenty, was soon traced to the home of Edith's parents. Brought in for questioning, he seemed arrogant and irritable; in spite of his youth, he was obviously a highly dominant character. But when some spots on the sleeve of his jacket were identified as blood, Wensley informed him that he was going to be detained. He insisted he knew nothing of the death of Percy Thompson.

Dr Arnold Axilrod, a Minneapolis dentist, broke one of the major rules of dental surgeons and often administered anaesthetic to female patients without the presence of a nurse. One seventeen-year-old girl complained that she had been given a pill that knocked her out for several hours.

On 23 April, 1955, the body of twenty-one-year-old Mary Moonen was discovered lying by the side of the road. She had been strangled. Medical examination revealed that she had recently had sexual relations, and that she was three months pregnant. Her husband, a soldier, had been in Korea for more than three months. When it was discovered that Mrs Moonen had had an appointment with Axilrod the evening before, he was arrested. Axilrod admitted that she had been to see him the previous evening, to tell him she was pregnant, then claimed he had "blacked out". When newspapers reported the case, twenty more women came forward to complain that they had been put to sleep by Dr. Axilrod for a period of hours. And Mary Moonen's sister, who had recommended Dr Axilrod to Mary, admitted that Axilrod had anaesthetized her for long periods, then talked "suggestively" to her. "I thought he was kidding".

In court, the prosecution accused Axilrod of habitually having sex with female patients under anaesthetic. Axilrod was sentenced to a period of from five to twenty years in prison.

By this time, the police had obtained a search warrant; and what they found in Edith Thompson's home would eventually condemn her to death: a series of letters written by Edith Thompson to Frederick Bywaters, and signed "Peidi". They made it clear that these two were lovers.

It was Edith who broke first. Crossing the yard at the Ilford police station, she caught a glimpse of Bywaters through the library window. She suddenly cried: "Oh God, what can I do? Why did he do it? I didn't want him to do it. I must tell the truth." And minutes later, in the CID office, she had admitted that the man who stabbed her husband to death was Frederick Bywaters. Soon afterwards, Bywaters also confessed. He admitted waiting for the couple at the end of the road, then grabbing Thompson and asking him to divorce his wife. They grappled, he said, and he pulled out a knife. "He got the worst of it." Mrs Thompson, he insisted, knew nothing about the murder; she had been standing at some distance, "spellbound", at the time ...

If that had been all, Frederick Bywaters would have hanged alone for the murder of Percy Thompson. But the letters shed an altogether more sinister complexion on the affair. For, if they were to be believed, Edith had been attempting to get rid of her husband by poisoning him with ground glass - a light bulb pounded into pieces - "big pieces too" - but he had found one of them in his porridge.

The dead man was exhumed, and his stomach examined - by Bernard Spilsbury - for signs of poisoning with powdered glass. Spilsbury concluded that Edith's account was pure imagination.

Nevertheless, when the trial opened on 6 December 1922, Edith Thompson stood beside her lover in the dock. The jury heard how, in the summer of the previous, year - 1921 - the love affair had started on holiday on the Isle of Wight. The Thompsons had gone there with Edith's younger sister Avis Graydon, and her boyfriend Freddy Bywaters, who was a friend of her brothers. Edith had known him since he was a schoolboy (even now he was only eighteen).

Edith had married Percy Thompson when she was twenty-two, in 1915; her husband, a shipping clerk was two years her senior. Percy had joined the London Scottish Regiment, and his wife, who was a romantic young woman, inclined to hysteria, had taken to her bed. However, Thompson proved to have heart trouble, and was soon invalided out. Thompson seems to have been dull but reliable, and his pay was poor; in fact, Edith contributed more to the family budget with her pay as the manageress of a millinery firm in the City, for which she received the generous (for 1922) salary of £6 a week.

It seems that the lovers were first attracted to one another on the Isle of Wight holiday, and when Bywaters kissed Edith, she made no protest. But Thompson noticed nothing of the flirtation ~ he probably regarded Bywaters as little more than a child - and liked the young man enough to suggest that he come and lodge with them. Freddy accepted the suggestion, and a week later told Edith he was in love with her. They sealed their love with a kiss - but, at this stage, went no further.

In the 1920s many major criminals in London tended to be men renowned tor their sheer masculine toughness rather than as businessmen-gangsters. East End villains such as Jew Jack "The Chopper King", Wassle Newman, Jimmy Spinks and Dodger Mullins (who was later to become something of a mentor to the Krays) were legendary for their displays of brute force. Newman was reputed to toughen his fists by tossing bricks in the air and punching them as they came down; but he was no master of organized crime. He simply enjoyed being a bully, and would go into pubs and take away the customers' beer, daring them to protest. Mullins was notorious for his perfunctory views on the fairer sex, and once disposed of a girlfriend he had tired of by pushing her out of a moving car. She broke her back. Spinks was a bully like Newman; when actually asked to pay tor some fish and chips he was guzzling, he tossed the cat belonging to the shop's owners into the chip-fryer. One Glasgow "hard man", Jimmy "Razzle Dazzle" Dalziel, was so afraid of having his masculinity questioned that he would always dance with a member of his gang, the "Parlour Boys", rather than be seen being sentimental with a woman.

Two months later - in August - Percy Thompson realized that he had made a mistake in inviting Bywaters to live with them. The young man was unmistakably sweet on Edith, and she encouraged him by allowing him to fetch and carry for her. In fact, this was what led to the quarrel that caused Freddy Bywaters to leave their home. One warm afternoon, as they sat in the garden waiting for the arrival of Avis Graydon, Edith, who was sewing, asked for a pin. Bywaters rushed in to get one. Percy Thompson was in a grumpy mood, and made some sarcastic remark about her desire to have people at her beck and call. The two began to bicker. Later, at tea, (Avis was late) Thompson continued to be grumpy, and made some critical remarks about Edith's family. In the garden, Freddy heard a crash as a chair overturned, and a gasp of pain from Edith as she was thrown across the room. Bywaters made the mistake of interfering, and was told to pack his bags and get out.

How the love affair continued is not clear - except that the lovers now had to meet secretly. Neither is it known when she cast aside her inhibitions and became the young man's mistress. But from 9 September, Bywaters was away at sea, and "Peidi" wrote to him at every opportunity ("darling your old pal is getting quite a sport. On Saturday I was first in the Egg and Spoon race and first in the 100-yard Flat race and third in the 50-yards last race . . .") When he returned, they began to meet secretly again. Percy Thompson, now thoroughly suspicious, waited at the station one day, and saw Edith get off the train with Bywaters. He waited until later, at home, to upbraid her, sneering that Bywaters had seen him at the station and "run away". When Edith reported this aspersion to her lover, he lost no time in calling at the house and insisting that he had not run away - he had simply not seen Thompson. When Bywaters told Percy Thompson that he was making Edith's life hell, the husband replied with asperity: "I've got her and I'll keep her."

In November Bywaters went back to sea in the *Morea*, and there were more letters. Thompson wanted his wife to have a baby; she refused angrily. Then she suddenly decided she preferred domestic peace, and told her lover that she had given way and "surrendered to him unconditionally" - a phrase that sounds as if it was intended to arouse jealousy. Now the letters begin to contain daydreams of getting rid of her husband. How about poisoned chocolates? Or hyoscine, the drug Crippen had used? She might poison him with gas if they had gas in the house . . . But perhaps a ground electric light bulb would serve just as well? Or an overdose of opium? It was soon after this that she told her lover that she had tried powdered glass three times, but that she had decided to give up these attempts at murder after her husband found a large piece of glass in his porridge; further attempts could wait until Bywaters returned. She reassured Bywaters that if Percy died, there would be no suspicion because of his bad heart.

In 1918, as we shall see, New Orleans had its own series of "Ripper murders": an individual who became known, as "the Mad Axe Man" broke into houses and attacked sleepers with a hatchet; he also cut their throats with a razor. He was never caught; but, like the Ripper murders, this series of crimes suddenly ceased. The Axe Man crimes simply fail to fit the pattern of murder as it had been known up till then. He was not even a "degenerate" - at least, there were no sexual attacks on the victims. A new age of murder had begun.

This is apparent even to the most casual student of crime. The Crippen murder is basically the "old fashioned" type of crime; it might have been dramatised by an Elizabethan playwright. It is essentially a drama of good against evil, of a fairly decent human under the strain of temptation, giving way to "diabolic impulses" - like Macbeth. This element can be found in most classic murder cases - the Red Barn murder, Lizzie Borden, Crippen, William Herbert Wallace. The Victorians found it necessary to apply the same explanation to the strange crimes of Jack the Ripper who killed and disembowelled five prostitutes in 1888; the favourite theory was that he was some sort of religious maniac - perhaps also a surgeon - driven mad by brooding on sin and prostitution. Now, more than a century later, we can see that he was an ordinary sadist, a man who - probably when drunk had an overwhelming urge to cut open women. And our knowledge of modem murderers of this type - we now call them "serial killers" - enables us to say with a fair degree of confidence that he was a member of the working class, not some unbalanced doctor or lawyer (or member of the royal family, as a recent theory has it).

The *Morea* was away on a long voyage - to Australia - so Edith had plenty of time to daydream. But finally - on 23 September, 1922 - the long wait was over. They met at a restaurant opposite her office in Aldersgate Street. On Saturday morning she got time off from work and they spent the morning in the park. They even seem to have found an opportunity to make love, for she writes tenderly about "what happened last night". She was remorseful about going to the theatre with her husband, and advised her lover to "do something to make you forget" - perhaps take Avis out. "I'll be hurt I know, but I want you to hurt me - I do really ..."

In fact, Bywaters spent the evening with her parents in Upper Norwood. Then, with a sheath knife in his pocket, he had made his way to Ilford to meet them on their return from the theatre ...

This, then, was the evidence presented before Mr Justice Shearman, who was clearly horrified by the letters and all they implied. "Right-minded persons will be filled with disgust", he told the jury. The Solicitor General, Sir Thomas Inskip, who presented the case for the prosecution, found it an easy task to convince the jury that Edith Thompson was a wicked and abandoned woman who had planned the murder of her husband. The letters - presented by the prosecution in telling but misleading extracts - left no doubt of it.

Edith spoke in her own defence, alleging that that she was deliberately misleading her lover into thinking she wanted to kill her husband when her real motive was to keep his love. (She might have been more honest if she had said "keep him interested".)

After a hostile summing-up from the judge, the jury took only two hours to find both defendants guilty. When Mr Justice Shearman read aloud the death sentence, Edith cried: "I am not guilty. Oh God, I am not guilty." The date of the execution was set for 6 January, 1923. Three days before this, Bywaters told his mother that although *he* was guilty and deserved to hang, Edith had no idea he intended to attack her husband that night.

But a last minute appeal - based on this "confession" - to the Home Secretary was rejected only hours before the execution. Both were hanged at precisely 9 a.m., she in Holloway, he in Pentonville. Edith Thompson was in such a state of collapse that she had to be carried to the scaffold.

Was she guilty? Certainly not of planning the events of the night of 4 October. But although the sixty-two letters fail to prove that she really intended her husband to die, they leave no doubt that it was she who put the idea of killing Percy Thompson into her lover's head. Her letters about ground glass and poison, whether fantasy or not, undoubtedly convinced Frederick Bywaters that Percy Thompson had to die. Whether or not that constitutes guilt must be left to the judgement of the reader.

COLD-BLOODED CRIMES OF PASSION

WHAT brings a person to commit murder - high emotion, unrequited love, monetary gain? Certainly in the case of Albert Guay, who had a bomb planted on a plane which not only killed his wife but twenty-two other people as well; or when you kill someone that you don't really even love, as in the case of Ruth Ellis, just because they were refusing to speak to you, the answer is sheer cold-bloodedness. The reasoning behind these sort of crimes of passion surely cannot be explained in any other terms.

THE GUAY CASE

IF there was a prize for the most cold-blooded of all crimes of passion, it would probably go to Albert Guay.

On 9 September, 1949, a Quebec Airways Dakota DC-3 on a flight from Montreal to Seven Islands exploded in mid-air, only minutes after take-off. The plane dived into inaccessible forest near Sault-au-Cochon, forty miles northeast of Quebec. All twenty-three passengers were killed. Since witnesses noticed that the engines were still running as it crashed, engine failure was clearly not the cause of the disaster. But there was scorched metal in the luggage compartment, suggesting an explosion. Chemical analysis revealed minute traces of dynamite.

A careful check of every item of freight against the company's list revealed that only one seemed to be missing, a "religious statuette" weighing twenty-six pounds. But there was no record of its sender; all the reception could remember about the person who delivered it was that it was a woman dressed in black. An appeal through the news media failed to trace her. But ten days later, a taxi driver came forward to say that he had picked up a woman of this description on the day of the explosion. And he could also remember the address from which he had picked her up. This proved to be the home of a woman named Marie Pitre. But when the police tried to call on her, they learned that she was in hospital, recovering from the effects of an overdose of sleeping tablets.

As soon as she was able to give an interview, Marie Pitre told them how she had come to take the parcel to the airport. For many years she had been the mistress of a Quebec jeweller named Joseph Albert Guay, who was married. He had, she said, virtually blackmailed her into taking the statue to the airport by offering to cancel some of her promissory notes that he held. Their love affair had been over ever since he met an attractive nineteen year old night club cigarette girl named Marie-Ange Robitaille, who preferred to be called Mary Angel.

Then Marie Pitre dropped her bombshell. "I didn't know his wife would be on that flight." And she went on to describe how, some weeks before, Guay had telephoned her and asked her to purchase ten pounds of dynamite, which he needed for landscape gardening.

Assuming that it was this dynamite that had blown up the Dakota, how had it been detonated? It would need a timing mechanism. And Marie, they discovered, had a brother named Genereux Ruest who was an expert clock repairer ... In fact, Ruest, who was a cripple, admitted that he had made the timing mechanism; Guay, he said, had told him that he needed it for exploding the dynamite to blow some rocks out of the ground.

Albert Guay, a thin-faced man with a pencil-line moustache, was arrested, and the newspapers headlined the "love bomb murder" - since it was by now plain that he had decided to kill his wife Rita in order to marry the pretty waitress Mary Angel. The crime caused such indignation that police had to hold back crowds who wanted to lynch the jeweller on the spot.

At the trial, Guay's defence lawyer had an impossible task; he was found guilty and sentenced to death. He met the hangman on 10 January, 1951. Eighteen months later, Marie Pitre and her brother also went to the gallows - new evidence had revealed that they had willingly participated in the murder plot that had killed twenty-two other people besides the intended victim.

RUTH ELLIS

ON the evening of Easter Sunday, 10 April, 1955, two men emerged from the Magdala public house in Hampstead, and walked towards the grey-green Vanguard parked outside. They were David Blakely, twenty-five, the manager of a small engineering firm in Penn, and a car salesman, Clive Gunnell, thirty. Both were carrying quarts of light ale, for they were about to return to a party which they had left to buy more beer. As Blakely fumbled for his keys, a small peroxide blonde woman approached him, calling out: "David". Blakely failed to hear her. Moments later she stood beside him, took a revolver from her handbag, and pointed it at him. Blakely gave a cry of alarm and ran towards the back of the car. Two shots hit him in the back. He started to run uphill, and another shot hit him. Even as he lay on the pavement, with Clive Gunnell bending over him, the woman went on firing over Gunnell's shoulder; one shot hit a female pedestrian in the thumb. When the hammer clicked on an empty chamber, the woman turned and said unemotionally:

"Go and call the police." A man strode out of the pub. "I *am* a police officer." He took the revolver away from her. David Blakely was dead when the ambulance arrived.

The killer was twenty-eight-year-old Ruth Ellis, and she and David Blakely had been lovers for two years, ever since they met at a London club. Blakely was something of a playboy; he had a well paid job, an inheritance of £7,000 (a considerable sum in 1953) and an allowance from his stepfather. His passion in life was racing cars.

Their relationship had been stormy; both were inclined to be jealous and possessive. Both were also emotionally unstable. Ruth hungered for constant flattery and attention; Blakely was immature, and inclined to become so rude when drunk that he drove away many regular customers at the Little Club, of which Ruth was the manageress. Eventually, the proprietor fired Ruth, largely because of her relationship with Blakely. A businessman named Desmond Cussen took her - and her two small children ~ into his flat in Devonshire Place and financed her; he was so devoted to her that he even allowed her to continue to sleep with Blakely.

Ruth's intensely possessive attitude to Blakely was due partly to insecurity. Born into a relatively poor family in Rhyl, North Wales, (her father was a musician), Ruth Neilson had left school at fifteen and worked as a machinist in a factory and a Woolworth's shopgirl. At seventeen she had become a photographer's assistant, and soon fell in love with a French Canadian soldier named Clare. She learned she was pregnant soon after Christmas 1944. Clare had promised to marry her, but a letter to his C.O. revealed that he already had a wife and children in Canada. Ruth got herself a job as a cashier, and a daughter was born in 1944. Clare paid maintainence, but it stopped when he returned to Canada.

She became a photographer's model and often posed in the nude. In a Mayfair club she met vice-boss Morris Conley, who was soon sleeping with her, and persuaded her to work for him as a hostess in the Court Club. She did not *have to* sleep with customers, but it helped her take-home pay. In 1950 she became pregnant again; she had an abortion. In November that year she married a recently divorced dentist, George Ellis - another customer - who was an alcoholic. He was forty-one, she twenty-four. A daughter was born in 1951, but by then her husband's alcoholism had been intensified by endless quarrels, often ending in violence, and they separated. She returned to being a club hostess for Maurice Conley, and in 1953, he made her manageress of the Little Club in Brompton Road, Knightsbridge. She received £25 a week and a rent-free flat. One client gave her £400 for going on holiday with him.

Her first meeting with the weakly handsome David Blakely was not a success - she remarked afterwards "I hope I never see that little shit again." But although Ruth had a violent temper she knew - as a hostess - how to keep it. Blakely had just become engaged to an heiress, but he was an incorrigible philanderer. Since Ruth made a habit of being available to customers of her choice, it was not too difficult to persuade her to let him sleep with her. He understood that he was not her "lover" - merely a customer who was being allowed to spend nights in her bed, as many others did. And, according to Ruth Ellis, she was not particularly in love with him either. Nevertheless, they seem to have found one another exciting in bed, and Blakely was soon sleeping in her flat five nights a week. They became lovers almost as a matter of habit. It was also a matter of vanity; Ruth liked the idea of having an affair with this ex-public schoolboy with his private income and racing car, and he liked the idea of having a sexy blonde mistress whose bed was right above the club.

In February 1954, she had an abortion - this time Blakely's baby. But while Blakely was away racing at Le Mans, she slept with her devoted admirer Desmond Cussen. He lent her money - she was insatiable where cash was concerned - and pressed her to marry him. Ruth was not interested - not because she preferred Blakely, for both of them slept with other people, but because she was not deeply attracted to Cussen. She may also have preferred Cussen as an adoring swain rather than a husband who might take her for granted. Cussen even arranged to send her son Andy to a private school.

Ruth and Blakely quarrelled after she noticed love-scratches on his back. He was the one who made it up, and the affair continued. Both of them were now drinking much more heavily. He often hit her when he lost his temper, on one occasion knocking her down the stairs. One night, she went back home with a man who had picked her up, and took off all her clothes to reveal bruises all over her body. Profits at the Club were sagging, and when Conley finally fired her at the end of 1954, she moved in with Desmond Cussen. But she often spent the night in a hotel with Blakely.

It was clear to their friends that the couple were bad for one another. Blakely was aggressive when drunk, and he was drunk much of the time. Ruth was less aggressive but gave as good as she got. They often quarrelled, but always made up in bed. Even when she knew he was having an affair with a married woman in Perm, she continued to let him sleep with her. Towards the end of January 1955, they went on a nine day drinking spree that ended with quarrels and hysteria. On another occasion Ruth hid his car keys, and when Clive Gunnell and another friend arrived to pick him up, Ruth had a black eye and many bruises. There was another hysterical scene when Blakely found his car keys and tried to drive off. Yet after more bitter recriminations, he sent her red carnations with a note: "Sorry darling. I love you. David." When she decided to leave Cussen's flat, the faithful admirer lent her the money to rent a new one in Kensington. When Blakely told her he had broken off his affair with the married woman, she allowed him to stay there with her. She then persuaded Cussen to take her down to a pub in Penn, and found Blakely in there with the woman. Back in Kensington, after another violent quarrel, he hit her in the stomach and caused a miscarriage.

In spite of this, they spent the night before Good Friday, 1955, in her flat. Ruth had become extremely sexually demanding, and Blakely was taking amyl nitrite, a sexual stimulant. He left the flat early because he found her son Andy (now ten) too noisy. Later that day he told friends - a married couple named Findlater - that he couldn't stand it any longer, and had to get away from her. Carole Findlater, who had once been Blakely's girlfriend, was glad to hear it; she disliked Ruth intensely. She persuaded Blakely to come home for lunch, and that night he stood Ruth up and went out with them. Late at night, Ruth repeatedly rang the Findlaters demanding to talk to him. When they refused -or hung up when they recognized her voice - she drove around to their flat and smashed in all the windows of Blakely's car. The police arrived, and Ruth was finally driven back home by Desmond Cussen.

The following day - Saturday - was spent unsuccessfully pursuing Blakely - Ruth was now convinced he was making love to the nursemaid of the Findlaters. Until late that night she hung around opposite the Findlaters' flat. She went home in the early hours of the morning, and telephoned the Findlaters; again she failed to speak to Blakely.

On Sunday, there was another party at the Findlaters, after a lunchtime drink at the Magdala public house. At 9 that evening, Carole Findlater ran out of cigarettes, and asked Blakely to go and get her some. Blakely decided they also needed more beer, and asked Clive Gunnell to go with him to the Magdala public house. . .

According to Ruth Ellis - speaking shortly before her execution - she had been pouring out her fury to Desmond Cussen when he had handed her a loaded revolver. He had then driven her to woodland where she practised shooting. And later, she alleged, he drove her to the Magdala public house. She arrived minutes before David Blakely came out with Clive Gunnel. Soon after that, David Blakely lay dead on the pavement, and Ruth Ellis was taken into custody.

On Monday 20 June, 1955, Ruth Ellis stood in the dock at the Old Bailey. And when she told the prosecuting Q.C, Christmas Humphreys, that she had intended to kill Blakely, the judge warned the jury that only one verdict was possible: murder. They took only fourteen minutes to arrive at the guilty verdict.

The campaign for the abolition of capital punishment was then in full swing, and many petitions for her reprieve were sent to the Home Secretary, one with 50,000 signatures. But the bank manager's wife who had been wounded in the hand by Ruth Ellis wrote a letter to a newspaper pointing out that if Ruth was reprieved, "other vindictive and jealous young women" might begin gunning down their boyfriends. She had actually witnessed the murder, and obviously felt that a woman who could shoot someone with such deliberate intent deserved to die.

The knowledge that her reprieve had been turned down did not seem to bother Ruth Ellis; she wrote to one friend that being hanged would be no worse than having a tooth out.

On 13 July, 1955, she drank a hot brandy, then walked firmly the few steps to the execution shed. She was the last woman to be hanged in England - ten years later, in 1965, capital punishment was abolished.

Clive Gunnell had a nervous breakdown after witnessing his friend being shot at close range. He told the present author that he rejected the idea that Ruth killed David Blakely because she was so much in love with him. He felt she was an exhibitionist who wanted to "become known", and that the murder was a theatrical performance as much as a *crime passionel.* Years of drunken parties and prostitution (for she was basically a high class call girl) had led to states of depression and boredom when she needed emotional stimulants. She killed Blakely because she was infuriated at his refusal to speak to her or see her after their last lovemaking session on Good Friday; there may also have been an element of self-disgust in her decision to make the break final by killing him. Her death, Gunnell argued, was a spectacular form of suicide.

THE DE KAPLANY CASE

WHAT is the most horrific crime of passion on record? There is a body of opinion in favour of a French case of 1958, which the press labelled "the demon lovers". Dr Yves Evenou was to all appearances a happily married man, who sometimes referred to his wife Marie-Claire as an angel. But Evenou harboured peculiar sexual tastes of which his wife knew nothing. In 1953, when a dressmaker named Simone Deschamps came to his surgery, Evenou divined instantly that this rather plain forty-three year old woman was a masochist, and therefore his ideal sex partner. They became lovers, and she submitted to sexual demands that included flagellation and semi-public strip-tease. In 1958, Evenou decided his wife had to die, and that the crime should be performed by his mistress - in the nude. By now, Simone Deschamps had moved into a flat directly underneath that occupied by the Evenous. On the evening of the murder, Evenou telephoned her, and she mounted the stairs wearing only a coat and shoes. In his flat she removed these. He then led her to the bed where his wife - a semi-invalid - lay half drugged. Evenou pulled back the bedclothes and ordered his mistress to strike. But Simone's hands were weak, and the first blow only awakened Marie-Claire. Evenou held her down while Simone completed the butchery, stabbing her eleven times. The murder of Marie-Claire Evenou was less an attempt to dispose of an unwanted wife than an act of sexual perversion by two lovers who had tried everything.

There was hardly any attempt to cover up the crime, and the lovers were arrested almost immediately. Evenou died before the trial - a life of excess had drained his vitality. Simone Deschamps escaped the death penalty, but received life imprisonment with hard labour.

But even the crime of Simone Deschamps sounds humane in comparison with the murder committed by the Hungarian doctor Geza de Kaplany. He had fled from communist persecution in Hungary, and took up practice in San Jose, California, in 1962, as an anaesthesiologist in a hospital. Kaplany was good looking in a cold, thin-lipped way. He soon fell violently in love with a beauty queen who was more than ten years his junior, and married her in 1962. But only a few days after he and Hajna moved into their apartment, he became impotent with his wife. He convinced himself that all the men in the apartment building were pursuing her, and that she was encouraging them. This, at all events, is the excuse he gave for what followed.

Kaplany bought himself a record player, and on the morning of 28 August, 1962, neighbours became indignant at the tremendous volume at which Kaplany was playing his new toy. They could also hear a woman's piercing screams above the music. Finally, the police arrived, and pounded on the door until it opened. Kaplany stood there in bloodstained underwear, and wearing rubber gloves. On the bed lay Hajna de Kaplany, so mutilated that the police were sickened. Kaplany had tied her hands and feet to the bedposts, then made razor cuts all over her body, into which he poured hydrochloric, sulphuric and nitric acid. He mutilated her face, her genitals, her breasts. His aim, he explained later, was not to kill her but to make sure that she ceased to be attractive to males.

Hajna died twenty-four hours later in hospital, while her mother knelt beside the bed and prayed - not for her to live, but to die.

The Denise Labbé case is perhaps one of the most sinister crimes of passion on record. Twenty-year-old Denise, a secretary, enjoyed mixing - and sleeping - with students at Rennes, and had a baby daughter, Catherine, by one of them. Then she met officer cadet Jacques Algarron, a brilliant mathematician who believed ardently in Nietzsche's theory of the superman. He decided that he and Denise were a "super-couple", and that to prove that she was above conventional morality, she should kill her daughter. She was so besotted with him that she agreed. Delays brought threats to break off the affair. Eventually, she tried to throw Catherine from a high window, but found she could not bring herself to do it. Then she pushed her into the canal, but relented, and summoned help. A second attempt at drowning was frustrated when neighbours heard the child's cries and pulled her out of the river. On 8 November, 1954, Denise Labbé finally drowned Catherine in a stone wash basin. Friends were suspicious, and Denise was questioned by police. Finally, she confessed, implicating her lover. "It was a ritual murder". She was sentenced to life imprisonment, Algarron to twenty years hard labour.

At the trial, Kaplany became hysterical as he viewed the photographs of his wife's mutilated body. He was found guilty and sentenced to life imprisonment.

In fact, Kaplany was released after only eleven years, even before he was due for parole. Then he was virtually smuggled out of the country, to take up duties in Taiwan as a "cardiac specialist" - a position for which he was unqualified. The parole board never explained its strange decision - it may have been due to the feeling that his life would have been in danger if he had been released in the normal way.

This seems highly probable, since his crime was probably the most sadistic in American criminal history.

HOLLYWOOD SCANDALS

ONE of the first great successes to come out of the west coast village called Hollywood was The Life of an American Fireman (made in 1902 - The Great Train Robbery came the following year). The excited patrons saw a house on fire, a man being rescued from an upstairs window, then a woman and a child,-coughing and staggering as they are overcome with smoke. The firemen dash through the streets on their horse-drawn wagons. As the mother and child collapse, unconscious, a fireman bursts in thorough the door. He carries the unconscious mother to a ladder that appears at the window; she wakes and begs him to save her baby. He carries her down, then goes back into the burning building, and gets the child.

Mother and child are united as the house blazes. There wasn't a dry eye in the cinema. It had only lasted a few minutes, but people felt as if they'd been through a crisis together; they smiled through their tears at their next door neighbour. What a noble, interesting thing life is, after all! And the cinema could suddenly bring it home to you . . . It deserves to be classified with the novel as one of the greatest imaginative advances in human history.

Then there was Chaplin, the comic but game little tramp, always in trouble, always fighting against the odds, always looking shyly and adoringly at the pretty girl in the spring dress - and often getting her in the end. People could certainly identify with him. Chaplin records his amazement when he left Hollywood, where he'd been churning out two-reelers for years, to visit

England and other towns in the United States, to realize that he was world famous. It wasn't just because Chaplin was a great performer. It was because he came from Hollywood - a word that was acquiring a dubious quality called "glamour". Hollywood was a magic land, a kind of Fairyland on earth.

Many of its inhabitants held the same view, though for different reasons. It was soon clear that there was as much money in movies as in oil. Even the most successful actors and comedians could only play in one theatre at a time; but a movie could be shown in a hundred vaudeville theatres and Nickelodeons all over the country. One of the earliest successes, Rescued by Rover (made in England), cost seven pounds thirteen shillings and ninepence to produce (in 1905). The prints - 400 of them - sold for a little over £10 each, so the producer, Hepworth, multiplied his investment by five hundred or so. The Dream of a Rarebit Fiend cost $350 to make, and made $30,000.

When the full length "drama" came in, around 1915, a movie might cost $50,000 and make a million. Producers found themselves unimaginably rich, rich on the scale of an eastern potentate. Their way of spending their money was to shower it on stars, directors and sets. In 1905, $10 a week was regarded as a reasonable wage for an actor; by 1920, a star could receive $100,000 for a movie that took ten weeks to make. Hollywood had the glamour of immense riches.

It was the Arbuckle case of 1921 that shocked the general public into realizing that many of its celluloid heroines and saints were nymphomaniacs and sinners. The studios had always done their best to hush up divorces and similar scandals. But now the jolly, fat-boy of the screen, who looked so completely amiable (as, indeed, he was), was suddenly associated with a rape ending in death. The lid was off Hollywood, and the stench was like a graveyard. In her best known photograph, Virginia Rappe looked so sweet and wholesome, the kind of girl every decent American boy wanted to marry. The thought of the manner of her death aroused a kind of morbid fascination; the grinning Fatty Arbuckle became a real life Dracula or Jack the Ripper. He was acquitted, and the jury foreman at his last trial said: "We feel a great injustice has been done him." Arbuckle chortled with delight; the studio bosses announced more Arbuckle pictures. They had simply failed to understand that once an idol has been de-glamorized, there can be no come-back. Possibly Arbuckle might have made a new career as an actor in horror movies, to fit his new image; but no one thought of that. He died of a heart attack in 1933, a tired and disappointed man.

THE MURDER OF WILLIAM DESMOND TAYLOR

AND in the year after the Arbuckle scandal, while the fat clown was still on trial, another scandal struck Hollywood like an earth tremor. The victim was the suave, handsome British film director William Desmond Taylor. Taylor was a cultured man who was enthusiastic about the works of Freud. No doubt he found himself in agreement with Freud's thesis that the libido is the basic animal drive, for he himself had an insatiable sexual appetite. And as the $100,000 a year chief-director of Lasky Studios (later Paramount), he had no difficulty in keeping himself supplied with a stream of young girls, all of whom wanted to marry him. Taylor had no intention of marrying anyone for a long time; he was enjoying life too much. Then, on 21 February 1922, it came to a sudden end. His valet, Peavy, returning to Taylor's expensive Westlake Park home at 7.30 in the morning, found his master lying on his back, quite dead.

The death was assumed to be natural until Taylor was turned over, and two bullet holes were seen. The police searching the house found evidence of Taylor's incredible love-life, including a note from a popular star of the day, Mary Miles

Minter -a Chaplin leading lady - which read "Dearest, I love you, I love you, I love you" with a whole row of kisses. At Taylor's funeral, she kissed the corpse on the lips. Like Arbuckle, she was unaware of the attitude of the outside world to the idols who inhabited their dream paradise. They were supposed to live up to their screen image of purity and innocence. Miss Minter's career came to an end with the scandal. So did that of Mabel Normand, a comedienne who, next to Mary Pickford, was Hollywood's most popular actress. Miss Normand had spent an hour or so with Taylor the evening before his death, although she had left early. She claimed to be his fiancee. But police discovered that the angelic-looking Miss Normand had been experimenting with drugs, and that Taylor had been doing his best to track down whoever was supplying her.

Hollywood began as a ranch near the small town of Los Angeles in 1886. In 1913, a New York film company run by two men named Schmuel Gelbfisz and Jesse Lasky sent their new employee Cecil B. DeMille to Flagstaff, Arizona, looking for a place to make westerns. Flagstaff was too flat, so he got back on the train and went on to Los Angeles, where he rented a barn on the Hollywood ranch, and made a smash hit called The Squaw Man.
Schmel Gelbfisz was already calling himself Samuel Goldfish, but he then decided on a further change - to Samuel Goldwyn. Under that name he is known as the author of some famous remarks, such as "Include me out", and "My film Hans Christian Andersen is full of charmth and warmth". He always referred to the classic film made by his own studio as Withering Heights. When told that he could not make The Well of Loneliness because it was about lesbians, he said, "Ok, make 'em Austrians."

In fact, the aftermath of Taylor's death was almost worse than the murder itself. It emerged that Miss Minter was not twenty, as she was supposed to be, but thirty. Peavy, the valet, was very obviously homosexual, and for a while, this seemed to supply a possible motive for the crime. For Taylor's previous valet, a man named Sands, had been forging cheques in Taylor's name while his master was in Europe, and smashing his cars. Yet when he returned, Taylor only fired him. Since then, Taylor had been burgled twice. Was it possible that Sands was Taylor's lover, and had killed him out of jealousy or revenge? This notion was exploded when it was revealed that "Sands" was actually Taylor's disreputable brother Denis, who had come to America with him years before. Denis was never located.

In 1967, the famous director King Vidor decided to turn the Taylor mystery into a film. What he learned about the power of the studios and the corruption of the Los Angeles police department shocked him. To begin with, Adolph Zukor and other executives of Famous Players Lasky had descended on Taylor's house immediately after the murder and destroyed a quantity of letters and papers. But according to information leaked to the press, the police had no difficulty finding out that Taylor had been having affairs with half the celebrated beauties of Hollywood. They also found quantities of silk knickers in Taylor's bedroom - souvenirs, apparently, of his many conquests, as well as pornographic photographs showing Taylor in the act of lovemaking with various ladies, and a pink silk nightie monogrammed MMM.

Mary Miles Minter and Mabel Norman were naturally among the suspects. So was Mary's mother, Charlotte Shelby, a tough Hollywood Mom who may have been in love with Taylor herself. But she, apparently, had a good alibi.

When Vidor's biographer, Sidney Kirkpatrick, began gathering material for his book, he discovered that a whole year seemed to be missing from his papers: 1967. When he found the missing papers in a locked strongbox in the garage, he discovered that they concerned Vidor's investigations of the Taylor case. And when he read them, he saw why Vidor had decided to abandon the whole project.

It seemed that Vidor had soon discovered that Taylor was not what he pretended to be; the evidence indicated that the insatiable Don Juan was, in fact, a bisexual, with a distinct preference for men, and (quite possibly) for young boys, who were procured by his valet. And at least one Hollywood journalist was able to tell Vidor authoritatively that the killer was the mother of Mary Miles Minter, the ambitious and ruthless Charlotte Shelby who, like everyone else, was unaware of Taylor's true sexual inclinations. Charlotte was not only fixated on Taylor; she was also quite determined that her daughter - who was also her meal ticket - should not get involved with any man. It seems that on the evening in question, Mary was having a tête-a-tête with Taylor when Mabel Norman turned up; so Mary fled into hiding. Her mother became increasingly irritable, and finally went looking for her with a pistol. She saw Mabel Normand emerge from Taylor's house, then peered in through the window and saw her daughter coming out of hiding. This was too much and she stalked in and shot the dastardly seducer - in the back, having made him raise his arms.

So what about all the stories of underwear and pornographic pictures? These, apparently, were the work of the film studio, which promptly went into action to throw up a heavy smoke screen. Hollywood had enough scandals - Fatty Arbuckle had just been arrested - and they had no intention of this one reaching court. So the press was fed with scandalous stories about silk nighties. The careers of Mary Miles Minter and Mabel Normand were ruined, but the wicked Charlotte lived on and prospered.

Mabel Normand's career experienced a setback as a result of the William Desmond Taylor affair, but it was wrecked by a further scandal in 1924. She was visiting Chaplin's leading lady Edna Puviance and her oilman lover Cortland S. Dines; all got very drunk. When Edna's chauffeur came to pick her up, he and Dines got into an argument and the chauffeur shot Dines, slightly wounding him. (The chauffeur was obviously her lover.) At a hearing, it was revealed that the chauffeur was a convicted criminal and a drug addict. This, combined with the fact that the women were drunk on bootleg liquor (1924 was the middle of the Prohibition) and that everyone was rumoured to be naked, was the final nail in the coffin of Mabel's career.

According to Kirkpatrick, Vidor decided to give up the film because he didn't want to taint the lives of the stars concerned. He may also have been worried about libel. But surely the true answer is that even in 1967, a film about a Don Juan who turned out to be a homosexual pedophile was just not good Hollywood material. That particular can of worms was just a little too putrid.

THE JEAN HARLOW MYSTERY

IN the early Thirties, some Hollywood producers decided they might as well cash in on the bad reputation of the movie capital. So while some studios were making fortunes with films like *Little Women* and *Rebecca of Sunnybrook Farm,* others introduced a new frankness to the screen. Mae West's line "Come up, see me sometime" became the great catch phrase of the day. Middle-aged men and women chuckled appreciatively when she sang: "I Like a Man Who Takes His Time". And the latest screen idol was a blonde newcomer called Harlean Carpenter, who chose the screen name Jean Harlow.

Harlow replaced Clara Bow, the "It" girl, in the public's estimation; Clara Bow lost her reputation in 1930, when her ex-secretary testified in court that she was virtually a nymphomaniac, spending her large income on good-looking gigolos. Yet even Harlow - whose screen personality was nearly as uninhibited as Mae West's - felt the chilly breath of scandal when her husband, the director and movie-supervisor Paul Bern, was found shot dead under mysterious circumstances in September 1932.

Amusingly enough, what alarmed the studios was not that the public might feel Harlow was as wicked as her screen parts, but that she might arouse pity - and contempt. She had been married to Bern - who was regarded as a Hollywood "genius" - for only two months, and reports said they were ideally happy. But police investigation revealed that, for many years before marrying Harlow, Bern had lived with another lovely blonde,

Dorothy Millette. After a nervous breakdown, Dorothy had spent some time in a mental home, then continued to live in the Algonquin Hotel in New York, at Bern's expense. She killed herself the day after Paul's death - she was in San Francisco at the time. Was it she who had killed Bern? Bern was naked when he was found, and a woman's wet swimsuit had been found beside the swimming pool. Hollywood was afraid that Harlow might arouse pity as a woman who could not keep her husband -and that would ruin her screen image just as surely as the Taylor scandal had ruined Mabel Normand's.

There were whispers of an even more embarrassing nature. Jean Harlow told friends, in the strictest confidence, that Bern was impotent. On the night before his death, he had come into her bedroom wearing a huge artificial phallus, and had pranced around the room with it on, until the two of them, shrieking with laughter, tore it to pieces with scissors and flushed it down the lavatory.

In 1960, the Hollywood screenwriter Ben Hecht wrote an article in *Playboy* claiming that Bern *had* been murdered by another woman, probably Dorothy Millette. The studio had forged the suicide note. Yet in retrospect, Hecht's version seems unlikely. Why did Dorothy Millette have a nervous breakdown in the first place - was it because Bern was impotent? Why did she and Bern never live together again, although they remained fond of one another? (The tone of the letters exchanged between them makes it unlikely that she would kill him.)

On September 23, 1935, two decapitated bodies were found in the area of Kingsbury Run and East 45th Street, a slum area. Both had been mutilated with a knife; both were men - one, a 28-year-old medical orderly, the other, a 40-year-old vagrant, who was never identified. The fact that both victims were male suggested that the killer was homosexual, and a sadistic pervert. But when, four months later, the headless body of a 42-year-old prostitute was found not far from Kingsbury Run, the police became less sure that they were looking for a homosexual; the woman's body had been hacked as if in a frenzy, and the head was never found.

The man who was then in charge of Cleveland's Police department was Eliott Ness - hero of T.V. 's 'Untouchables'. Ness recognized that the usual methods of detection were of doubtful value here. But he realized that the mad killer was finding most of his victims among prostitutes and down-and-outs. The latter congregated in a shanty-town area in the centre of the city, near the market. One night in August, Ness raided the place, forced its inhabitants to leave, and burnt it down. This had the desired effect of depriving the killer of his victims; there were no more murders.

Ness also reasoned that the 'Mad Butcher' must be of a certain type. He must be big and powerful to overpower his victims. He must own a car, to transport the bodies. He must live alone, and in some quiet area - perhaps an unfrequented cul de sac - in order not to arouse the curiosity of his neighbours. And in order to fit this pattern, he must be rich, or at least well off.

Ness's team made painstaking enquiries in Cleveland society and, according to Oscar Fraley, chronicler of the 'Untouchables', soon found a suspect who fitted. He was physically huge, homosexual, sullen and paranoid, and well-to-do. Ness had the man brought in for questioning, and for months played a cat and mouse game with him. The man, confident he was cleverer than the police eventually admitted the murders.

The note itself sounds too authentic to be a forgery. It said: "Unfortunately, this is the only way to make good the frightful wrong I have done you and to wipe out my abject humiliation. I love you"; a postscript added, "You understand last night was only a comedy". That has the ring of authenticity, and it fits the story of impotence and the dildo episode. The fact that Bern was naked when he was shot also suggests self-humiliation.

Four years later, in 1936, Jean Harlow also died, of a gall bladder infection. She was twenty-six. There were many American matrons who felt it was divine justice.

THE DEATH OF THELMA TODD

IN 1935, another Hollywood tragedy ended in murder - although it is still officially listed as suicide. Thelma Todd became Miss Massachusetts at the age of sixteen, and shortly thereafter, she threw up a job as a teacher to go to Hollywood. In 1926, when she was twenty-one, she appeared with fifteen other promising "starlets" in a film called *Fascinating Youth,* and her career was launched. Her real talent proved to be in comedy, and the beautiful and statuesque blonde appeared with Laurel and Hardy and the Marx Brothers. ("Madame, you're making history. Madame, you're making me, I wish you'd keep your hands to yourself.") She was a kind, good-natured, popular girl, with an odd touch of sadness, a feeling that life - or perhaps just her life - was unreal. In 1932 - when she was twenty-seven - she married an agent named Di Cicco, but two years later they were divorced. She had already decided to retire from films and go into the restaurant business in 1935 when Stanley Lupino and his daughter Ida decided to give a party for her.

Di Cicco came to the restaurant and there was a quarrel. In the early hours of a Sunday morning in December 1935, she was driven to her home in Santa Monica. More than twenty-four hours later, she was found dead in her car, in the garage above the beach restaurant she owned. There was blood on her face, and she still wore the party clothes. She had died of carbon monoxide poisoning. The odd thing was that her evening slippers showed no sign of the wear they would have received climbing the rough concrete stairs - 270 of them - from the beach to the garage. All the evidence pointed to murder -particularly when it was discovered that she had been alive on the Sunday after the party, and had been seen in a car with a dark, foreign-looking man. It looked very much as if he had driven into the garage with her, knocked her unconscious, then turned on the exhaust and left her.

Again, the movie moguls went into a frantic scramble of panic. A scandal of this sort was the last thing the studio wanted. The police suddenly announced that, in spite of the blood on her face, they were treating Thelma Todd's death as a case of suicide. Even when they received a telegram from Ogden, Utah, saying that Thelma Todd's killer was in a hotel there, they did nothing about it. The case has remained as mysterious as when it happened.

By 1968, the golden days of Hollywood were only a distant memory, and a death that occurred in a Spanish-style hilltop home above Laurel Canyon may be regarded as a sad postscript to the history of the great years. Ramon Navarro, the handsome star of *Ben Hur* and *The Prisoner of Zenda,* was found, naked and beaten to death, on his bed, his hands tied behind him. The house was ransacked. Navarro's telephone bill revealed that a long call had been made to Chicago on 30 October, the evening of his death. It was easy to discover that the call had been made by a young man named Tom Ferguson. The police arrested Tom and his brother Paul, a male prostitute. When they discovered that seventy-year-old Navarro, the idol of American women, had been homosexual, they had solved the case. The Ferguson brothers admitted going to Navarro's house - at his request - and then tying him up and beating him to make him reveal the whereabouts of money. He died from swallowing blood. The robbery netted the brothers about $45. Both brothers received life imprisonment.

THE MYSTERY DEATH OF MARILYN MONROE

BUT by far the most famous of all Hollywood scandal stories is the mystery surrounding the death of Marilyn Monroe.

The life of Hollywood's most famous "sex symbol" had been a tale of hardship and misfortune. Norma Jeane Baker (or Jean, as she sometimes spelt it) was born in Los Angeles in 1926, the illegitimate daughter of Gladys Pearl Baker (née Monroe), a film cutter at the Columbia and RKO studios, and a fellow lodger called C. Stanley Gifford. There was a history of mental instability and suicide in Gladys's family. For most of Norma Jean's childhood, her mother was confined in mental institutions, and from the age of five, the child spent most of her life in foster homes - no less than twelve of them. At the age of seven her mother had her back home to live, but then had a nervous breakdown and was hospitalized yet again. At the age of eight (other biographical sources say eleven) she was persuaded to remove her dress by a gentlemanly old boarder who caressed her genitals; finally, troubled by his excitement, she put her clothes back on and went to tell her foster mother, who told her angrily to shut up. But she later admitted to a lover that the experience had not been traumatic - in fact, that she had found it oddly pleasant.

At sixteen, she married a twenty-one-year-old aircraft-worker, Jim Dougherty, mainly to gain her independence, but they had little in common; a year later, she made her first suicide attempt. In the same year she became a paint sprayer in a defence plant and was "discovered" by an army photographer; her "pin-ups" achieved great success among GIs, and the army medical corps voted her the girl they would most like to examine. During this period, she later confessed to Ted Jordan, an actor who became her lover, she often went out to bars, became acquainted with men, and allowed them to make love to her. It may be that her earlier sexual encounter with the boarder had established a pattern - the recognition that she could give men pleasure and excite their tenderness by removing her dress. She always seems to have been singularly frank about sex, describing it uninhibitedly in four-letter words.

By 1946 she had been to a charm school and become a successful model; soon afterwards she was signed on by 20th Century Fox at $125 a week, and her name changed to Marilyn Monroe.

The two years she spent as a Fox starlet were not a success; after two brief appearances she was dropped. Columbia signed her up, and she received good reviews playing the lead in a low budget musical. *Ladies of the Chorus*. But Columbia also allowed her contract to expire. While unemployed she posed for a nude calendar photograph, for which she was paid $50; it went on to make three quarters of a million dollars for the calendar company.

The police are continually being astonished by some of the strange forms of suicide they encounter. Wendel and Svensson's classic study Crime Detection has a description of a man who killed himself by placing the blade of a jack knife against his forehead, and then driving it in by beating his head against a tree; it also contains a photograph of the body of an old lady who carefully placed all her furniture in a pile in the middle of the room, lay down on it, and set it on fire.

Taylor's Medical Jurisprudence has an even stranger case of a man who burned himself to death by lying down on his mattress and setting it on fire; but as he burned to death, he periodically got up, and made notes about his sensations.

All healthy creatures loathe the thought of death; so we find such cases incomprehensible. We try to dismiss them by saying: 'They were insane' - and we are reassured by the usual coroner's verdict: 'Suicide while the balance of mind was disturbed.' Yet in recent years, criminologists have realized that this simplistic view is false, and that the truth about suicide brings us to the edge of some of the most disturbing and fascinating revelations in the whole field of criminology.

Expressed in crudely simple terms, you could say that most psychologists now accept that murder is a form of suicide. At first sight, this seems absurd. Take the case of a bank robber who shoots a policeman in the course of escape, or a rapist who strangles the girl to make sure she cannot identify him. Surely this is a matter of self-preservation rather than 'suicide'?

No. The impulse that makes a man capable of murder springs from his indifference to life: to others' and to his own.

In the 1950s, she returned to Fox, and although she always played the same dumb blonde, her popularity increased slowly but surely. She herself was frank about the extent to which her success was due to granting her sexual favours to directors and agents: she commented: "I spent a lot of time on my knees." But her sexual acquiescence was also the secret of her immense success on the screen: it was the combination of physical beauty and the hint of submissiveness, of availability, that made her every man's dream. It was also the basic cause of her downfall; every man wanted her, and her desire to please meant that she often said yes. The list of her lovers was immense, and one writer estimates that she had as many as fourteen abortions.

Her marriage to baseball star Joe Di Maggio in 1954 confirmed her status as Hollywood's latest "sex goddess". But he wanted a wife rather than a movie star, and they divorced only nine months later.

Deciding that she wanted to be a "real actress" she went to New York to study at the Actors Studio, where she met the playwright Arthur Miller. Back at Fox, she was now the most valuable property in Hollywood, and her salary reflected this. But she was also well known for her unpunctuality and unreliability. This was due mainly to her depressions, and their accompanying listlessness. Marriage to Arthur Miller in 1956 seemed to stabilize her, but after an affair with her co-star Yves Montand in 1960, they were divorced. After that she embarked on an affair with Frank Sinatra.

Miller had written a screenplay especially for her - *The Misfits, a* grim and depressing piece of work about drifters that contributed to the death of one of its male stars, dark Gable, and which increased her tendency to depression. A month after the premiere she had a total breakdown and entered a psychiatric hospital. On the set of her final film, *Something's Got to Give,* her behaviour became increasingly erratic, until she was finally sacked.

No one, therefore, was greatly surprised when, on 5 August 1962, her housekeeper found her naked and lifeless body on her bed, apparently a victim of suicide (although there was no suicide note). The coroner's verdict was death by an overdose of barbiturates - Nembutal. Yet there were some odd discrepancies. Although there were huge quantities of barbiturates in her bloodstream and liver, there was no sign of it in her stomach - an impossibility unless she had injected it. But no sign of needle punctures was found at the autopsy, and there was no syringe in the room.

Persistent rumours began to circulate that her death was not suicide, but murder. It had been widely known among journalists that Marilyn had had an affair with President Kennedy - a notorious womanizer - but it was less well known that she had later had an affair with his brother Robert, the Attorney General. A detective named Fred Otash later revealed that he had bugged the telephone in Marilyn's home at the behest of Bobby Kennedy. Kennedy spoke openly to Marilyn about some rather dangerous secrets, such as his intention of having Fidel Castro assassinated. (Thirteen years later, it was revealed that President Kennedy had authorized the CIA to try and assassinate Castro.) Kennedy also told her that he intended to get "that son of a bitch Jimmy Hoffa" into jail no matter what it cost him - Hoffa was head of the Teamsters Union and a man with known links to organized crime. Marilyn kept notes of these conversations because Kennedy was sometimes irritated by her failure to remember things he had said to her.

According to a man named Bob Slatzer, who claimed that he and Marilyn had been briefly married in 1946, Marilyn had been hoping to marry Bobby Kennedy, who had promised to divorce his wife. But Bobby Kennedy was warned off such an idea by his brother, and he accordingly broke with her not long before her death. She was bitter, and felt she had been used; she tried to ring Kennedy in Washington many times, without success. She hinted strongly to the actor Peter Lawford that she was pregnant with Bobby Kennedy's child. More dangerously, she told Slatzer that she was thinking of calling a press conference to "blow the lid off the whole damn thing". She repeated the same thing to Lawford, declaring that she had been "used . . . thrown from one man to another" (which obviously referred to the Kennedys) and that she was "going public with everything". Since Lawford was John Kennedy's brother-in-law, this was a sure way of getting her message through to the President.

On the weekend she died, Robert Kennedy travelled to San Francisco to address a law conference. In his Monroe biography *Goddess,* Anthony Summers argues convincingly that Robert Kennedy came over to see her that afternoon, to explain that their affair had come to an end. In fact, neighbours reported seeing Robert Kennedy arrive with another man carrying a bag like a doctor's bag. Kennedy himself is alleged to have testified in a secret deposition that he had been there, and that the doctor had given Marilyn an injection of a strong sedative to calm her nerves.

It later emerged that Marilyn's home had also been "bugged" by an electronics expert named Bernard Spindel, who was employed by Jimmy Hoffa. Spindel subsequently went to prison, and alleged that he had also bugged the home of Peter Lawford. Hoffa's intention was to get compromising material about Robert Kennedy. Kennedy found out about the tapes of his conversation with Marilyn, and offered Spindel $25,000 for them, which Spindel refused.

That some kind of "cover up" had happened became clear in the years following her death. Peter Lawford admitted that she had telephoned him - sounding tired and slurry - to say goodbye during that last evening, and that he had wanted to rush over to see she was all right. He was dissuaded because it would compromise him. What seems clear is that before her death was announced, someone rushed to her house to remove compromising material, such as the red notebook recording Kennedy's conversations - most writers on the case believe this was done by CIA agents on the orders of Robert Kennedy. The housekeeper, Mrs Murray, told two conflicting stories about the time she found Marilyn's body - that it was at midnight, and that it was at 3.30 a.m.

But there is one aspect of 'victimology' that has so far been totally neglected by the criminologist: the quession of the 'born victim': the person who seems to be 'destined' for murder.

Anyone who has read a biographical sketch of President Kennedy - with his childhood illnesses, his accident proneness, his wartime misadventures - feels that this was the type of president to be killed by an assassin's bullet. The same applied to his brother Robert. On the other hand, Lyndon Johnson somehow didn't look accident prone; a kind of invulnerability was a chart of his total personality.

It would be easy for speculations of this kind to turn into absurd hypotheses and preposterous guesses. However, the psychologist Carl Jung developed a valuable concept called 'synchronicity' which

could be defined as 'a coincidence that is not a coincidence Since President Kennedy's death, many writers have pointed out the number of strange similarities between the assassinations of Lincoln and Kennedy; both were shot in the head from behind, both succeeded by a southerner called Johnson, both advised by their -secretaries against the visit that led to the assassination, and so on. There is also the extraordinary fact-that ever since Lincoln, who was elected in 1860, all presidents elected at 20-year inervals have been assassinated or died in office: Garfield, 1880, McKinley, 1900, Harding, 1920, Roosevelt, 1940, Kennedy, 1960.

Most of this evidence seems to suggest suicide - except for the absence of barbiturates in her stomach. Is it possible that she injected herself with the drug, and that the telltale syringe was removed by the "searchers"? This is unlikely, since she is known to have been a "pill popper" who never used a syringe. Another possibility emerges from remarks made by Lawford's ex-wife Deborah Gould; she claims she asked her husband how Marilyn died, and that he replied: "She took her last big enema." This suggests that she was sometimes in the habit of taking drugs anally - which has a far quicker effect than taking them orally, since the drugs enter the large intestine immediately.

But if Marilyn sometimes took drugs by enema, then it is also possible that she was killed by the same method. People to whom she talked on the afternoon of her death say she sounded slurred. A neighbour who sometimes lent her sleeping pills says she asked to borrow some that afternoon; but there had been pills in the house in the morning. If she had been "popping pills" all day, she may have lapsed into unconsciousness, and been vulnerable to attack.

If she *was* murdered, then the chief suspect is bound to be Bobby Kennedy himself. The private detective Fred Otash claims that Lawford burst into his office at 3 a.m., announcing that Marilyn Monroe was dead, and that Bobby Kennedy was there - adding that Kennedy and Marilyn had "got into a big fight that evening". Otash went on to allege that he was then hired by Lawford to go to Marilyn's home and remove any evidence of links with the Kennedys.

Norman Mailer, in his biography of Marilyn Monroe, denies that the Kennedys could have been implicated in her death, because it would have been stupid of them to risk everything. His theory is that disaffected members of the CIA, angry about the bungled assassination attempt on Castro, killed Marilyn to destroy the Kennedy Administration. They left the room looking as if she had committed suicide, but knew that the lack of barbiturates in her stomach would point to murder. The finger would then be pointed at the Kennedys.

Since Jimmy Hoffa knew of the existence of the compromising tapes, he also had a motive for killing Marilyn Monroe. Her death, and the subsequent revelation of her affairs with both Kennedy brothers, would trigger a scandal, and would probably prevent Kennedy from being re-elected in 1964. In fact, Spindel's home was raided in 1966, on the orders of the Manhattan District Attorney, Frank Hogan, and all his equipment seized. He believed that this was inspired by Robert Kennedy. And members of the DA's staff subsequently told a reporter that the tapes contained evidence that "Marilyn had been murdered and that Bobby Kennedy was involved "if only as a catalyst causing someone else to do it." This "someone else" was presumably Jimmy Hoffa.

But if Marilyn Monroe was murdered in order to ruin the Kennedys, then why did the scandal never explode as planned? Was it because the cover-up by the Kennedys was too efficient? (It is known that Marilyn's phone records for August were illegally seized from the General Telephone Company, presumably to hide the number of calls she made to Washington in her last days.) Even so, it is hard to believe that the Kennedys' many underworld enemies would have failed to make use of compromising material.

Milo Speriglio, a private detective hired by Robert Slatzer, has stated unequivocally: "Marilyn Monroe was politically assassinated" - for the sake of the tapes of sessions with Robert Kennedy, and the red notebook containing his "secrets". Speriglio later changed his opinion and came to believe that she was killed at the behest of Mafia boss Sam Giancana, who wanted her dead because she knew of his involvement in the plot to kill Castro.

One man who may know more of the truth than most is Marilyn's doctor, Ralph Greenson, to whom she talked confidentially on the afternoon before her death. Greenson says he cannot reveal what she said, but that it leads him to believe that her death was not suicide. Pressed for more information, he said exasperatedly: "Listen . . . talk to Bobby Kennedy."

Asked if it was true that she had nothing on when the famous calendar photograph was taken, Marilyn Monroe replied: "I had the radio on."

Most of those who might have been able to tell the truth about Marilyn Monroe's death died without revealing it: President Kennedy in 1963, Robert Kennedy in 1965, Jimmy Hoffa in 1975. (Hoffa simply vanished, and has never been found.) The final verdict must be that Marilyn Monroe *could* have committed suicide - she had reason to do so - but that much of the evidence points towards murder. On the other hand, if Lawford's remark that she used enemas to administer drugs is correct, then suicide remains the likeliest possibility after all.

THE BLACK DAHLIA

NO account of Los Angeles murder mysteries would be complete without a mention of the most gruesome riddle of all: the death of aspiring actress Elizabeth Short. Known as the Black Dahlia because of her preference for black underwear, "Beth" had spent much of her short life (she was twenty-two when she was murdered) wandering aimlessly - from Massachusetts to Florida, from Florida to California, then Chicago, then California again. Like Marilyn Monroe, she spent her life seeking security and affection.

In January 1947, her body was found in a vacant lot in Los Angeles, severed in half at the waist; medical examination revealed that she had been suspended upside down and tortured to death over many hours - the body was covered with cigarette burns and small cuts. The letters "BD" had been cut into her thigh.

The killer sent the police some of her personal possessions-including her birth certificate and address book - together with a letter made up of words and letters clipped from newspapers. The horror of the crime made it headline news, and in due course, the police received twenty-eight confessions, all of which proved to be false. Two films have been made about the case, and a novel that suggests that she was involved in sadistic pornographic movies. But although more confessions have continued to pour in down the years, the case remains unsolved.

AN ADDICTION TO MURDER

THE term serial killer was invented in the early 1980s by FBI agent Robert Ressler, to describe someone who kills repeatedly and obsessively.

In the past we called anyone who killed several people a "mass murderer". But then, the mass murderer may be someone like the unknown killer who slaughtered the Evangelista family in Detroit on 2 July, 1929, chopping off the heads of all six.

Or like Charles Whitman, the sniper who shot eighteen people from a tower on the campus of the University of Texas in August 1966. These were clearly not serial killers - which means one after another - because the murders all happened on the same occasion.

Neither was the French "Bluebeard" Landru, because although he killed eleven women between 1914 and 1918, his crimes were coldly and carefully planned, and the motive was purely financial.

For, as we shall see, the modern serial killer tends to choose his victims at random, and the motive is usually sexual. Even more important is the fact that he (or she) becomes addicted to murder, exactly as if it were a drug.

EIGHTEENTH AND NINETEENTH CENTURY CRIMES

NOW oddly enough, sex crime is a relatively modem phenomenon. In the eighteenth century, the usual motive for most crime was money, and throughout most of the nineteenth century, the majority of murders were committed in the course of robbery -with a few during domestic quarrels. It was only towards the end of the century that "sex crime", in our modem sense of the word (that is, murder for rape) began to appear. In the eighteen and nineteenth centuries, prostitutes were so cheap -and almost any lower class girl could be had for a few pence -that sex crime would have been pointless.

But Victorian prudery gradually created a new attitude towards sex - as something rather wicked and forbidden. This was first reflected in the rise of pornography ("dirty books" were also an invention of the nineteenth century) which was often about rape or child-sex. And, inevitably, a time came when dreams of "the forbidden" turned into the real thing. In July 1867, a clerk named Frederick Baker persuaded eight year old Fanny Adams to go with him for a walk in the fields near Alton, Hampshire. Her dismembered body was found a few hours later in a hop garden. Baker had written in his diary: "Killed a young girl today. It was fine and hot." Baker was hanged at Winchester.

Two years later, in Boston, a bellringer named Thomas Piper began attacking and raping girls, battering them unconscious; in May 1875 he lured five year old Mabel Young into the belfry knocked her unconscious with a cricket bat, but was interrupted, The girl died in hospital and Piper was hanged after confessing to five sex murders and several rapes of children. Piper had some claim to be regarded as the first serial killer.

On the other hand, that dubious distinction might be claimd by a German murderess named Anna Zwanziger, a domestic servant who, in the first decade of the nineteenth century, developed a strange obsession with poisoning with arsenic. The wife of a judge named Glaser seems to have been her first victim in August 1808; the judge himself followed, probably because he resisted Anna's hints about marriage. Another judge named Grohmann died in May 1809. Weeks later she poisoned the wife of her latest employer, a magistrate named Gebhardt. When he dismissed her, most people in the house became violently ill, and it was discovered that someone had put arsenic in the salt cellars. Tests for arsenic had just been invented, and Anna was arrested in September 1809. Frau Glaser's body was exhumed and found to be full of arsenic. After being sentenced to death by beheading, Anna Zwanziger admitted that she frequently administered poison simply for her own entertainment. She is quoted as saying that "poison was her truest friend", and the German judge Feuerbach says that she trembled with rapture when she looked upon arsenic. This casual attitude towards her victims certainly entitles her to be labelled a serial killer rather than someone who murdered for profit.

Gesina Gottfried, another German, began by poisoning a brutal husband who beat her, then killed her second husband and his parents. In the course of her subsequent travels as a domestic servant she killed at least another half a dozen people. Her last intended victim, a man called Rumf, wondered about the white powder she had sprinkled on the leg of pork, and went to the police to get it analysed. When it was identified as arsenic, she confessed to her murders with a certain pride, and was executed in 1828. Like Anna Zwanziger, she had somehow become addicted to administering poison.

This is even more true of a Frenchwoman named Helene Jegado, a Breton peasant woman who went on a poisoning spree over a twenty year period, beginning around 1830. In one house where she worked, seven people died in agony, including her own sister; by 1851 the number of her victims had swelled to at least twenty-three, although a more probable estimate is sixty. Arrested for poisoning a fellow servant of whom she was jealous, she was executed in 1852.

A Dutch nurse named van der Linden - of whom, unfortunately, little is known - surpassed all three women by poisoning more than a hundred.

Here, then, we can see the true characteristics of the serial killer - a kind of obsessive *repetitiveness* that resembles a hiccup. What causes it? Some religiously-inclined people suggested that a demon had got into them (and many serial killers have, in fact, declared that they were possessed by the Devil). Whatever the answer, there seems to be no doubt that murder can become an addiction, and that most serial killers are, in some sense, "driven by a demon".

One of the oddest cases of "murder addiction" on record took place in the Lyon area of France in the mid-nineteenth century. In May 1861, an attractive twenty-seven year old servant girl named Marie Pichon was accosted by a peasant with a deformed upper lip, who asked her the way to the registry-office for servants. When the man learned that Marie was looking for work, he offered her a good job at a country house near Montlul. The girl agreed to accompany him there, and they travelled to Montlul by train. The peasant, who seemed a stolid but decent sort of man, told her that he was the gardener of a certain Madame Girard, and that another servant who was due to arrive the day before had fallen ill, so that Madame was in urgent need of a replacement.

At Montlul, the peasant took her box on his shoulder, and told her they would take a short cut across the fields. As night closed in, he stopped to take breath, and suggested that they should abandon her trunk until morning. Without waiting for her agreement, he dropped it in a ditch, then he plodded on into the darkness. The girl became increasingly nervous at his odd behaviour, and when they came to a hilltop, and there was still no sign of lights, she declared her unwillingness to go any further. The man then rounded on her suddenly and threw a noose round her neck. She pushed him and they both fell down. Marie was first on her feet, running into the darkness. She crashed through hedges, scratching herself and tearing her clothes, and frequently fell over. But eventually, the footsteps of her pursuer died away, and she almost collapsed with relief when she came to a house. Its owner, who was still unharnessing his horse after a journey, was startled by this bloodstained apparition, but he let her in, and sent for the local constable. Then she was taken to the police station, where she repeated her story. In spite of her exhaustion, she was taken back over the route she had traced with the murderous peasant. They eventually found the ditch where the man had dropped her trunk - but it had vanished.

The news caused a sensation in the Trevoux district - particularly when it was recollected that Marie Pichon was not the first girl to place her trust in a peasant with a deformed lip. Six years earlier, in 1855, a servant girl named Josephine Charloty had become suspicious as she plodded across the fields behind the squarely-built man who was carrying her trunk, and had finally fled and taken refuge in a farmhouse. Another girl, Victorine Perrin, had simply lost her trunk when the man had run off into the trees. In all, five girls had escape alive. But others had vanished and never been seen again. In February 1855, a few months before the escape of Josephine Charloty, hunters had found the battered corpse of a young woman hidden in a thicket; she was naked except for her bloodstained shoes and a piece of ribbon. The body was later identified as that of Marie Buday, who had left Lyon with a "countryman" a few days before she was found. Another girl, Marie Curt, had turned down the offer of a job from the man with the twisted lip, but recommended a friend named Olympe Alabert; Olympe had then vanished.

Now although the police had been aware that a peasant posing as a gardener was abducting and murdering girls, no one seems to have made a determined effort to find him. (The French police force was still in its infancy.) But the case of Marie Pichon was discussed all over the district. And three men in an inn at nearby Dayncux decided that the peasant with the deformed lip sounded like a local gardener known as Raymund, who lived nearby. Raymund kept himself to himself, spent a great deal of time in Lyon - where he was supposed to work as a porter -and had a lump on his upper lip. His real name, it seemed, was Martin Dumollard.

A local Justice of the Peace agreed that Dumollard certainly sounded as if he might be the wanted man, and issued a search warrant. This search was conducted by the magistrate himself, and it left no doubt that Dumollard was a major suspect. The house was found to contain many women's garments, and some of them were bloodstained. Dumollard was immediately arrested. He strenuously denied knowing anything about missing women, and went on denying it even when confronted by Marie Pichon herself, who identified him as her attacker.

Meanwhile, Dumollard's wife had decided to save her own neck by confessing. She admitted that her husband had brought home Marie Pichon's box, and that he had burned much of its contents in a wood - obviously concerned that if the police tracked him down the box would conclusively prove his guilt. The investigators went to the spot she indicated, and found buried ashes and fragments of books and clothes, which Marie Pichon identified.

Martin Dumollard continued to insist stolidly that he knew nothing about any crimes. But his wife Anne admitted that a woman's watch found in their house had been brought home one night four years earlier, with a quantity of bloodstained clothes. Dumollard had told her he had killed a girl in a wood at Mont Main, and was now going to bury her. He left the house with a spade. . .

A careful search of the wood revealed a depression that might be a grave. Two feet below the surface, the diggers found a female skeleton. The skull showed she had died from a violent blow on the head.

Dumollard continued to deny all knowledge of the crime. But his wife went on to describe another occasion when he had returned home and told her he had killed a girl. This body was also discovered buried in a wood, the Bois de Communes. The dry earth had preserved the flesh, and the position of the body made it clear that the girl had been buried alive and had suffocated while trying to claw her way out of the grave. She was identified as Marie Eulalie Bursod.

In the seven months that followed, it became clear that Martin Dumollard had killed at least six girls (clothes of ten were found in his home), and had unsuccessfully tried to lure another nine to their deaths. On 20 January, 1862, he and his wife were tried at the Assizes at Bourg (Ain), and he was found guilty and sentenced to death. Anne Dumollard was sentenced to twenty years imprisonment. He was guillotined on 20 March, 1862, and his head sent to be examined by phrenologists, who declared that, according to the shape of his skull, Dumollard should have been a man of the finest character.

Why did Dumollard kill? We do not know whether sex played any part in the crimes. But the notion that he murdered purely for profit seemed unlikely. The possessions of a servant girl would fetch very little money on the second-hand market, and it seems relatively certain that such girls would have very little money. So Dumollard's relative prosperity (his house was larger than that of most peasants) can hardly be explained by his crimes.

We know little of Dumollard's background except that his parents were tramps who wandered around Italy, and that his father was a murderer who was broken on the wheel. He was undoubtedly miserly, obsessed by money - his last words to his wife were to remind her that someone had failed to repay a debt - and it seems just possible that he killed the girls for their meagre possessions. But the likeliest explanation is that Dumollard became a "murder addict", and went on killing because it gave him pleasure to lure girls to their death. He has all the characteristics of the modern "serial killer".

JACK THE RIPPER

EARLY in the morning of 31 August 1888, a carter named George Cross was walking along Bucks Row, Whitechapel - in London's East End - when he saw what he thought was a bundle of tarpaulin lying on the pavement. It proved to be a woman with her skirt above her waist. In the local mortuary, it was discovered that she had been disembowelled. Mary Ann Nicholls was almost certainly the first victim of the sadistic killer who became known as Jack the Ripper. (He provided himself with the nickname in a series of letters that he wrote to the Central News Agency.)

Just over a week later, he killed and disembowelled a prostitute named Annie Chapman in a Whitechapel backyard. On the morning of 30 September, he was interrupted soon after he had cut the throat of a third victim - a woman called Elizabeth Stride - and immediately went and killed and then disembowelled another woman, Catherine Eddowes. On the morning of 9 November, he committed his last murder indoors, and spent hours dissecting the body of Mary Kelly by the light of a pile of rags burning in the grate. By this time Londoners were in a state of hysteria, and the Chief of Police was forced to resign. But the Whitechapel murders were at an end.

All theories suggesting that the Ripper was a "gentleman" - an insane doctor, a cricket-playing lawyer, a member of the royal family - are almost certainly wide of the mark. The kind of frustration that produced the Ripper murders is characteristic of someone who lacks other means of self-expression, someone who is illiterate or only semi-literate. Such a suspect came to the attention of Daniel Farson after he had directed a television programme about Jack the Ripper.

The Marquis de Sade, who gave his name to sadism, never actually killed anyone. He had a taste for whipping prostitutes on their bare behinds - for which he paid them well – but only harmed one of them inadvertently when he gave her an aphrodisiac called Spanish Fly which made her ill. It was his atheism and anticlerical views that first landed him in jail, and he was later imprisoned in an asylum for writing dirty books. Nowadays, in the company of Jean Genet and William Burroughs, he would simply be a respected writer.

He received a letter (signed G.W.B.) from a seventy-seven-year-old man in Melbourne, Australia, who claimed that his father had confessed to being the Ripper.

> My father was a terrible drunkard and night after night he would come home and kick my mother and us kids about, something cruelly. About the year 1902 I was taught boxing and after feeling proficient to hold my own I threatened my father that if he laid a hand on my

> mother or brothers I would thrash him. He never did after that, but we lived in the same house and never spoke to each other. Later, I emigrated to Australia. . . and my mother asked me to say goodbye to my father. It was then he told me his foul history and why he did these terrible murders, and advised me to change my name because he would confess before he died.

He goes on to explain: "He did not know what he was doing but his ambition was to get drunk and an urge to kill every prostitute that accosted him." Whether or not G.W.B.'s father -whose job was collecting horse-manure - was Jack the Ripper, he is certainly a far more likely suspect than a member of "Walter's" social class.

To us, it seems obvious that Jack the Ripper's murders were sex crimes (for example, the impulse that drove him to seek out another victim when he was interrupted while killing Elizabeth Stride). But it was by no means obvious to the Victorians, who preferred to think in terms of religious mania and "moral insanity". Sexual murders were a new phenomenon in the 1880s, and the average Victorian still found it puzzling that anyone should want to kill for the sake of sexual satisfaction.

The Whitechapel murders changed all this: they produced a deep disquiet, a morbid thrill of horror that made the name of Jack the Ripper a byword all over the world. It was an instinctive recognition that some strange and frightening change had taken place. In retrospect, we can see that the Ripper murders were a kind of watershed between the century of Victorian values and the age of violence that was to come.

THE PSYCHOPATHIC KILLER

IN 1970, an American publisher brought out a volume called Killer, A Journal of Murder, and made the world suddenly aware of one of the most dangerous serial killers of the first half of the twentieth century.

His name was Carl Pamram, and the book was his autobiography, written more than forty years earlier. It was regarded as too horrifying to publish at the time, but when it finally appeared, it was hailed as a revelation of the inner workings of the mind of a serial killer. However, Panzram belongs to a rare species that criminologists label "the resentment killer".

Far more common - particularly in the last decades of the twentieth century - is the travelling serial killer, the man who moves restlessly from place to place. In a country as large as America, this makes him particularly difficult to catch, since communication between police forces in different states is often less efficient than it should be.

Earle Nelson, the "Gorilla Murderer", is generally regarded as the first example of the "travelling serial killer".

CARL PANZRAM

PANZRAM was born in June 1891, on a small farm in Minnesota, in the American midwest. His father had deserted the family when Carl was a child, leaving his mother to care for a family of six. When Carl came home from school in the afternoon he was immediately put to working in the fields. "My portion of pay consisted of plenty of work and a sound beating every time I done anything that displeased anyone who was older and stronger. . ."

When he was eleven, Carl burgled the house of a well-to-do neighbour and was sent to reform school. He was a rebellious boy, and was often violently beaten. Because he was a highly "dominant" personality, the heatings only deepened the desire to avenge the injustice on "society". He would have agreed with the painter Gauguin who said: "Life being what it is, one dreams of revenge."

Travelling around the country on freight trains, the young Panzram was sexually violated by four hoboes. The experience suggested a new method of expressing his aggression. "... whenever I met [a hobo] who wasn't too rusty looking I would make him raise his hands and drop his pants. I wasn't very particular either. I rode them old and young, tall and short, white and black." When a brakesman caught Panzram and two other hoboes in a railway truck Panzram drew his revolver and raped the man, then forced the other two hoboes to do the same at gunpoint. It was his way of telling "authority" what he thought of it.

Panzram lived by burglary, mugging and robbing churches. He spent a great deal of time in prison, but became a skilled escapist. But he had his own peculiar sense of loyalty. After breaking jail in Salem, Oregon, he broke in again to try to rescue a safe blower named Cal Jordan; he was caught and got thirty days. "The thanks I got from old Cal was that he thought I was in love with him and he tried to mount me, but I wasn't broke to ride and he was, so I rode him. At that time he was about fifty years old and I was twenty or twenty-one, but I was strong and he was weak."

In Various prisons, he became known as one of the toughest troublemakers ever encountered. What drove him to his most violent frenzies was a sense of injustice. In Oregon he was offered a minimal sentence if he would reveal the whereabouts of the stolen goods; Panzram kept his side of the bargain but was sentenced to seven years. He managed to escape from his cell and wreck the jail, burning furniture and mattresses.

They beat him up and sent him to the toughest prison in the state. There he promptly threw the contents of a chamberpot in a guard's face; he was beaten unconscious and chained to the door of a dark cell for thirty days, where he screamed defiance. He aided another prisoner to escape, and in the hunt the warden was shot dead.

The new warden was tougher than ever. Panzram burned down the prison workshop and later a flax mill. Given a job in the kitchen, he went berserk with an axe. He incited the other prisoners to revolt, and the atmosphere became so tense that guards would not venture into the yard. Finally, the warden was dismissed.

The new warden, a man named Murphy, was an idealist who believed that prisoners would respond to kindness. When Panzram was caught trying to escape, Murphy sent for him and told him that, according to reports, he was "the meanest and most cowardly degenerate that they had ever seen."

When Panzram agreed, Murphy astonished him by telling him that he would let him walk out of the jail if he would swear to return in time for supper. Panzram agreed - with no intention of keeping his word; but when supper time came, something made him go back.

Gradually, Murphy increased his freedom, and that of the other prisoners. But one night Panzram got drunk with a pretty nurse and decided to abscond. Recaptured after a gun battle, he was thrown into the punishment cell, and Murphy's humanitarian regime came to an abrupt end.

This experience seems to have been something of a turning point. So far, Panzram had been against the world, but not against himself. His betrayal of Murphy's trust seems to have set up a reaction of self-hatred. He escaped from prison again, stole a yacht, and began his career of murder.

He would offer sailors a job and take them to the stolen yacht; there he would rob them, commit sodomy, and throw their bodies into the sea. "They are there yet, ten of 'em." Then he went to West Africa to work for an oil company, where he soon lost his job for committing sodomy on the table waiter. The US Consul declined to help him and he sat down in a park "to think things over". While I was sitting there, a little nigger boy about eleven or twelve years came bumming around.

He was looking for something. He found it too. I took him out to a gravel pit a quarter of a mile from the main camp . . . I left him there, but first I committed sodomy on him and then killed him. His brains were coming out of his ears when I left him and he will never be any deader . . .

"Then I went to town, bought a ticket on the Belgian steamer to Lobito Bay down the coast. There I hired a canoe and six niggers and went out hunting in the bay and backwaters. I was looking for crocodiles. I found them, plenty.

They were all hungry. I fed them. I shot all six of those niggers and dumped 'em in. The crocks done the rest. I stole their canoe and went back to town, tied the canoe to a dock, and that night someone stole the canoe from me."

Back in America he raped and killed three more boys, bringing his murders up to twenty. After five years of rape, robbery and arson, Panzram was caught as he robbed the express office in Larchmont, New York and sent to one of America's toughest prisons, Dannemora. "I hated everybody I saw."

And again more defiance, more boatings. Like a stubborn child, he had decided to turn his life into a competition to see whether he could take more boatings than society could hand out.

In Dannemora he leapt from a high gallery, fracturing a leg, and walked for the rest of his life with a limp. He spent his days brooding on schemes of revenge against the whole human race: how to blow up a railway tunnel with a train in it, how to poison a whole city by putting arsenic into the water supply, even how to cause a war between England and America by blowing up a British battleship in American waters.

It was during this period in jail that Panzram met a young Jewish guard named Henry Lesser. Lesser was a shy man who enjoyed prison work because it conferred automatic status, which eased his inferiority complex. Lesser was struck by Panzram's curious immobility, a quality of cold detachment. When he asked him: "What's your racket?" Panzram replied with a curious smile: "What I do is reform people."

After brooding on this, Lesser went back to ask him how he did it; Panzram replied that the only way to reform people is to kill them. He described himself as "the man who goes around doing good". He meant that life is so vile that to kill someone is to do him a favour.

When a loosened bar was discovered in his cell, Panzram received yet another brutal beating - perhaps the hundredth of his life. In the basement of the jail he was subjected to a torture that in medieval times was known as the strappado. His hands were tied behind his back; then a rope was passed over a beam and he was heaved up by the wrists so that his shoulder sockets bore the full weight of his body.

Twelve hours later, when the doctor checked his heart, Panzram shrieked and blasphemed, cursing his mother for bringing him into the world and declaring that he would kill every human being. He was allowed to lie on the floor of his cell all day, but when he cursed a guard, four guards knocked him unconscious with a blackjack and again suspended him from a beam. Lesser was so shocked by this treatment that he sent Panzram a dollar by a "trusty".

At first, Panzram thought it was a joke. When he realized that it was a gesture of sympathy, his eyes filled with tears. He told Lesser that if he could get him paper and a pencil, he would write him his life story. This is how Panzram's autobiography came to be written.

When Lesser read the opening pages, he was struck by the remarkable literacy and keen intelligence. Panzram made no excuses for himself:

> If any man was a habitual criminal, I am one. In my life time I have broken every law that was ever made by God and man. If either had made any more, I should very cheerfully have broken them also. The mere fact that I have done these things is quite sufficient for the average person.
>
> Very few people even consider it worthwhile to wonder why I am what I am and do what I do. All that they think is necessary to do is to catch me, try me, convict me and send me to prison for a few years, make life miserable for me while in prison and turn me loose again ... If someone had a young tiger cub in a cage and then mistreated it until it got savage and bloodthirsty and then turned it loose to prey on the rest of the world . . . there would be a hell of a roar . . . But if some people do the same thing to other people, then the world is surprised, shocked and offended because they get robbed, raped and killed. They done it to me and then don't like it when I give them the same dose they gave me.
>
> (From *Killer, a Journal of Murder,* edited by Thomas E. Gaddis and James O. Long, Macmillan, 1970.)

Panzram's confession is an attempt to justify himself to one other human being. Where others were concerned, he remained as savagely intractable as ever. At his trial he told the jury: "While you were trying me here, I was trying all of you too.

I've found you guilty. Some of you, I've already executed. If I live, I'll execute some more of you. I hate the whole human race." The judge sentenced him to twenty-five years.

Transferred to Leavenworth penitentiary, Panzram murdered the foreman of the working party with an iron bar and was sentenced to death. Meanwhile, Lesser had been showing the autobiography to various literary men, including H. L. Mencken, who were impressed.

But when Panzram heard there was a movement to get him reprieved, he protested violently: "I would not reform if the front gate was opened right now and I was given a million dollars when I stepped out. I have no desire to do good or become good." And in a letter to Henry Lesser he showed a wry self-knowledge: "I could not reform if I wanted to.

It has taken me all my life so far, thirty-eight years of it, to reach my present state of mind. In that time I have acquired some habits. It took me a lifetime to form these habits, and I believe it would take more than another lifetime to break myself of these same habits even if I wanted to . . ." ". . . what gets me is how in the heck any man of your intelligence and ability, knowing as much about me as you do, can still be friendly towards a thing like me when I even despise and detest my own self."

When he stepped onto the scaffold on the morning of 11 September 1930, the hangman asked him if he had anything to say. "Yes, hurry it up, you hoosier bastard. I could hang a dozen men while you're fooling around."